Praise for Deb Caletti's

the nature of jade

"Smooth, perceptive writing adds polish to an already compelling story. . . ."
—*BCCB*

"A sure hit for fans of Sarah Dessen. . . . All in all, a pleasure."
—*Kirkus Reviews*

"Full of heart, great twists and fully realized, soulful and flawed characters."
—*Romantic Times,* 4½ stars

"Caletti masterfully creates her character and setting with highly crafted, straight-to-the-heart prose."
—*VOYA*

the nature of jade

DEB CALETTI

SIMON PULSE
New York · London · Toronto · Sydney

This book is a work of fiction. Any references to historical events, real people, or real locales are used fictitiously. Other names, characters, places, and incidents are the product of the author's imagination, and any resemblance to actual events or locales or persons, living or dead, is entirely coincidental.

▧ SIMON PULSE
An imprint of Simon & Schuster Children's Publishing Division
1230 Avenue of the Americas, New York, New York 10020
Copyright © 2007 by Deb Caletti
All rights reserved, including the right of reproduction in whole or in part in any form.
SIMON PULSE and colophon are registered trademarks of Simon & Schuster, Inc.
Also available in a Simon & Schuster Books for Young Readers hardcover edition.
Designed by Lucy Ruth Cummins
The text of this book was set in Garamond Infant.
Manufactured in the United States of America
First Simon Pulse edition March 2008
10 9 8 7 6 5 4 3 2 1
The Library of Congress has cataloged the hardcover edition as follows:
Caletti, Deb.
The nature of Jade / Deb Caletti.—1st ed.
p. cm.
Summary: Seattle high school senior Jade's life is defined by her anxiety disorder and dysfunctional family, until she spies a mysterious boy with a baby who seems to share her fascination with the elephants at a nearby zoo.
ISBN-13: 978-1-4169-1005-3 (hc)
ISBN-10: 1-4169-1005-0 (hc)
[1. Coming of age—Fiction. 2. Elephants—Fiction. 3. Zoos—Fiction.
4. Family problems—Fiction. 5. Anxiety—Fiction. 6. Seattle (Wash.)—Fiction.] I. Title.
PZ7.C127437Nat 2007
[Fic]—dc22
2006004632
ISBN-13: 978-1-4169-1006-0 (pbk)
ISBN-10: 1-4169-1006-9 (pbk)

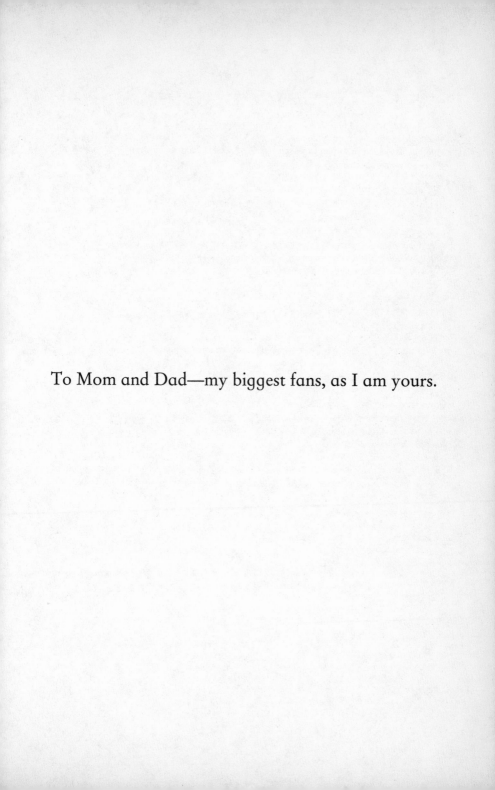

To Mom and Dad—my biggest fans, as I am yours.

ACKNOWLEDGMENTS

Gratitude first to Ben Camardi and Jen Klonsky, as ever. My work is better because of you, but so is life in general.

Thanks as well to the superb folks and my happy family at Simon & Schuster, particularly Jennifer Zatorski, Jodie Cohen (woman of a thousand shoes), and Kimberly Lauber. Appreciation, too, to U.K. Scholastic and Amanda Punter. Love and admiration also go to my favorite local and not-so-local independent bookstores. Thank you for your continued and priceless support. Special thanks, as well, to the Washington Center for the Book and Eulalie and Carlo Scandiuzzi for their acknowledgment of my work.

I owe a debt of gratitude to the work of Frans de Waal, Jeffrey Moussaieff Masson, Cynthia Moss, and Jane Goodall, which helped me better understand evolutionary processes and the emotional lives of animals. Appreciation, too, to Dr. Jerry Kear, who provided essential information on therapeutic methods, along with just plain fascinating conversation.

Finally, love and gratefulness to my family, who are there through every bump and joy and storm of chaos. You are very patient people. And to Sam and Nick—as always—it is a privilege to be your mom.

the nature of jade

PART ONE:
Sea Boy and Desert Girl

Humans may watch animals, but animals also watch humans. The Australian Lyrebird not only observes humans, but from its forest perch, imitates them, as well. It's been known to make the sound of trains, horns, motors, alarms, and even chainsaws . . .

—Dr. Jerome R. Clade, *The Fundamentals of Animal Behavior*

When you live one and a half blocks away from a zoo like I do, you can hear the baboons screeching after it gets dark. It can scare the crap out of you when you're not used to it, as I found out one night right after we moved in. I thought a woman was being strangled. I actually screamed, and my mom came running in my room and so did my dad, wearing these hideous boxers with Santas on them, which meant he'd gotten to the bottom of his underwear drawer. Even Oliver stumbled in, half asleep in his football pajamas, with his eyes squinched from the light my parents flicked on.

The conversation went something like this:

Dad: God, Jade. Zoo animals! *Baboons*, for Christ's sake.

Mom: I knew we should never have moved to the city.

Oliver (peering at Dad with a dazed expression): Isn't it August?

I was told once, though, that we really would have something to fear if there ever were a big earthquake, like they're always saying is going to happen at any moment here in

Seattle. Then we'd be living in the most dangerous part of the city. See, all the electrical fences are, well, *electrical*, and so if the power went out for any length of time there'd be lions and tigers (and bears, oh my) running loose, panicked and hungry. You hear a lot of false facts around the zoo—you've got the husbands incorrectly correcting wives ("No, ha ha. Only the *males* have tusks, honey"), and you've got those annoying eight-year-olds you can find at nearly any exhibit, who know entirely too much about mole rats, for example, and who can't wait for the chance to insert their superior knowledge into any overheard conversation ("Actually, those teeth are his incisors, and they're used for protection against his greatest enemy, the rufous-beaked snake"). But this bit of frightening trivia came from one of the Woodland Park zookeepers, so I knew it was true.

That's one of the reasons I have the live zoo webcam on in my room to begin with, and why I see the boy that day. I don't mean I keep it on to be on alert for disaster or anything like that, but because I find it calming to watch the elephants. I also take this medicine that sometimes revs me up a little at night, and they're good company when no one else is awake. Besides, elephants are just cool. They've got all the range of human emotion, from jealousy and love to rage and depression and playfulness. They have one-night stands and then kick the guy out. They get pissed off at their friends and relatives or the people who care for them, and hold a grudge until they get a sincere apology. They are there for each other during all the phases of their lives. A baby is born, and they help it into the world, trumpeting and stamping their feet in celebration. A family member dies, and they bury the body with sticks and then mourn with

4   deb caletti

terrible cries, sometimes returning years later to revisit the bones and touch them lovingly with their trunks. They're just this group of normally abnormal creatures going through the ups and downs of life with big hearts, mood swings, and huge, swingy-assed togetherness.

When we moved into our brick townhouse in Hawthorne Square by the zoo during my first year of high school, I had this plan that I'd go there every day to watch the gorillas and take notes about their behavior. I'd notice things no one else had, make some amazing discovery. I had this romantic idea of being Diane Fossey/Jane Goodall/Joy Adamson. I liked the idea of bouncy, open-air Jeeps and I liked the outfits with all the pockets, only I didn't really want to live in Africa and be shot by poachers/get malaria/get stabbed to death. Bars between gorillas and me sounded reasonable.

I went over to the zoo and brought this little foldout chair Dad used for all of Oliver's soccer and baseball and basketball games, and I sat and watched the gorillas a few times. The only problem was, it felt more like they were watching me. They gave me the creeps. The male was the worst. His name is Vip, which sounds like some breezy nickname a bunch of Ivy Leaguers might give their jock buddy, but Vip was more like those freaky men you see at the downtown bus stops. The ones who silently watch you walk past and whose eyes you can still feel on you a block later. Vip would hold this stalk of bark in his Naugahyde hand, chewing slowly, keeping his gaze firmly on me. I'd move, and just his eyes would follow me, same as those paintings in haunted-house movies. If that wasn't bad enough, Vip was also involved in a tempestuous love triangle. A while back, Vip got gorilla Amanda pregnant, and when she lost the baby, he ditched her for Jumoke. He got her pregnant too, and after Jumoke had the baby, Amanda went nuts and stole it and the authorities had to intervene. It was like a bad episode of *All My Primates*.

So I moved on to the elephants, and as soon as I saw Chai and baby Hansa and Bamboo and Tombi and Flora, I couldn't get enough of them. Baby Hansa's goofy fluff of hair is enough to hook you all by itself. They are all just so peaceful and funny that they get into your heart. When you look in their eyes, you see sweet thoughts. And then there's Onyx, too, of course. One notched ear, somber face. Always off by herself in a way that makes you feel sad for her.

I didn't even need the little soccer chair, because there's a nice bench right by the elephants. I went once a week for a few months, but after a while I got busy with school and it was winter, and so I decided to just watch them from home most of the time. There are two live webcams for the elephants, one inside the elephant house and one in their outdoor environment, so even when the elephants were brought in at night, I could see them. Twenty-four hours a day, the cam is on, for the pachyderm obsessed. I got in the habit of just leaving the screen up when I wasn't using my computer to write a paper or to IM my friends. Now I switch back and forth between the cams so I can always see what's going on, even if the gang is just standing around sleeping.

I never did really write anything in my "research notebook" (how embarrassing—I even wrote that on the front); making some great discovery about elephant behavior kind of went in the big-ideas-that-fizzled-out department of my brain. But the elephants got to be a regular part of my life. Watching them

6   deb caletti

isn't always thrilling and action packed, but I don't care. See, what I really like is that no matter what high-stress thing is going on in my world or in the world as a whole (Christmas, SATs, natural disasters, plane crashes, having to give a speech and being worried to death I might puke), there are the elephants, doing their thing. Just being themselves. Eating, walking around. They aren't having Christmas, or giving a speech, or stressing over horrible things in the news. They're just having another regular elephant day. Not worrying, only *being*.

That's why the elephant site is up on my computer right then, when I see the boy. I am stretched out on my bed and the elephants are cruising around on the screen, but I'm not even really watching them. My room's on the second floor of our townhouse, and if you lie there and look out the window, all you see is sky—this square of glass filled with moving sky, like a cloud lava lamp. Sometimes it's pink and orange and purples, unreal colors, and other times it's backlit white cotton candy, and other times it's just a sea of slow-moving monochrome. I'm just lying there thinking lazy, hazy cloudlike thoughts when I sit up and the computer catches my eye. The outdoor cam is on, which includes a view of the elephants' sprawling natural habitat. Chai is there with baby Hansa, and they are both rooting around in a pile of hay. But what I see is a flash of color, red, and I stop, same as a fish stops at the flash of a lure underwater.

The red—it's a jacket. A boy's jacket. When the outdoor cam is on, you can see part of the viewing area, too, and the people walking through it. At first it's this great big voyeuristic thrill to realize you can see people who are right there, right then, people who are unaware that you're watching them from your bedroom. There's probably even some law that the zoo is breaking that they don't know about. But trust me, the people get boring soon enough. It's like when you read blogs and you get this snooping-in-diaries kind of rush, until you realize that all they talk about is how they should write more often. People's patterns of behavior are so predictable. At the zoo, they stay in front of the elephants for about twelve seconds, point to different things, take a photo, move on. The most excitement you get is some kid trying to climb over the fence or couples who are obviously arguing.

But this time, the red jacket compels me to watch. And I see this guy, and he has a baby in a backpack. The thing is, he's young. He can't be more than a year or two older than I am, although I'm pathetic at guessing age, height, and distance, and still can't grasp the how-many-quarts-in-a-liter type question, in spite of the fact that I'm usually a neurotic over-achiever. So maybe he's not so young, but I'm sure he is. And that brings up a bunch of questions: Is he babysitting this kid? Is it his huge-age-difference brother? It can't be *his*, can it?

The boy turns sideways so that the baby can see the elephants better. Baby? Or would you call him a toddler? I can't tell—somewhere in between, maybe. The boy is talking to the baby, I can see. The baby looks happy. Here is what I notice. There is an ease between them, a calm, same as with zebras grazing in a herd, or swallows flying in a neat triangle. Nature has given them a rightness with each other.

My friend Hannah, who I've known since I first moved to Seattle, would say I am interested in the boy on the screen only because he's cute. Hannah, though, seemed to wake up one day late in junior year with a guy obsession so intense

deb caletti

that it transformed her from this reasonable, sane person into a male-seeking missile. God, sorry if this is crude, but she had begun to remind me of those baboons that flaunt their red butts around when they're in heat. Talking to her lately, it goes like this:

Me: How did you do on the test? I couldn't think of anything to write on that second essay question.

Hannah: God, Jason Espanero is hot.

Me: I don't think it's fair to give an essay question based on a *footnote* no one even read.

Hannah: He must work out.

Me: I heard on the news that a fiery comet is about to crash into the earth and kill us all sometime this afternoon.

Hannah: He's just got the sweetest ass.

It *is* true that the guy on the screen's cute—tousled, curly brown hair, tall and thin, shy-looking—but that's not what keeps me watching. What keeps me there are the questions, his *story*. It's The Airport Game: Who are those people in those seats over there? Why are they going to San Francisco? Are they married? She's reading a poetry book, he's writing in a journal. Married literature professors? Writers? Weekend fling?

The boy doesn't take a photo and move on. Already, he is not following a predictable path. He stands there for a long time. The baby wears this blue cloth hat with a brim over his little blond head. The boy leans down over the rail, crosses his arms in front of himself. The baby likes this, pats the boy's head, though the boy is probably leaning only to relieve the weight of the backpack. The boy watches Hansa and Chai, and then Hansa wanders off. Still, he stands with his arms crossed, staring and thinking. What is on his mind? His too-youthful marriage? His nephew/brother on his back? The college courses he is taking in between the nanny job?

Finally, the boy stands straight again. Arches his back to stretch. I realize I have just done the same, as if I can feel the weight of that backpack. You pass a bunch of people in a day—people in their cars, in the grocery store, waiting for their coffee at an espresso stand. You look at apartment buildings and streets, the comings and goings, elevators crawling up and down, and each person has their own story going on right then, with its cast of characters; they've got their own frustrations and their happiness and the things they're looking forward to and dreading. And sometimes you wonder if you've crossed paths with any of them before without knowing it, or will one day cross their path again. But sometimes, too, you have this little feeling of knowing, this fuzzy, gnawing sense that someone will become a major something in your life. You just know that theirs will be a life you will enter and become part of. I feel that sense, that knowing, when I look at this boy and this baby. It is a sense of the significant.

He stands and the baby does something that makes me laugh. He grabs a chunk of the boy's hair in each of his hands, yanks the boy's head back. Man, that has to hurt. Oh, ouch. But the baby thinks it is a real crack-up, and starts to laugh. He puts his open mouth down to the boy's head in some baby version of a kiss.

The boy's head is tilted to the sky. He reaches his arms back and unclenches the baby's fingers from his hair. But once he is free, he keeps his chin pointed up, just keeps staring up above. He watches the backlit cotton candy clouds in a lava-lamp sky, and it is then I am sure this is a story I'll be part of.

deb caletti

In the animal world, sisters are frequently caretakers. Wolf sisters become babysitters when their parents leave to find food. Sister acorn woodpeckers take care of their siblings from birth, even giving up their first year of adult freedom to stay behind in the nest and look after them . . .

—Dr. Jerome R. Clade, *The Fundamentals of Animal Behavior*

You are wondering about the medicine I take, so let's just get that part out of the way so you don't think I'm dying or something. I'm going to describe it logically, but there's really nothing logical about it. My illness is like instinct gone awry, and there's not too much sense you can make of that.

So, number one: When I was fourteen, my grandmother died. If you want to know the truth, she wasn't even a particularly nice person, which you can tell by the fact that we called her Grandmother Barbara and not the more cozy things you call the relatives you like, such as Granny, Nana, Grams, et cetera. Grandmother Barbara would give you horrible clothes for presents and then ask why you weren't wearing them the next time you saw her. She was impatient with Oliver when he was little, wore a nuclear cloud of perfume, and hugged like she wished she could do it without touching. Once I caught her snooping in my room during a visit, looking for evidence of my rampant sex life or my hidden stash of drugs and alcohol, I guess. God, I still wore Hello Kitty underwear at the time.

She was also the kind of relative that had a bizarre, inexplicable obsession about your romantic success. Starting somewhere around the age of five, up until the last visit I had with her, our conversations went like this:

Me: So, lately, school's been great and I've been getting straight A's and I'm the vice president of Key Club and a member of the Honor Society and do ten hours of community service a week and have discovered a cure for cancer and successfully surgically implanted the kidney of a guppy into a human and . . .

Grandmother Barbara: Do you have a boyfriend?

Still, she was my grandmother, and she was dead. She'd had a heart attack. She had been overcome with this shooting pain down her chest and arm—she told my father on the phone before he called the ambulance—and that was that. Alive; not alive. There was a funeral and this box she was supposedly in, this ground. Her body was there in the dirt, the same body that walked around and snooped in my stuff and stunk of Chanel. See, it suddenly struck me that there was such a thing as dead, and all of the ways one could get dead. I'd wake up in the night and think about it and become so frightened at the idea that I wasn't going to be here one day that I could barely breathe.

Then, number two: A few months later, my parents went away on a trip. Hawaii. Second honeymoon, because they were fighting too much after it had been decided that we were moving from Sering Island, which Mom loved, to the city, which she already hated. She was pissed and he was trying to buy her good mood with a swim-up bar and a couple cans of macadamia nuts and "memories to last a lifetime." Or so the hotel brochure said.

My mom was nervous about leaving—she wrote pages of instructions for my aunt who was staying with us, and just before they left for the airport I caught Mom in the kitchen. She was holding a paper lunch bag up to her mouth.

"Mom?"

I startled her. The bag came down. "Jade," she said, as if I'd caught her at something.

"What are you doing?"

"Planes. I'm just. Having jitters. About. Flying. It's supposed to help. Breathing in a bag." She had gotten an electric starter-tan, but her face was pale. My dad walked in then.

"Nancy. We're going to be late."

"I'm coming."

"What are you *doing*?" Dad looked crisp, competent. He had a golf shirt on, tucked into khakis, a travel bag over his shoulder.

"Nothing," she said. She put the bag on the counter.

"Thousands of people fly every day," he said. "I, for one, don't want to miss the plane."

Hugs good-bye, off they went. My aunt looked slightly lost at first, clapped her hands together and said, "Well! Here we are!" with too much cheer and a dose of desperation. She's got that nervous thing around kids that childless people have. Like if they turn their backs, you're going to blow something up. And they're not sure quite what to say to you—either they ask what you're learning in school, or they talk about the economy.

The evening was going along fine. Aunt Beth made macaroni and cheese, with very little butter because she was on a diet, so it wasn't so great, but oh, well. We watched a video she brought over, some National Geographic thing about pyramids, which Oliver loved but I was about snoozing through. I decided to go to bed but I wanted to get a snack first, so I walked into the kitchen. I don't know what had been going on in my subconscious for the last few hours, but here's what happened:

I see the bag on the counter. It has my mother's lipstick around the edges. Something about that blown-up bag makes me think of those oxygen masks that pop down from the ceiling of airplanes. I think about those airplanes that crashed into the World Trade Center, the hijackers, and my parents on an airplane. I think of those people on that burning plane, and the ones jumping out of the buildings, and suddenly I get this sharpness in my chest, like my grandmother had, and I can't breathe. I literally can't catch my breath, and I feel like I'm in some really small box I've got to get out of or I'm gonna die, and there's no way out of the box.

I clutch the counter. I almost feel like I could throw up, because suddenly I'm hot and clammy and lightheaded. I can't really be dying, right? Fourteen-year-olds don't have heart attacks, but even though I'm telling myself this, my body isn't listening, because I need out of this box and there is no out and I'm *gonna die*.

I'm gasping and I don't even have enough air to cry out, same as the time in second grade when I landed hard on my back after falling off the jungle gym. I am aware, too aware, of my heartbeat, and then Oliver comes in. I'm panicking, shit, because I can't breathe, and Oliver must see this in my eyes and he goes and runs and gets Aunt Beth. I hear him call her name, but it's really far off, and I'm in this other world where there's

deb caletti

only this fear and this pain in my chest and no air and this feeling of Need Out!

"Jade? Jade, are you choking?" Aunt Beth is there, and she takes hold of my shoulders and I don't want her to touch me, but on the other hand I want her to put her arms around me and make me breathe again. "Water," she says, and lets me go. "Get a glass of water, Oliver."

I am so cold and hot and clammy all at the same time, that pass-out feeling. But instead of passing out, I throw up. Right on the kitchen floor, and I'm sorry for the gory details. I hate throwing up. No one likes it, I know, but I detest it, and that feeling of choking is the worst. My heart is beating a million miles an hour, and I'm shaking and Aunt Beth gets me to the couch to sit down. The pyramid show is still going on, I remember that.

Oliver stands there looking worried and holding a glass of water.

"It was that macaroni and cheese," Aunt Beth says.

Only it wasn't.

Because it kept happening. Three years later, it still happens sometimes. The medicine helps it happen less. That week, though, I succeeded in doing two things—I convinced everyone that I was nuts, and I convinced Aunt Beth never to have children.

My parents came home early from their trip. My father seemed pissed, my mother, sort of relieved. They took me to a doctor, who found nothing wrong. They took me again and again, because I *knew* something was wrong. They kept saying I was fine, but, excuse me, I know when my own body isn't acting like it should. I *felt* the symptoms in my heart, my chest, this shortness of breath. Maybe it was a cardiac problem. I could have a hole in my heart or a murmur, whatever that was, or *something*. I know what I felt. And what I felt was a real, physical happening.

I only threw up that one time, but the other feelings kept coming, at night in bed, and in school—God, once right during PE. I held onto the gym wall feeling like I was going to pass out, sweat running down my face and the jocks staring at me and then going right on playing basketball. The male teacher (twit) thought I had cramps and sent me to the nurse's room. Ms. Sandstrom, she's the one who called my mom and told her I had what she thought was a panic attack. She said we should see a psychologist. Actually, she said this after about my sixth or seventh visit to the nurse's room. See, I kept avoiding the gym, in particular, because I thought it would keep happening there since it happened there once, so Ms. Sandstrom was seeing a lot of me. This same thing had happened to Ms. Sandstrom, she told me, when she first moved away from home and went to college. Panic disorder. Anxiety. She had her first attack in the campus dining hall and didn't go back there for five months.

I saw a psychologist, and then also a psychiatrist, who I only visit now if my medication seems messed up. I see the psychologist every two to four weeks, depending on how things are going. I really like the guy I have now, Abe, which is what I'm supposed to call him. His last name is Breakhart, so you can understand the first-name-basis insistence. For a guy that's supposed to be fixing people, it seems like a bad omen. The psychiatrist finally put me on medicine because these episodes were making my life hell. I was sure I was dying, only no one knew it yet except me.

deb caletti

Nothing made sense. I tried to logic myself out of it, not to have the thoughts, but it wasn't like it was always thoughts = attack anyway. Sometimes it was more like attack = thoughts. Once I had attacks, I started worrying about getting more. After I had the first episode, I started listening hyper-carefully to see if it was going to happen again. Was my chest tight? Did I feel short of breath? Could I feel my heart beating? Was I about to lose all control in public? Was I going to die after all, and were all those people who said I wasn't going to feel horrible that they were wrong? Your body does all kinds of things that are disturbing when you start really paying attention, believe me.

And I had no idea when it might kick into gear. It wasn't like I panicked every time I was somewhere high up, or in an enclosed space, or during a storm. It could be none of those things, or all of them. I could (*can*) panic in a car, a new situation, any time a person feels a twinge of nerves. It's a twisted version of *Green Eggs and Ham: I could panic in a train! I could panic on a plane! I could panic on the stairs—I could panic any-where!*

I didn't even want to go to school, because what if it happened there again? In class or something, when we were taking a test? How many cramps can you have? What if I threw up during an assembly, with the whole school there? People who have these panic attacks sometimes have "social anxiety," which means, basically, you don't want to go out in the world. But I think sometimes they've got their cause and effect screwed up. Would you want to get on a bus if you thought your body might do this? Would you want to be in a crowd of people? Sitting in Math? That kind of fear, that kind of physical out-of-control is . . . well, private.

Anyway, I am not my illness. "Girl with Anxiety," "Trauma of the Week"—no. I hate stuff like that. Everyone, *everyone*, has their issue. But the one thing my illness did make me realize is how necessary it is to ignore the dangers of living in order to live. And how much trouble you can get into if you can't. We all have to get up every morning and go outside and pretend we aren't going to die. We've got to get totally involved with what we're going to wear that day, and how pissed we are that another car cut us off, and how we wish we were in better shape, so we don't have to think about how little any of that really matters. Or so we don't think about how we're just vulnerable specks trying to survive on a violent, tumultuous planet, at the mercy of hurricanes and volcanoes and asteroids and terrorists and disease and a million other things. We concentrate on having little thoughts so we don't have BIG THOUGHTS. It's like those days when you've got a really bad pimple but you still have to go to school. You've got to convince yourself it's not so bad just so you can leave the house and actually talk to people face-to-face. You've got to ignore the one big truth—life is fatal.

I hurry home after school the day after I see the red-jacket boy. I want to see if he and the baby will reappear. I drop my backpack at the foot of the stairs as I come in, head up to my room.

"Jade?" Mom calls from upstairs. She's in her bathroom, I'm guessing, judging by the muffled sound of her voice.

"Yeah, it's me."

"How was school?"

"Fine."

"The day went all right?"

"Uh-huh."

"I got my dress for homecoming," she says.

Yeah, you read that right.

My mom has gone to more homecomings than I have—four for four. I went once, with one of my best friends, Michael Jacobs, during a time we thought we liked each other more than friends but didn't really. As vice president of the PTSA, my mother chaperones the dances, which means she goes when I don't. I swear, she's got more pictures taken in front of phony sunsets and palm trees and fake porches than I do (with Mr. Robinson, my math teacher; Mitch Greenbaum, Booster Club president; Mr. Swenson, P.E., etc.), more corsages pressed between pages of our *Webster's* dictionary, more shoes dyed to odd colors. She's involved in every other committee and program my school has, too, from fund-raising to tree planting to graduation ceremonies to teacher appreciation days. Most irritating is The Walkabout Program, where "concerned parents" walk the school hallways in between classes to promote safety and good behavior, i.e., to spy. They even wear badges around their necks that read SAS—Safety for All Students. One time, some kid got into the badge drawer with a Magic Marker and swapped all the first and second letters, giving you an idea of how appreciated the program is.

Don't get me wrong. I love my mother, and I feel bad having these mean thoughts. Because Mom, she's one of the few people I can really talk to, who understands me. Sometimes she knows what I'm feeling before I even realize it. And we have a great time together. We make fun of the really bad clothes in the discount stores, and put ugly and embarrassing things into each other's carts when the other person's not looking. We tell each other about good books and talk each other into ordering a milk shake with our cheeseburger. But sometimes it just feels like she's this barnacle we learned about in biology. It discards its own body to live inside of a crab (read: *me*), growing and spreading until it finally takes over the crab's body, stealing its life, reaching its tentacles everywhere, even around its eyes. Well, you get the idea.

"Wanna see?" Mom calls.

"In a sec," I say.

I want to get to my computer. I want to be there if the red-jacket boy happens to come back. I knock on my doorframe three times, which is just this thing I like to do for good luck, then I go in. I log on, and sit down. Then there's a knock at my door.

"What do you think of the color?" Mom asks. Rose-colored taffeta, no sleeves, sash around the middle. The dress actually swishes as she walks. "With the right bra . . ."

"It's real nice, Mom." It screams homecoming. Or brides-maid.

"You don't like it."

"Not for myself, but it's great on you."

She checks herself out in the mirror on the back of my door. She lifts her blond hair up in the back, even though there's not much to lift. She tilts her chin, sucks in her stomach. Something about this makes me sad, the way women with eighties-style permed hair make me sad. The way old ladies in short-shorts make me sad.

"I think it makes me look slimmer," she says. She's always worrying about this—pretty needlessly, because she's average weight. Still, we've got low-fat and "lite" everything, and tons of those magazines with articles like "Swimsuits That Flatter Every Figure" and "Five Minutes a Day to a Tight Tummy." It makes you realize how basically everything we do comes down to a) mating or b) competing for resources. It's just like *Animal Planet*, only we've got Cover Girl and Victoria's Secret instead of colored feathers and fancy markings, and the violence occurs at the Nordstrom's Half-Yearly Sale.

"You don't have to look slimmer. You're fine."

"God, I'm just glad for fabric with spandex. Just shove in the jiggly parts and zip. Are these considered unhealthy weight issues that'll make your daughter turn anorexic?"

"Nah," I said. "I think they're completely normally abnormal. Besides, you know how I hate throwing up."

"Okay, whew. I can chalk that off my list of concerns."

"Yeah, stick to worrying about me robbing banks."

"Or your drug dealing. I've been thinking that it's something you should quit. I know you like the money, honey, but it's just not right."

I laugh. "You're not going to make me give *that* up," I faux-groan. This is my favorite version of Mom. The relaxed, watch-romantic-movies-together Mom. The let's-stay-in-our-pj's-all-day Mom.

But suddenly she takes a sharp left turn into the version I'm not so thrilled with. The I-want-more-for-you Mom. I hear it in her voice, which goes up a few octaves. "So? How was school today?" she asks.

"Fine. I told you." I'm trying to keep the edge off of my words, but it's creeping in anyway. "And, no, no one asked me to homecoming."

"Jade. Jeez. I didn't say anything."

But I know it's what she's really asking. It's in the way she says "So?" As if it can unlock a secret.

"Are you getting your period?" She narrows her eyes.

"No! God. I hate that. I hate when every negative act is blamed on your period." Sometimes bitchiness is just bitchiness, happily unattached to anything hormonal. It should get full credit.

"I'm sorry. I hate that too. It's just . . . You. I want you to have a great year," Mom says.

"I don't even *want* to go to homecoming. And no, it's not because of anxiety." We'd been mother and daughter long enough that I hear *that* in her voice too. When you've got a situation like mine, people are always looking at you sideways, trying to figure out what's you and what's the illness, as if there's some distinct line down the center of my body they should see but don't. "It's because of people dancing like they're having sex while you're trying not to feel weird about it and everyone all made up and phoniness and because somewhere inside you're always wishing you were home, eating popcorn and watching TV." In my opinion, dances like that are one of those painful things we all pretend are fun but really aren't.

Mom sighs. Her dress rustles. "I hear you. I do. Wait, what am I saying? I never even *went* to a dance when I was your age. But your *senior year*. It should be fun. It should be one of the happiest in your life."

"You always tell me how much you hated your senior year," I say.

"I hated *all* of high school," she admits. "I was so glad to get to college, I cannot tell you. Let's just say, I was a late

deb caletti

bloomer. College, now, that was a good time. College, I was good at. I had friends, went to parties, got good grades—the whole thing. But high school. Oh, my God."

"Ha-ha. You ate lunch in the *library*."

"Don't remind me. Not that there's anything wrong with the library."

"*I* don't eat lunch in the library. I'm happy," I say. "Look." I put on a huge, toothy smile. Wiggle my index fingers in the air. "See? Yay, happiness is flowing throughout me."

Mom smiles. "You goof."

"Happy happy, joy joy. Three cheers for late bloomers."

"What do you keep looking at? It feels like you, me, and your computer are having this conversation."

"Nothing." I focus on her. "Just elephants."

"All right. Okay. I'm going to go change." She says this reluctantly, as if getting back into her jeans will change everything back, coach to pumpkin, glass slippers to the big yellow Donald Duck ones we gave her for her birthday and I think she actually hated.

I'm glad when Mom leaves, because I don't want to miss that red jacket. I was so sure he'd be back that I'm bummed when I finally realize I must be wrong. No boy. No anyone, except for the Indian man in charge of the elephants.

I try to do homework—Advanced Placement American Government, Advanced Placement English, Calculus, Spanish, and Biology, which shows why I barely have a life. It's hard to concentrate, though. I keep peeking up, still holding out impossible hope for the nonexistent red jacket.

Another knock—Oliver, this time. You wouldn't believe how many years it took to train that kid to knock. He's ten years old, so minus one before he could walk—nine years. See, I'm not in Calculus for nothing.

"What?" I say, and he comes in. I bust up when he comes through the door. I could never quite get over the sight of Oliver in a football uniform. Oliver's kind of small for his age, and he has this narrow face and thoughtful, pointy chin. His hair is a soft blond like Mom's, where mine is black like Dad's. He looks too sweet for football. He is too sweet for football. That's why he's coming to see me.

"Don't laugh," he says. "I hate it. Help me." He holds his helmet under one beefed-up arm, just like you see the real football guys do. He waddles over, sits on my bed.

"Talk to him. Tell him how much you can't stand it." Him, meaning Dad. My father, Bruce DeLuna, is a financial officer for Eddie Bauer, and a bit sports obsessed. To him, there's nothing that can't be cured by a brisk jog or vigorous game of touch football, even anxiety. He had this whole "cure" mapped out for me once, which actually included calisthenics. Dad's the kind of person who thinks he knows "what is what" and how exactly things should be, which means he misses the point about most everything. I've gotten him off my back, though, mainly by using his narrow-minded female stereotyping to my benefit. Shameless, but it's a survival tactic. See, I'm a *girl* (the "just" hovers somewhere nearby in his mind, you can tell), and even though he constantly reminds me that I should be doing my "cardio," he lets me off the hook on the team-sports thing. He tried me in softball for a while, but I'm one of those wusses that flinch when a baseball flies at my face. A ball hit me in the leg once, and after that, all I could do was crouch and hover and wonder when it was going to happen again. I'm sorry, it's not my idea of a good time to stand alone

deb caletti

while someone pelts a hard object my way, with basically only a stick and my bad hand-eye coordination for protection.

I know I'm making Dad sound like a dad stereotype, but it's how he is. He loves sports and understands sports, and I see him as viewing the world in this sports-themed way—win/lose, right/wrong, yes/no. The garage needs cleaning: yes. I should buy you your own car: no. You can slack off on your grades every now and then: wrong. Sports are a good idea for girls and mandatory for boys: right.

So I can get off the athletic hook, but Oliver, who is a *guy*, can't. Even if he hates sports and just wants to play his viola and read his Narnia books, he's constantly signed up for soccer, basketball, Little League, and even the Lil' Dragons karate course in town. I swear, the kid has so many uniforms, I don't remember the last time I saw him in regular clothes.

"You know talking to him doesn't do any good."

"'Being accountable to a team builds character.'" One of Dad's expressions.

"I hate it."

"'There's no 'I' in *team*.'"

"These other guys—they're *machines*."

"'Sports are good practice for life. You've got to be able to hang tough.'"

"Please, Jade." He's almost crying. I can see fat tears gathering in the corners of his eyes. "He's going to be home any minute to take me to practice. It's so stupid. Guys smashing into each other, shoving each other down. What's the *point*? The coach calls us men. 'Okay men, in formation.' We know we're not men. And why? Why are we doing it? I've got *homework*."

"'A good athlete makes time for work and sport.'"

"Please. I can't do this. I can't." A tear releases itself, slides down his nose. "What can I do?"

My brother was born when I was seven. I was old enough that I can still remember him as a baby, with his tiny toes like corn kernels and chubby wrists with lines around them, as if a rubber band had been placed there too tightly. Ever since he first grasped my finger and held on (a reflex, I was told, but who cares), I felt a responsibility toward him. He was my brother, which meant I both loved him and wanted to kill him often, but that there was no way I'd ever let anyone else lay a finger on him. "Okay, Oliver. Let me think."

"Hurry."

"Okay, okay." Broken arm, broken leg—too drastic. Run away? Nah, he'd have to come home sometime.

"Help me, Jade."

Sick. Yeah. Really sick. Undeniably sick. "Meet me in the bathroom."

"He's gonna be here in five minutes."

"Just meet me there."

I hop off my bed, tromp downstairs to the kitchen. Root around in the fridge. Even if we don't have any, I can whip up a batch with some catsup and mayo. But, no, the phony-illness gods are with me. There, behind the milk and the jam and the single dill pickle floating in a huge jar of green juice, is the Thousand Island dressing.

I head up the stairs, and halfway up, I hear the garage door rising. Dad is never late when it comes to taking Oliver to sports practice. Once, I had to drive Oliver to soccer, was ten minutes late, and learned that there had apparently been a mis-

26   deb caletti

print in the Bible on the Ten Commandments thing: Thou shalt not murder, thou shalt not commit adultery, thou shalt not be late to soccer. My father was so pissed, I practically had to get the lightning bolt surgically removed from my back.

I shut the bathroom door behind us. Oliver rises from where he was perched on the edge of the tub, the shower curtain a plastic ocean behind him. "You're going to have to do some groaning, look bad," I say as I unscrew the cap.

"Okay."

I squirt a blob of the dressing down the front of the football uniform. Smear it around. Perfect.

"Oh, gross, it looks like I threw up."

"That's the idea, Tiger."

"It looks so real," Oliver says.

"Smush your bangs up with some hot water. But get a move on. He's coming. Call out for Mom. You're so sick, remember? *Bleh.*" I hurry. Screw the cap back on. Hide the dressing bottle in a towel.

"You're a genius, Jade," he says.

I smile. Feel a rush of sisterly competence and good will. It makes me happy to help him. He's my brother, after all, and I love the little guy. It's important I stick by him. Your sibling, after all, is the only other person in the world who understands how fucked up your parents made you.

Dad is ticked off that night, you can tell, probably because he got off work early for football practice for nothing. His dark eyes look as flat and hard as asphalt, his jaw line stone. Even his black hair looks angry, if that's possible. It's like he knows he can't get mad at a sick child, so the anger just simmers around in there and presses from the inside out, making his face tight and his footsteps heavy on the stairs after dinner. He stays in the basement all evening, working on his train set, something he's been building for a couple of years now, since we moved to Seattle. He's got a mountain with a tunnel and the start of a town, and a place for a river sketched out on the big board that's the base. His own world. He can move mountains, and no one complains. If he goes downstairs, you don't bother him, or rather, it's just pointless to try. The conversation goes something like this:

Me: Hi, Dad.

Dad: Hi.

Me: How's it going?

Dad: Good.

Me: I got a ninety-six on my calculus test.

Dad: Oh, mmhmm. Great. Can you hand me that glue bottle over there?

Me: I also built a bomb in a Coke can and set it off in the cafeteria during lunch.

Dad: Oh, super.

So we leave him alone there, and it's my personal opinion that he's immersed in the project just to get away from us anyway. I love my dad. And he's not always a father stereotype—sports fanatic, go-to-work-then-come-home-and-disappear. Sometimes he just cracks me up when he's really relaxed and he is laughing so hard at his own jokes. He's a lot of fun when he goes off his healthy eating regimen and buys a big bag of Doritos that we munch happily, our fingers orange and salty. He's an incredible basketball player, even if he's just average height, and makes the best fried chicken I've ever eaten, even if it's the only thing he

deb caletti

cooks. And I really like it when he watches dog shows on TV and talks to our dog, Milo. Milo's a beagle and is a bit on the insecure side. He always walks around with his blankie in his mouth. It's like he's perpetually lovelorn, without the love part. Cover boy for Dogs Who Love Too Much. But Dad tries to boost his self-esteem. He'll watch the parading boxers and terriers combed to perfection and he'll scruff Milo under his chin and around his floppy ears and tell him what a good-looking dog he is, even if he's a bit overweight. How he is the best dog, and if there were ever a dog show around here, there wouldn't even be a contest. All the other dogs would just have to go home.

And Dad wasn't always . . . missing in action. He used to come home when we were little and we'd all ride bikes together or he'd play board games or we'd roughhouse. Lately, though, I have the feeling he's been taking single pieces of himself out of the house, one at a time. One, and then another, and another, until all of a sudden, you notice he's not there anymore. Sure, he's busy—he gets up in the morning, goes to the gym or for a run before he heads off to work, and then after work, he plays basketball a few evenings or stays late at his office or goes downstairs to do some more building on the train. But he's most missing when he's right there having dinner with us, or when we're all driving in the car together, or watching TV. When you have a conversation with him, it's less like he's listening than he's being quiet while you talk. His eyes are looking your way, but he's not really with you. It makes me wonder if his absence is really just concealed disappointment. I get this feeling that he's lived by all these rules all his life and tried to get us to live by them too, just like he was supposed to, but now it's turned out to be something of a letdown. As if he'd followed step-by-step instructions on how to build an entertainment center and ended up with a nightstand instead.

The bad part about my Oliver-saving plan is that Oliver doesn't get dinner—his stomach needs to settle, according to Mom, so all he has is ginger ale and a couple of saltines. After we eat, I bring him up some confiscated slices of that thin, rubbery orange cheese wrapped in cellophane, a couple of peanut-butter granola bars, and a banana. He is sitting up in bed, looking as happy as a released prisoner. He's reading *The Narnia Fact Book* by the light of the clip-on lamp attached to his headboard. A shelf of trophies (for participation, not skill) is directly opposite him, the frozen figures packed tight and looking on the verge of a golden war, with their upraised arms and kicking feet and swinging bats.

Oliver thanks me for the food, folds a piece of shiny cheese into his mouth. "What was Lucy's gift from Father Christmas?" he asks.

"Days-of-the-week underwear."

"Come on, Sis."

"Okay. Magic potion."

"Close."

"Magic dust."

"No. Flask of Healing."

"Sounds handy. Okay. I've got to go finish my homework."

"Who was the 'sea girl'?"

"Oliver, I've got a ton of math."

"'Sea girl,'" he reads. "'An undersea girl in *Voyage of the Dawn Treader* that Lucy sees as the ship passes. They become friends, just by meeting eyes, though their worlds cannot meet.'"

deb caletti

I shut the door behind me. I pass Mom and Dad's room, see Mom sitting on her bed in her sweats, watching a travel show on television, small squares of construction paper around her. Everything in the room matches—floral duvet, matching floral bed skirt and valance above the window. It's take-no-chances decorating.

"Jade! Come here for a sec."

I pop my head into the room.

"Invitations for the principal's tea next week. What do you think?" Blue on yellow, green on blue, yellow on green, green on yellow. *Come meet Mr. Hunter, your principle pal at Ballard High!* It's funny how we've developed tool-making skills over billions of years only to use them for invitations for teas and wrapping Christmas presents and folding napkins into swans.

"I like the green on blue," I say. I'm used to these decisions. Valentine faculty parties and mother-daughter teas and graduation cruises. I've seen more invitations than the White House mailman.

"Really? It seems a little dark. I was thinking maybe yellow on blue."

"Sure."

"That'd be zingier. Is that a word? More zingy."

"Uh-huh." I remind myself a little of Dad right then. The travel show is visiting some amazing beach with beautiful, clear water and women in tiny bathing suits walking on the sand. "Where's this?" I ask.

"I've lost track. Australia?"

It doesn't look like Australia, but oh, well. I watch for a minute.

"You should have seen the pool they just showed. Wow. Water slides, swim-up bars, a lagoon."

"You should go. You and Dad."

"Australia's got *sharks*. You can't even swim in the ocean. No, thanks."

"Then don't go in the ocean. Just tan by the pool and sip drinks with umbrellas in them. Or go to London." We'd heard the story a thousand times about how she'd planned to live in London for a year with a bunch of her girlfriends after they all got their business degrees, but how she'd married Dad straight out of college instead.

"Jade, all *right*. If I want to go, I'll go, okay?" Her voice prickles. And I guess I understand. It's a role reversal from her wanting me to go to the dance. Mom sighs, looks down at the paper in her hands. It's the way I sometimes catch her looking out of the window. As if she's staring somewhere way beyond, to a place I can't see. "I'm sorry I snapped," she says. "I guess . . . It just makes me feel you expect more of me, and I already expect more of me enough for the both of us."

"Man, we're hard on ourselves," I say.

"You're so right," she says. "Let's make it a way-after-New-Year's resolution not to be."

"Deal," I say.

She sets the invitations on the bed. Looks at them a long while. "Yeah, yellow on blue," she says finally.

I tap my doorframe three times, same as always, and go into my room. I let myself be swallowed up in the comfort of my deep blue walls, the warm light of my paper lanterns, and my patron saint candles (long glass cylinders decorated with pictures of

deb caletti

saints, lit when you feel in need of a little protection and good luck) on top of my dresser. It occurs to me, then: four people, four different rooms. We are in our own cages, unlike the elephants, who stay all together in their adopted family.

I do a mind-blowing two hours on calculus and another brain-frying hour on research notes on Faulkner. I spend forty minutes on essays for my college applications. I spend ten minutes online talking to Michael Jacobs about how much work we have to do. I spend five minutes thinking of things I could do if I weren't such a freaking overachiever. I could read something without a theme. I could paint my fingernails. I could make an igloo out of sugar cubes.

All the while I keep checking out the computer screen, hoping the guy in the red jacket will appear but knowing it is too late, past the hours the zoo is even open, for God's sake. I'm just so disappointed at how he hadn't come when I'd been so sure he'd be back. It was one of those times you feel a sense of loss, even though you didn't have something in the first place. I guess that's what disappointment is—a sense of loss for something you never had.

Dad is still in the basement, Oliver is asleep, Milo is cuddled with his blankie, and Mom's light is off when I go to bed.

I shut off my own light, prop up on one arm. The moon is almost full, bright and round in my window, illuminating the blue-black clouds hanging around while deciding on a direction. The computer screen glows an eerie greenish gray. The image on my desk is of an empty viewing area, a still, dark night. Only the trees sway a bit; that is the only movement, until I see the bulk of a figure enter the bottom corner of the screen.

I sit up in bed, get up, and bend down over the computer. Yes. It's true. A figure is there. I can only see shoulders—the night zookeeper, maybe? A watchman of some kind? At night I usually switch to the elephant house, where they sleep, so it's possible this is routine. That's what my front-stage mind is saying. My backstage mind is thinking something else. Accelerating just a small bit with crazy-but-maybe possibility.

I send the figure a mental request: *Turn around! Let me see you!* If he turns around, I will know if it is the boy. Maybe if he looks toward the camera our eyes will meet, him a sea boy, same as Oliver's sea girl. Our eyes will meet from different worlds and still we'll connect. Two points in need of a line.

The figure goes to the rail, leans over, and rests on his elbows. This is not what a watchman would do. Not what anyone who worked there would do. It is a visitor's pose, so whoever it is had snuck in. The man does not have a baby in a backpack, and it is too dark to see a jacket color. But he just leans there for a long time, gazing into the darkness of the elephant pen.

It is when he leans back, tilts his head up to the moonlit clouds, that I know it is him. It is that same profile, full of questions, full of thought. My heart *ba-bamps* in my chest. I feel this surge of happy. My inside voice too often screams unreliable things at me, misinformation—that I am in danger, that someone I love is in danger, that now is the time to panic, to flee. I am happy, because it is just so good to know that it can give a whispered message, a simple, quiet knowing, and that it can be right.

CHAPTER THREE

Animals have anxiety. Primates will pluck their hairs or injure them-selves in times of stress. Dogs are also very vulnerable. They are pack animals, and rely on the others in their pack for a feeling of safety. Separation and death are innately intertwined. When they are left alone, without their human "pack" some dogs become anxious that their owner may never return. They bark, chew, urinate, or try to escape by scratching. If left alone frequently or for long periods, some become ill, in a form of depression . . .

—Dr. Jerome R. Clade, *The Fundamentals of Animal Behavior*

Jenna's the only one of my friends with her own car, so she's the designated driver to take us to Starbucks for lunch. As seniors, we can go off campus to eat, and so we all leave, because no one wants to sit in the cafeteria that smells like gravy and tuna fish and cut apples turning brown when you don't have to. Plus, that's when Mom and the other "concerned parents" (read: *bored PTA mothers*) roam around and see which kids were raised badly so they have something to talk to each other about. I know how mean this makes me sound, and I'll probably be either unable to have children of my own or end up roaming the cafeteria myself one day for saying so, but you'll notice that none of the parents of the kids who really need spying on are ever part of these things.

The first time I drove with one of my friends, my chest got

so tight and my palms so sweaty that I thought for sure I was going to have an attack. I had to crack the window and ride like one of those dogs with his nose stuck out, even though it was January and freezing. It was nuts at first, because I kept thinking of all those teen driving accidents you see on the news, where there's this really handsome guy in his football uniform and crying girls interviewed by news reporters saying how he was the nicest person. I had to increase my exposure to the whole situation bit by bit, like Abe, my psychologist, has said, and that worked for the most part. I had to remember to breathe from my diaphragm and not my chest (hyperventilation causes a lot of the symptoms of anxiety), and I had to tell myself (a zillion times) that what I was feeling was not dangerous, just a nuisance. A problem I was making, not a real one. Restructure my thoughts. I still bring my cough drops along on the ride, because I find that if I've got a really strong flavor in my mouth, it helps me keep both my front-stage and my backstage mind off of plotting any ambush. I don't know why it works, but it does. Plus, it keeps my breath fresh.

Anyway, I don't mind driving with Jenna too much because she's a careful driver, and she's also got this cross hanging from her rearview mirror. I'm not a hugely religious person—the members of my family are Christmas Eve Catholics—but the cross does make you think that maybe this gives you a few safety points. Probably like if you saw a sweet old lady reading a Bible on an airplane you're on, you'd feel a tiny bit better about flying—that kind of thing. God couldn't kill her off, right? They say religion is about love, but you wonder how much of it really is about fear.

"Do you realize how many calories are in those butter-

deb caletti

scotch bars?" Hannah asks me. I've got a small brown bag in one hand, a cup of chai tea in the other. We settle into a table surrounded by coffee mugs and espresso machines for sale. Today it's me, Michael, Jenna, Hannah, and Akello, this friend of Michael's from Uganda who hangs out with us sometimes.

"Frappuccinos have more calories than a Big Mac," I say as Hannah sips hers. I don't particularly care how many calories it has, anyway. I love those butterscotch things, and besides, I'm too skinny. My mom says it's nervous energy, and I'm thinking she's right. I've probably burnt the calories I've set down on the table just by worrying about the grade I'm going to get on the Faulkner paper I've just turned in.

We pull a couple of chairs over so everyone can sit. Michael's been reading my mind. "That Faulkner paper killed me. I was up till two in the morning doing the citations."

"Like you won't get an A," Hannah says.

"What's that supposed to mean?" Michael says.

"Michael, have you ever *not* gotten an A?"

"Yes," he says, a guilty yes that really means no. He probably hasn't, but so what. "Some of us want to get into a good college. Some of us want to go to med school and become doctors and not just meet some guy and have sex." He's noticed about Hannah too.

"Some of us actually want to have a social life. You've been more intimate with your laptop than an actual female."

"I don't own a laptop," Michael says.

"For God's sake, you'll still be a successful adult one day if you get an A minus," Hannah says.

"Please," Jenna says. "Don't."

"What?" Hannah says. "He's getting obsessed. He started

his American Government project practically before the teacher finished handing out the worksheets. We had two weeks to do it. He's like the teacher's pet in the Kiss-Ass School of Life."

Michael looks murderous.

"Not that," Jenna says.

"What?"

"For blank's sake. I wish you wouldn't say that."

"What?" Hannah says. She squinches up her face.

"Who's blank?" Akello says, twisting open the cap from his juice bottle.

"You know. What you just said. 'For blank's sake.' Taking the Lord's name in vain."

"Oh, fuck," Hannah laughs. "You're kidding me."

"It's offensive."

"You're kidding me," Hannah says again.

"Maybe we should change the subject," I offer.

"Yeah. Back off, Hannah," Michael says.

"Me? God," she says.

"Hannah!" Jenna says.

"What? Jeez. I'm sorry! I can't help it! I say 'God' all the time. You never had a problem with me saying 'God' before. I don't think it makes me a bad person."

"It's sacrilegious. You just shouldn't do it," Jenna says.

"Like, 'Thou shalt not fight in Starbucks,'" Akello says. I'm beginning to like him.

"Oh, for Christ's sake."

"That's enough," Jenna says. "That's it." She shoves back her chair. Gets up, slams her balled-up napkin into the garbage can, and walks out.

deb caletti

"Great," Michael says. "That's our ride. If I'm late to Physics, Mr. Geurnley's gonna kill me."

"She's gotten psycho lately with the whole Christian thing," Hannah says. "Shit, it's annoying." She's right, really. Jenna had gone from this really cool, fun person to someone who wouldn't listen to rock music. We went together to my first concert, an alternative band that played at the Sit 'n Spin, the Laundromat–concert place downtown. Two years ago, she'd had the side of her nose pierced, and that's gone too, ever since she started going to this Bible study group at the end of last year.

Then again, my group of best friends, these people sitting around this tiny round table who are now realizing we'll have to walk back to school, these people I'd done every memorable thing with over the last three years, have all gotten a bit extreme. It is true, Michael is grade obsessed—he even has one of those shower curtains at home decorated with the vocab words and definitions that most often appear on the SATs. And Hannah is so guy magnetized that I even saw her flirt with Jake Gillette the other day, who's this seventh-grader who comes over from the middle school to be part of my calculus class. He's about four-foot-seven and sixty-eight pounds, and rides over on his skateboard that has a parachute attached to the back. The other day, Jake raised his hand to answer a problem, and then gave an answer to which Ms. Arnold responded, "Uh, these guys don't know about that yet. Let's hear from someone who doesn't know as much."

Akello starts reading a newspaper. He is bored with us. I can't blame him. I'm bored with us too.

"I don't think it was very Christian to leave us stranded here," Hannah says.

"It's your fault. If I get marked down, I'm blaming you," Michael says.

"I thought she was Buddhist," Hannah says.

"Just because she's Asian, doesn't mean she's Buddhist," Michael says.

"Yeah, just because I'm Italian, doesn't mean I'm in the mob," I say.

"I'm not in a tribe, but at the moment, it sounds kinda nice," Akello says.

Michael tilts his head back, drinks the last of his coffee. "We'd better get walking. Next time you piss off my ride, you can pay for a cab," he says to Hannah. He crushes the paper cup in a manly fashion, causing the plastic lid to pop off and go flying onto the floor. After he retrieves it under the table of two businesswomen, we walk outside.

"Did you get their shoe size?" Akello says.

"Shut up," Michael says.

I realize it's cool, suddenly, almost seriously chilly, and I'm in a T-shirt. Fall is like that. It's the only season that sneaks up on you. Every other season gives you advance notice, builds up, but fall—even if you're determined to see it coming, it's not there and then it is. The leaves are orange, bam, the air is cool, the furnace goes on, and there's that sad, something-finished feeling. I rub my arms for warmth. Great, and I'm feeling like I'm getting a sore throat. I'll probably get strep and miss a ton of school right at the start.

We walk about a block, and there's Jenna, waiting for us with the car idling.

"Get in," she says. "But no more garbage."

Everyone keeps quiet on the ride. Jenna turns on the

Christian rock station and we listen to some frenzied, pounding song about loving Him being easy, and no one even says a word.

"So, how're you feeling," Abe says.

"Like shit," I say. I put my hand to my throat. "Ach."

"Lovely," he says.

"I was out in the cold. I'm probably going to catch pneumonia," I say.

Abe works with teens mostly. Or, as he says, "The Jung and the Restless." He's pretty young himself, for a psychologist, at least compared to the others I've seen there. He doesn't wear doctorish clothes, just his jeans and a khaki shirt with the sleeves rolled up, with some T-shirt on underneath. It looks like he gets dressed in five minutes. He barely shaves, either, so he's always got a face half-full of bristles. "Do you think you're going to catch pneumonia?" he asks. He peers at me with his eyes, set a little too close together on his face. But they're twinkling. He's testing to see if I'm bullshitting him.

"My great-grandmother's sister died from pneumonia," I say. This is true. Whenever we look at the old pictures, that's what they say about her. She was only twenty-two. I look in her face, wonder what she was like when she was twenty-one and only had a year to live but didn't know it.

"Yeah, that was a billion years ago, before they invented good drugs," Abe says. "And speaking of, how are yours? Any more insomnia?"

"No. A little zingy at night, but it's okay. Things have been good." Here, he writes a few things down in my chart. He shares some of this information with my psychiatrist, Dr.

Kaninski, who works down the hall and who I can skip visiting if my medication is okay.

"School?"

"Yeah, I go to school."

"Great, terrible, mildly crappy?"

"Somewhere in between." I tell him about school. How my friends have all been going their own directions lately.

Abe listens. He leans back in his chair, folds his hands and rests them on his chest. Behind him are pictures he took from a trip to Tibet. Prayer flags flapping, the brown, eager faces of a group of children, tents at a mountain base. "Why do you think you're feeling this separation now?" Abe asks.

"Distancing?" I guess. "Kind of distancing beforehand?"

"I think you got that exactly right."

"When I was in the fourth grade, I had this best friend—April Barker," I tell him. "We did everything together. Made forts, baked our own recipes." Blue cupcakes, I especially remember. "Then, in the fifth grade, she moved. We got in a big fight the day she left. I guess it's like that. Same as you've said before about Mom and me—trying to get to our own territory."

"Senior year," Abe says. "Everyone gets thinking about going their own way. . . . Everyone starts bugging you, huh? Best friends, parents. Everyone is themselves in the extreme, which is annoying as hell, right?"

I laugh. "Really right."

"What's the latest on your college applications?"

"I've been working on them."

"Which 'them'?"

"Same as I told you last time. University of Washington, Seattle University, SPU. You know. The ones around here."

deb caletti

"The applications your mom sent away for." Abe rips open a tea-bag package on his desk, plunks the bag into his cup of hot water, and dips it up and down, up and down. His cup says WORLD'S GREATEST GOLFER on it, which is a crack-up. Abe's just not the golfing kind. Golf sweaters? Abe? Ha-ha. I can't see him in any sport that involves matched clothing. I'm guessing he's snitched it from Dr. Kaninski, who I know for a fact is big on golf. I once saw him get out of his Lexus in the parking lot. His license plate read BO-GEE, and the plate holder, "I'd rather be driving my club," which probably has Freudian undertones.

"Yeah," I say. "But I'm filling them out."

Abe takes a sip of his tea. "Last time, we talked about the upsides and the downsides of going to school so close to home. You were going to consider applying to other schools. How did that go?"

"I thought about it . . ."

"Mmhmm."

"It just seems like such a hassle."

"You have a common application, right? What's the hassle of applying to other schools? Maybe you'll have to write an extra essay question?"

"It's not just that. Mom'll freak if I go out of state. And it's expensive."

"With your grades? Read my lips. *Scholarship.* All those AP courses? You just breaking your butt for your good health?"

"No . . ."

"You'll be applying for scholarships anyway?"

"Yeah."

"Is Mom getting a degree, or are you?"

"Shut up, Abe." I appreciate the fact that I can tell my psychologist to shut up and he won't scribble notes in my chart.

"Whose job is it to make this decision?" Abe thinks I try too hard to please people. He's trying to get me to do it less, but he doesn't understand that sometimes fighting is just not worth the hassle. It's too much pain and effort. Maybe Abe doesn't mind climbing a mountain to see the view on top, but I'm happy with a postcard.

"Mine." I bite an annoying bit of skin at the edge of my fingernail. "I was thinking I'd just live at home and go to school."

"And if that's your decision, I applaud you one hundred percent. Just, *your decision*, right? There's no magic here. If you don't change direction, you'll go where you're heading."

"Okay." I know he's right, but I still feel the battle inside—Oliver's White Witch and Aslan going at it.

"I'm going to give you a little homework. For us to discuss next time."

"You want me to get a scholarship *and* you're giving me more homework? I already have no life."

"Do a little research. Bop on the Web and look around. Find three schools that look cool. Away from home. And then let's try applying to one."

"Oh, God, Abe." I groan.

"What's the worst that can happen?"

"Mom refuses to write the check and starts crying hysterically. No, wait. I actually *get in*."

"Dad can write the check?" Abe suggests. I nod. "If you get in, do you have to go?" he asks.

"No," I say.

deb caletti

"We've tried things in the past and it's worked out all right, yes? You've trusted me."

"Of course I trust you. Even if you have no fashion sense."

"Hey . . ." He mock-scowls. "This is about you. You pretending you can go anywhere you want. Palm trees? Homework on a beach? No problem. Bring me pictures. Tell me what you like about them."

"Fine," I say.

"All right," he says. Abe always finishes up by looking at his watch, which he does now. Then he says, "Anything else I should know?"

"No," I answer. I'm not going to tell him about the guy with the baby. I'm not telling him that I've seen the boy appear at the elephant exhibit for eight days in a row now, enough to know there's a pattern. He comes with the baby at three thirty most weekdays, and if not, he comes at night, alone. Then, he just stares, lost in thought, like he's trying to work something out. It doesn't even matter if it's raining or not, he still comes. I don't tell Abe how much I look forward to seeing the boy appear, how much I think about why he's there and who that baby is, because that's all mine. It's like a little present I can count on—a happy something to look forward to.

"You know how to handle anything," Abe says. "You can take any step you want and be okay. I'm proud of you."

He always gives me that rah-rah right before I leave, no matter what kind of bad shape I'm in, but that's all right. I kind of like it, even if I can see through it.

"And you," I say. "Work on your klepto tendencies." I point to the cup. Abe looks down. Smiles.

"Fore!" he says.

When I get home, I start my Abe homework. I'm not going to see him for another week, but he'd made college hunting sound like a quest for a vacation spot, and it sounds better to dream a while with an excuse than to do my AP English. Also, it requires me to be at my computer. Flicking back and forth between websites and the elephants. On the screen, I can see Chai rubbing her side against a tree, and baby Hansa nearby. They're never far from each other. A nine-year-old elephant still spends half of its time only five yards from its mother. If they were in the wild, Chai and Hansa as mother and daughter would have a bond that would last fifty years or more, just like a lot of humans. They are the most fun to watch, because Chai just loves that Hansa so much. She puts her trunk under Hansa's butt to help boost her up the hillside, and she tucks Hansa underneath her on a hot day to keep her cool. She'll steer Hansa around by holding her tail, or Hansa will follow behind, holding Chai's.

The Abe homework is harder than it seems. I narrow it down to the west coast (no way I want to go farther), choose only sunny climates (I like Abe's palm tree idea, and besides, I'm one of those people who are cold all the time). I narrow it further to colleges with animal studies programs. It's all getting complicated and overwhelming. *University of California Davis*, I write down, though it looks huge and busy and crowded. *University of Arizona*, smaller, thank God, and because I love the desert. *University of New Mexico*. Same reasons, smaller yet. Animal studies and cool adobe architecture. And I write down *University of Hawaii*, just because it sounds warm and daring, though it's a bit like those posters in hair salons—hip, unusual styles that look possible in the hair spray scented, pop music

deb caletti

fortified moment of why-not, but that you know have nothing to do with your real life.

By the time I'm done, my head hurts and my nose has gotten so clogged my sinuses feel like the human body equivalent of a sofa cushion. I think I might have a fever. I go downstairs to find Mom, who has ingredients for tacos spread across the counter. She's grating cheese onto a paper towel, the shredded orange growing into a pyramid.

"Am I hot?" I ask.

"Not you, too. Just when Oliver's feeling okay . . . Boy, I thought he'd never get better."

Oliver had used the alibi as long as he could, but now he was back at practice. Maybe that's what you get for faking someone's illness—a real one. Mom sets down the grater, wipes her hand on a kitchen towel. She sets her hand to my head. "Nope. You feel fine."

I have the small, backstage thought, *If I'm sick, it might be the flu, and if it's the flu, am I nauseous?* Just this small thought, which begins as a spiral somewhere inside, a wide circle, which will grow ever smaller. Smaller and tighter. Tighter and faster.

"Are you sure I'm not hot?" See, my chest. Got tight. Like I was running. Out of air. Like I'd just. Run up. This huge hill. In the cold.

"You're fine, Jade. You've got a cold," Mom says. "An annoying but harmless cold."

"I've got to . . ."

"Are you all right?"

"Lie down."

I head back up to my room, knock three times, sit on my bed. See, you come to understand this thing, come to notice it when

the circle of thought is still wide. You catch it, before it starts spi-
raling so fast, so fast upward to where it clutches your heart and
grabs your throat so you can't breathe and you're sweating and
about to pass out. I find the quiet place in my mind that Abe
taught me about. For me it is the desert, empty and calm. No sea,
no tidal waves that sometimes visit my dreams. Just the desert,
and cacti, and other plants and animals that have adapted to a
harsh environment, hardy and long living, from the time of the
dinosaurs. I breathe in, and out. Picture red and rolling forever
desert. I knock out of my thoughts the huge cement campuses
and pictures of shiny glass buildings and enormous libraries.
Enrollment forms, campus tours—out. I knock out the secret
thoughts that still visit, even if I know they're illogical. That I
really am about to die. That I've been right all along, only no
one's discovered what's wrong yet. Desert. Just the dry desert,
sprawling and timeless. Creatures evolving and surviving
throughout thousands and thousands of years.

Breathe in and out, and the shakiness subsides, and the sense
that I can feel and hear my own heartbeat diminishes. In and out,
now is all that matters, and now, this minute, everything is okay.

I decide not to have dinner, and then decide to eat a little. If I
don't eat, I will certainly feel more nauseous. So, dinner and
then my homework while I watch for the boy. I'm guessing this
will be a night-visit day, as it was last week.

"You know, you need to be more aggressive out there,
Oliver," Dad says at the table. His head is tilted sideways as he
bites his taco. Oliver still has his football shoulders on. "You've
got to hustle if you want to stay open."

"Bruce," my mom says.

deb caletti

"What? I don't see the point in us going out there to practice and play if he's going to hang back and not give it everything he's got," Dad says. He eats his taco in twenty seconds flat, which is the way you've got to do it. Still, he ends up with a plate littered with bits of meat and lettuce. Milo's under the table, wearing his wishing-and-hoping eyes.

"Maybe football's not his thing," Mom says.

"Football's not my thing," Oliver says.

"I don't think basketball's his thing either. Or soccer," I say.

"I'm not going to have my son be one of those kids who sits in front of the TV or computer all day," Dad says. "You guys really have no idea of the importance of athletics." He holds up a finger. "Social skills." A second finger. "Mental well-being." A third. "Physical health."

I take my Kleenex out of my sweatshirt pocket and blow my nose loudly.

"God," Dad says. "You guys don't have a clue."

"Uh-oh. You said 'God,'" I say.

Dad looks at me like I'm nuts.

"I certainly must need some basketball myself, since right now my mental well-being is suffering," Mom says. Her mouth is cinched upward in a sarcastic smile, but her eyes look hurt at the way he included her in the clueless camp. I feel a pang of sadness for her. Sports Dad can be such an asshole. I pet Milo with my foot. Drop him a bit of meat, though I know I shouldn't. I blow my nose again, meanly wishing the germs toward Dad's perfect, athletic, physically and mentally healthy self.

"Sis, you need the Flask of Healing," Oliver says.

I help Oliver with the dishes and listen to him explain how Aslan means lion in Turkish, and how Lucy spends more time in Narnia than any of the other human characters, four hours longer than Edmund. I hear the *shi-shu, shi-shu* of Dad sawing something downstairs. Mom leaves for a PTA meeting, leaving dueling puffs of perfume and mint in the air. Milo is turning in circles, waiting for the right view before he plops down.

I do my homework, then lie on my bed with the light out, watching the computer. I think about the day, about Jenna and Michael and Hannah, about Mom and Dad and Oliver and anxiety and palm trees and deserts. It seems right then that my world is very small. Small enough to fit inside a cage, small enough that it's as if it has a lock that I cannot see.

The boy finally comes into view on the screen, that known/unknown figure, wrestling with his own questions. I close my eyes, so it feels like we are just two people in a room, thinking quietly together. The sea boy and the desert girl. We both have decisions to make, it seems.

And so I decide something. I decide that I don't want to live in a cage. I decide my world should be bigger than that. That's when I know that after school tomorrow I am going to the elephant house. I am going to go and see what happens if we meet, because I can handle it. I can take any step I want and be okay.

deb caletti

In captivity, an animal will sometimes create unnecessary problems or challenges for himself to solve. A lion will pretend to "chase" its food by throwing it in the air. A raccoon will search for food in a stream, even if he lacks a stream. He'll drop his food in his water bowl, hunt for it as if it is not right there in front of him. Then he'll pummel it, "kill" it, and finally fish it out . . .

—Dr. Jerome R. Clade, *The Fundamentals of Animal Behavior*

When I get home from school, I whip my shirt off and change. It's a cold, rainy day, and they'd had the heat turned up too high in the building and I feel sweaty and damp. I'm thinking maybe I should just wait and go to the zoo another day. One, it's raining, and by the time I walk over there my hair will look like shit. Two, I still have my cold, and my eyes are hot and tired and I have to blow my nose every two seconds. Three, I have a lot of homework, which isn't unusual, but still. Four, the shirt I just put on looks bad and is wrinkled, and figuring out what else to wear suddenly seems as monumental as a death in the family.

So, I plunk on my bed and take my shoes off, and this little feeling of self-disgust starts to creep up my insides. I try to ignore it by popping a few of those miniature Halloween chocolate bars that my Mom has bought early. I'd seen them on the counter and wouldn't have had any without asking, except I'd noticed that she'd already poked a hole through the bag herself.

I'm opening up my third baby Snickers and the self-disgust is not drowning out as it's supposed to, but getting worse. It makes me more restless, and damn it, I get my shoes back on. Oh, man, I get up and look in my closet again and try to find something that I don't hate myself in, because I guess I'm going to the zoo after all. Me and myself try to talk I into not going, but uh-uh. Black sweater. Armpits smell fresh. No wrinkles. I look pretty good in it. To the bathroom, brush the chocolate out of my teeth reluctantly. It's tough to go from all of that gooey, chewy comfort to the businesslike sharpness of tooth-paste. Comb out my long hair. Pull it back? Keep it down. Ponytail? I look at myself as if I've never seen me before, or else I try to. Black hair, dark eyes, narrow face. I keep my hair down, as I look older that way. He's got a baby. He might have a wife. *Wife* is a word that means that all of this dress-up is just teenage playacting. I feel the difference between teen and adult, a difference that usually just seems like an annoying technicality. But now it feels real enough that I get this jolt of stupid-and-ashamed at the fact that I'm putting on lip gloss.

Actually, this is stupid, I'm sure. He's got a baby. What does this mean for his life that he has a baby at his age? And what if he's not as young as he looks? What kind of fool would I be then? What if he asks me to babysit, like the old Brady Bunch episode where Marsha gets a crush on the dentist?

Mom's downstairs, looking for something in the coat closet. She's got that pissy, can't-find-it distraction.

"Where're you going?" she asks.

"Just the zoo. Fresh air."

"Drive carefully," she says.

"I'm walking. The zoo." It's two blocks away. I don't know if she wasn't really listening, or if she's doing the suburban thing again. Where we used to live, Sering Island (a suburb of Seattle), people drive their cars everywhere they go. If they have to mail a letter a block away, they drive. In the city, you walk. In the time it takes to find a parking space, you can go on foot, do whatever you're planning to do, and get home.

I'm not sure my mother has ever forgiven my father for the move from Sering Island, and I'm not sure he's ever forgiven her for not forgiving him. We moved to the city when my father got a new job with Eddie Bauer. It's not like Sering Island is far enough from Seattle to make commuting an issue (it's only a twenty-minute drive in good traffic), but my dad had always wanted to live in the city. He had this idea of us broadening our cultural scope (being buddies with people who have henna tattoos), seeing *films* (instead of just going to the movies), eating fine food (not fast food). This was a way to build a healthy intellect along with our healthy bodies. He wanted it so badly that he pushed the issue hard, and so we moved.

My mother had a full-blown passive-aggressive episode about us going—Sering Island has the best schools in the area, and the only serious crime occurred in 1983, when the ex–Mrs. Drummond brought home a young drifter she'd met in a bar and ended up getting murdered. Several decades later, people still talked about it. The only other crime news to gossip about was the two hundred dollars that got stolen from Janey Edwards's BMW, and everyone knew her son Zenith did it anyway. Sering Island was *safe*. Besides that, Mom had channeled the energy and organizational skills from her left-behind business degree and had become PTA vice president at my middle school. A move meant she'd have to build up her reputation from the bottom, the CEO going back to the mailroom, as she put it. She'd have to attend every poster-making meeting and chaperone every field trip, even the inevitable one to the Puyallup Fair, which she hated. Her friends at school didn't like going in to the city. Besides that, she'd have to find a new post office and craft store. Figure out which grocery store had the best produce. Leave the comfort and reassurance of the suburbs.

Funny thing is, three years after our move, Mom is busier with school projects than ever, and Dad only comes out of the basement for his own or Oliver's sporting events. I don't think he really likes the city. We went to one foreign film, got there late, and had to sit in the back. Dad forgot his glasses, so he couldn't read the subtitles. We went to one Ethiopian restaurant, and Dad seemed vaguely uncomfortable eating with his hands, using up more napkins than the rest of us combined. The food was actually good, even the pile of brown stuff that looked like what Milo used to leave on the carpet when he was a puppy. I think city life just turned out not to be Dad's thing after all, but now he can't admit he was wrong about moving, and Mom can't admit she was wrong about moving either.

"Take the car," Mom says to the inside of the closet. "It's raining. You don't want to catch pneumonia."

Milo trots to the door, gives me a pleading look. "I'm sorry," I say. Milo's the kind of dog you are always apologizing to. I close the front door behind me, ignore Mom about the car. We live in a brick townhouse built in the 1920s, one of ten joined together in an open oval, which surrounds a center rose garden and fountain. It's smaller than my old house—less

deb caletti

modern, but more charming, with its intricate molding around the ceilings and windows, and its elaborate fireplace and stair-well. Everyone knows one another. There are the Chens next door, with little Natalie and the new baby, Sarah; old Mrs. Simpson, with her bird feeders and favorite Energizer Bunny sweatshirt her kids gave her for her eightieth birthday; and Ken Nicholsen, with the perfect house, inside and out. Hank and Sally Berger, who treat their parrot like a kid. It's a comfort-able, safe place.

I walk down the porch steps and through the garden. When you leave our enclave, it's city houses and the Union 76 station and Total Vid, the video store where Titus, one of the guys who works there, always tries to rent you his favorite movie, even if you've seen it before. *Riding Giants* is this surfing movie, and Dad's brought it home three times now because Titus is so con-vincing, even with his bleach-blond hair and favorite/only attire of jeans and a T-shirt with a large pineapple on it that crypti-cally reads JUICY PINEAPPLE. Total Vid has, I swear, a hundred copies of *Riding Giants*, since Titus tells everyone how gnarly and bitchin' it is. Anyone in Total Vid's radius knows more about surfing history than the average person.

One more block over, and you hit the zoo parking lot. That's how close we are. I walk, counting my steps in groups of eight. I show our family pass to the older lady with the big but-ton that reads ASK ME ABOUT BECOMING A ZOO PAL, then push through the revolving metal gates. Someone who had snuck in would have had to climb the stone border around the zoo's perimeter.

My cell phone rings—Jenna—but I ignore it. I'm feeling too nervous to talk. I look at the face of my phone, though, to see the time. Three fifteen. He usually appears about three thirty.

I take the path past the giraffes and zebras, around the African savannah. I hear weird bird calls, exotic messages. Hippos, the meanest and most dangerous animals on earth, are off on their own, like we put away prisoners. Down the path a bit farther is the elephant house, and the outdoor enclosure, a large, mostly flat area of bamboo fields with its own "watering hole" and a few trees. As far as the rain Mom warned me about, it is more of a drizzle, a sprinkle, a mist. We've got a thousand words for rain here, same as Eskimos have for snow.

I duck my chin down and walk fast. The rain means the zoo is nearly empty of visitors, except for this one mother, who looks slightly dazed and is pulling on the hand of her sticky toddler. God, I'm nervous. I have this wound-up, hyper feeling, energized fear, and I'm thinking this is about the nuttiest thing I've ever done. And stupid. And maybe dangerous. He's a stranger. He has a baby, which makes him seem unlikely as a rapist, but come on. I don't know him and here I am going to meet him, and I barely feel good about talking to guys I don't know at my own school. This could be one of those horrible stories you hear about, where some dumb girl meets some guy she's talked to on the Internet. It's either the bravest thing I have ever done or the most idiotic, and I suddenly realize how hard it is to tell the difference.

There is an overhang by the outdoor viewing area where I can stay dry, and that's where I head. I sit on the bench for a few minutes; I look out at Onyx, an Asian elephant and the only animal I see out there, except for a few pigeons pecking at the ground in a bored, halfhearted manner. My stomach is flopping around in anticipation. I watch Onyx for calm, her swaying body, her trunk that rises to explore the upper leaves of a tree. Onyx isn't the best choice for calm. Onyx is pretty old, I think—at least she looks old and acts old. She moves more slowly than the others, her movements dull and cranky. Her eyes look sad and sweet, dark and down-turned, as if she's asking for something but would refuse it if you offered. She makes me think of those days you have sometimes, when you're pissed off and driving everyone away with your mood, but what you most need is for someone to love you in spite of yourself. I've seen Onyx be aggressive with the others—shoving and nudging with her trunk, refusing to move when it would be the friendly thing to do. I know it sounds silly, like those people who have their dogs analyzed, but she seems depressed.

I'm getting cold just sitting, so I stand and lean against the railing. Just because it's three thirty, I shouldn't panic. He could be late. I'm sure he's still coming. I hope my hair still looks okay. I search off in the distance, hoping to see a red jacket. My heart thumps around at the thought of actually seeing and maybe talking to the real him. No one is around at all, and it's just me and all of the sounds around me. Rain falling, a strange twittering of some bird, the eerie warbling of another. I can hear water rushing somewhere, maybe from the brown bears' river, I'm not sure. I look back at the camera where it is perched at the corner of the elephant house, and I give a small wave to the me's out there who are watching.

Red jacket! I mentally call. Where are you? Only five minutes, but forever passes. I take out a Kleenex, blow my nose again, which is when he'll probably come.

But no.

I blow it again, just to give him a second chance to meet me at a bad time. I hear an elephant trumpet, not Onyx, who is just standing under that tree, sniffing its bark. More twittering. The trees *shh-shush* with a bit of wind. One of the pigeons hops around by my feet and pecks at pieces of dropped, soggy popcorn. God damn it, red jacket!

I sit back down. Go through the list in my head again. He's babysitting. It's his sister's baby. It's his baby, and he's married. Too young, unhappily. Happily married. Divorced, raising a baby alone. What I am doing here today is a stupid thing. It's a brave and bold thing. I say the phrase over again, It's a brave and bold thing, count off the words using the fingers of one hand. *It's* is my thumb, *a* my forefinger, et cetera. I start again from the next finger and count until the sentence ends on my pinkie.

My butt is cold sitting on the bench, and so are my hands, shoved in my pockets. My Kleenex supply is dwindling. It's three forty-five, which doesn't necessarily mean anything, but probably does mean something.

I stand up again, hold the railing and lean back, face to the sky like he does, rain falling on my cheeks and eyes and chin. Maybe he's done with elephants, moved on to a different animal. Maybe he's just moved on, period. Maybe I'd missed my chance by waiting too long. By just watching and not doing.

Four o'clock. He'd never been this late before, unless he came at night. I see the green pants and green shirt of the zookeeper who seems to be in charge of the elephants, an Indian man with a curving mustache and beard. He catches me watching him and waves and I smile. He disappears into the elephant house. I walk over to the house, peer inside at the glass windows of the huge stalls where Hansa and Chai and Tombi

deb caletti

are snuggled, eating. The zookeeper isn't there, but a young woman feeds them something out of a metal bucket.

Outside again, the rain has turned from drizzly to insistent, consistent, drenching. I think maybe my chest feels heavy, a bit heavy—does it? From standing outside in the cold that long? That kind of heavy means a chest-heaving cough is coming on. Bronchitis, maybe. *Pneumonia*, my backstage mind says. There is not a red jacket anywhere, and my Kleenex is now a small, basically unusable wet ball, a soggy clump.

I walk away from the elephant house. My stupidity and I head home. We are both dripping wet, my hair becoming plastered to my face. In the zoo parking lot, I see Jake Gillette, the idiot genius, riding around on his skateboard in the rain, doing tricks, the parachute still attached to the back. That parachute looks optimistic in the gray wetness—trying hard even as it becomes heavy with rain—and something about this pitiful sight annoys me. I pass Total Vid, see Titus in his pineapple shirt behind the counter.

My shoes are sopping, my hair is too; even my pant legs are drenched when I get home. I don't want to see Mom, or for her to see me, so I close the front door very quietly, avoid the squeaky parts of the stairs. I knock on my doorframe softly three times. I take off my clothes, which an hour ago were confident and daring but are now soaked and humiliated. I drop them on the floor in a heap, leave them there where they belong. I have a bad headache. So bad that my headache has a headache.

I put on my robe. The only item of clothing that gives you unconditional love. I have dinner with my family, do my homework. The rumble in my chest is getting worse, I am sure. It feels dark, deep. I eat about ten cough drops to keep any anxiety under control, and because they have medicinal purposes.

And, yes, I watch the screen, in case he appears that night. But he doesn't. He's gone.

I turn the light off in my cage. Watch the screen. There are no flickering images. Just the muddy black of darkness lying on bamboo fields.

The next day, there's excitement in the air. It is a cliché to say so, I know, but it's true. And the reason there's excitement in the air is because the homecoming dance has finally arrived. Oh, yay. My mom is up early making breakfast for us on a school day, French toast, when we usually just have cereal. She's got the kind of looking-forward-to-it excitement that gives you culinary energy. Mom, though, doesn't eat any of it herself, she says, because she has to fit into her dress—like one piece of French toast is going to suddenly split her zipper. I know I'm just pissed off and am acting horrible and will probably get struck by lightning for all the awful thoughts I'm having. And I know none of the homecoming stuff is meant to hurt me—Mom's explained that she has to go as one of the dance coordinators. Still, she's obviously revved up, and her cheery anticipation makes me want to fling French-toast triangles like boomerangs.

"I'm just glad I finally found my beaded purse," Mom says, as she flips a couple more pieces of toast onto Oliver's plate. They're perfect, too. Browned, yet still fluffy. Buttery, but not heavy with grease. "In the coat closet! With Oliver's dirty cleats and soccer socks and your old school backpack piled on top. It's a metaphor for my life. Buried under everyone else's."

"I wish there was a dance every day," Oliver says, and pours more syrup on his breakfast.

I glare at him. "Don't even joke," I say.

"What?" he says.

Mom doesn't hear us. "I've got a hair appointment at one, so you'd better pick up your brother after school in case I'm late," she says.

"Cretin," I say.

"It's not my fault," Oliver says, which is true, but who cares.

Ordinarily, I might have been sick enough to stay home, but there's no way I can deal with this all day. Calculus even sounds like more fun. Dad must have felt the same way, because he'd left for work early.

"Dad took the bus so we'd have the car. In fact, if you can take Oliver this morning, too, that'd be great. I've got so much to do yet to get ready."

"Fine."

"Jade? Is there a problem?" Her spatula stops midair.

"No, Mom. I said fine."

"It's just your *tone*."

Ah, yes—the tone. The nasty traitor. My tone has gotten me into more trouble over the years than any actual behavior. And as much as I knew she'd hassle me about it, I couldn't help but let it slip. My tone is like one of those guys who commit crimes right under a surveillance camera.

"I'm sorry," I say, not in the least sorry, or maybe just a small bit sorry. I give Milo the rest of my French toast, even though he's too fat already. "Hurry up, Oliver. If you make me late, I'm going to hurt you."

"God, I didn't *do* anything."

I change all the radio stations in Mom's car. We drive along to rap music, which I actually hate. I hate it all the way to Oliver's school.

"Sis, do you ever get the feeling our parents are wacko?" Oliver asks.

"All the time, Tiger." I pull up in front of Oliver's school, past the flag whipping on the flag pole and the little kids with drooping backpacks waiting obediently at the crosswalk. I am feeling a little bad about how I treated him, though, because I really do like him. He's my brother, and we go through things together that no one else will ever understand. I have the thought that he's sure to get hit by a school bus or be killed in a school shooting now that I'd been mean to him. He'd be dead and I'd have guilt forever and never have the chance to make it up to him. "Have a good day, okay?" I say.

"It'll be a good day since it's the last one I'll have with all my limbs. The first football game is tomorrow." He scoots across the seat, opens the door.

"Oh, man. I'm sorry, Oliver."

"Not as sorry as I am."

He shuts the car door. I watch him walk toward the building. From behind, Oliver, too, is mostly all backpack. He seems too small for a big world. Which is funny, because I'm feeling too big for my small one.

"Why don't you come hang with Akello and me tonight," Michael says. "Forget all this homecoming crap."

It sounds good, but I don't like how Michael drives. And I'd never driven with Akello before, so he might be reckless. He's nice, but that doesn't necessarily tell you everything you need to know. I could always meet them wherever they were going,

deb caletti

though. "Sure," I say. "What are you guys doing?"

"Movies?"

"Okay."

"Should we ask Jenna?" Michael asks. Hannah's going to homecoming, with this guy named Jordan from another school, so she won't be there.

"Nah. If we ask Jenna, we'll have to watch *Mary Poppins*," I say. It isn't nice, but I'm not feeling nice. I have this bone-deep ticked-offness, like those days when no clothes look right and your jeans are too tight, and you feel so negative you know you're going to end up working in a 7-Eleven the rest of your life, with only an occasional robbery to look forward to for excitement. I get a 96 percent on my Faulkner paper (big deal), am asked by Ms. Deninslaw to run for an Honor Society office (so what). No way in hell I'd do it anyway, as it would mean giving a speech in front of the club, and I'd rather walk around naked in Costco during free-sample hour than give a speech. I smiled and thanked her, though, and told her I'd think it over. Just another moment brought to you by the Politeness Equals Bullshit network.

After school, I pick up Oliver, who isn't dead, and we head home. Now that he is still alive, he's annoying me again, telling me that Narnia is the name of an Italian town, that J. R. R. Tolkien criticized *The Lion, the Witch and the Wardrobe* so much that C. S. Lewis almost didn't finish it, something Oliver's told me at least three times. The house smells all perfumey when I get in, and it isn't even time for Mom to leave yet. This can only mean she is back from the hairdresser's. Hairspray fumes. If aerosol could destroy ozone, God knows what it could do to our insides, so I hold my breath. Mom's dress hangs on the back of her door, and the sight of it, plus my extreme, bordering-onhomicidal mood, makes me go into my room and hunt around in my box of patron saint candles.

We're not devout Catholic or anything, but I like the patron saint idea. There's a saint for everything. There are patron saints for rain (Gratus of Aosta), rats (Servatus), respiratory problems (Bernadine of Sienna), riots (Andrew Corsini), and ruptures (Florentius of Strasburg), and that's only the Rs. They've got these cool candles for each different one, a column of tall glass with a picture of the saint on the front, and a matching prayer on the back, one in English and one in Spanish. They are pretty in-depth prayers and do a way better job of kissing up to God than you could ever think up on your own. For example, a prayer to Anthony of Padua, a full-service saint who protects against shipwrecks and starvation, helps you find lost things, and protects old people, pregnant women, and fishermen, reads like this: *Glorious Saint Anthony, my friend and special protector, I come to you with full confidence in my present necessity. In your overflowing generosity you hear all those who turn to you. Your influence before the throne of God is so effective that the Lord readily grants favors at your request, in spite of my unworthiness.*

Or, for the Spanish among you, *Santo Glorioso Anthony, mi amigo y protector especial, Vengo a usted con confianza completa en mi actual necesidad. En su generosidad . . .* You get the idea. The grammar isn't always the best, but who cares. It's like Cliffs Notes for praying. You light one up, and if anyone is listening and in need of a lot of flattery, voilà.

It's tricky to choose, because I don't really have any candles for Intrusive Mothers Who Can't Live Their Own Lives. So I pick Saint Philomena, Patron Saint of Lost and Desperate

Causes. Anyway, her picture is one of my favorites. She seems like a really nice person.

I move a few other saints over on my dresser (saints wouldn't mind) and put Philomena front and center and light her up. Hopefully, the match won't set off the fire alarm, causing Mom to come running in with her hair just done from the hairdresser's, and her nails all long and glossy. That, I do not want.

I wave my hand around to dissipate the small poof of smoke. And then I have this realization, and that is, I just don't want to be here at all as Mom is getting ready to go. I know she has to leave early to help set up, but I still have a good hour and a half or more where she is bound to come out and want me to take her picture and admire her and be excited for the fun she's going to have at my senior-year homecoming. I know I should be a bigger person about this, but that knowing and what I feel are in enemy camps. Maybe I'm just an awful person, but I'm not in the mood to be one of the mice that helps Cinderella before the ball. Abe says I have to stop trying to please everyone, so fine.

I watch Philomena burn for a while as I figure out what I want to do. I know there's a little piece of me already working on the possibility of going back to the zoo in the hope that the red-jacket guy just missed one day and isn't really gone after all. It isn't like stalking or something if I go back again, is it? My brain starts negotiations. If I go, I can't torture myself with humiliation and embarrassment if he isn't there. If I go, I can't get all invested in the idea of seeing him. Besides, I do want to go to the zoo, just because I admire and appreciate the zoo.

Something about this still seems obsessed-fan like, so I cut-

and-paste the plan. I won't exactly go to the zoo again, I decide. I'll just take Milo for a walk. Past the zoo entrance. Past the zoo entrance he'd have to go through, right around the time he'd have to go through it. I check the clock. I'll have to hurry if there's going to be a coincidence.

Milo is so thrilled when he sees his leash that he leaps around and starts barking, tripping over himself with excitement. It makes me feel a little guilty because, honestly, he's just being used. His little black lips are smiling. His pudgy rear end is waddling back and forth, back and forth with joy.

I clip Milo to his leash and escape out the door. I don't even check to see how I look before I leave, so I'm really not even expecting to cross paths with the boy in the red jacket, and that way I'll hardly be disappointed when we don't. I've discovered this about things you look forward to or dread. Fate likes the surprising detour, the trick ending. When you're really excited and looking forward to something is when it turns out ho-hum or completely and devastatingly horrible. And when you think you are about to have the worst day of your life, things generally turn out okay. So I play this trick, and when I'm excited about something, I tell myself it's going to be lousy, and I think of all that might go wrong. Which is what I didn't do last time when I was going to meet the boy in the red jacket. Stupid me, I let myself get all excited, and look what happened.

Milo is walking me, instead of me walking him. For a small dog, he's really strong. Since he's a beagle, he's basically a nose on legs. Supposedly, he can pick up a jillion more scents than we can. He puts his nose to the ground and just goes. It's like he's reading a bunch of stories, following timelines in history. If you are in a car and reading a map, tracing a path with your

deb caletti

finger, you are doing exactly what Milo does with his nose—he even takes these little sudden turns and then veers back again. He stops for a while when the story gets a little longer or more interesting. Or else it's just where another dog peed.

I have to really yank on Milo's leash to get him to break focus and go where I want him to go, and then he gets settled on a new trail and I have to yank him again. Walking him is a whole lot of work, a constant battle of forcing someone to stop doing what they're really into. Like those poor mothers trying to get their kid out of the McDonald's play tubes.

We arrive at the zoo, and the same round woman with the ASK ME ABOUT BECOMING A ZOO PAL button is at the window, and she smiles at me this time. I feel kind of funny hanging around there with her watching, as if I've done something wrong already. Even though she's smiling, it's the same feeling you get in some stores when the saleswoman follows you around as if you are about to shoplift at any moment. So I decide on another plan, which is to walk Milo around the zoo's rose garden, where dogs are allowed and where there's a clear view of the zoo entrance.

I haul Milo into the garden, which turns out to be a huge mistake because there are a couple of squirrels jetting around, which drives Milo into a frenzy of pulling and barking and straining at the leash and straining at my patience. I can barely hang on to him, he is yanking so hard, and I get worried he might win the tug-of-war and break the metal clip that connects him to his leash. Let me just tell you in case you don't know— letting a beagle off his leash can have disastrous consequences. They are at the mercy of their nose and this screaming drive to follow the scent to wherever some animal might be. They will follow it into eternity or into a busy intersection or into the wilds or into the path of a truck or a ferocious dog simply because they can't help themselves. Beagles have to be protected from their own instinct. One time Milo got off his leash and flew his fat self like a speeding train through the Chens' yard, across the street, past the center fountain. Mom was chasing him in her robe. Luckily, he got pinned in the corner of the front gate, his face bent down in captured shame. He could easily have been Squashed Milo in morning traffic.

Anyway, he is behaving atrociously. He really needs more practice getting out. It has to be right around three thirty now. It'd be just great if the boy in the red jacket came now. Milo is straining and barking and bulgy eyed and practically frothing at the mouth. He starts making that horrible *heck-heck* sound, that dying cough he gets when he practically strangles himself. He's so loud, Mom can probably hear him from home. I lean down and pick him up, cart his heavy, squirming self out of the garden, away from the squirrels who make that creepy semi-squeak at him as they cling vertically to the tree trunks.

Now I am sweaty and covered in dog hair and drool. Milo is not generally a drooler, but get him near an animal and he's a Saint Bernard. I set him down back near the zoo entrance. I decide to handle the whole ticket-saleslady-worry with authority. I give my face that look of determined searching, check my cell phone clock with annoyance as if I'm waiting for someone who hasn't shown, which I guess I am. Milo sits politely and stares off in the distance as if waiting for his bus, as if that crazed, frenzied fiend back there was someone he didn't know and wouldn't care to.

I look around and fold my arms, pissed at the faux friend

who hasn't shown, but actually searching for the red-jacket boy. I'm half-hoping he really won't show, because I'm sure I smell of sour underarms and a situation out of control. Me looking like shit, and smelling bad—I am giving him his best shot to appear. Milo and I stare toward the parking lot, at an assortment of minivans with baby seats, Fords and Subarus and who knows what; I'm not so good at car identification. A big RV with a license plate that reads CAPTAIN ED and a bumper sticker HOME OF THE BIG REDWOODS takes up two spots.

Three forty-five. Three fifty. Jake Gillette shows up with his skateboard under his arm, sets it down carefully on a large, empty patch of parking spaces. He whips around with exaggerated style, showing off. I see our neighbor, Ken Nicholsen, go into Total Vid and come out a few moments later carrying a copy of *Riding Giants*, the big white wave on the cover obvious even from across the street. Milo starts to pant, which isn't too surprising after all the barking he'd done back at the squirrels.

Four ten.

He isn't coming.

In spite of my resolve, I feel an avalanche of disappointment. God, it's been a shitty day. And Mom is still home, no doubt, putting on her nylons and more mascara.

I decide to leave, but before I do, I notice the elephant keeper in his green shirt and pants, coming out toward the parking lot, carrying what looks to be a file box out to a truck parked in a front space. He sets the box on the hood, fishes for his keys in his pocket and unlocks the door. He puts the box inside, then looks up suddenly and catches me staring at him for the second time in two days.

"Elephant girl," he says. His voice is deep, almost musical

from his accent. I smile. "He's a fat one," the keeper says, and nods his chin toward Milo. It might have been not nice, except he then pats his own stomach and smiles. "Like me. Like my wife at home. Too many treats."

Ordinarily, I'd have felt a little more wary—adult man, unknown. But I don't get any creepy vibes, and I'd seen him so many times with the elephants. He's all right, I can tell. He has smiley crinkles by his eyes, a kindly brown face, black beard and mustache turning gray. "Have to watch those treats," I say.

"Ah, such a shame," he says with a sigh. "So, you like the elephants? I've seen you come and stay."

I'm embarrassed. The kind of embarrassed you feel when you've been watched and didn't know it. "Chai, Hansa, Bamboo, Flora, Tombi . . ." I count on my fingers. "Who'd I forget?"

"Onyx," he fills in.

"Oops."

"Onyx hates to be forgotten."

Milo's manners are impeccable. Or maybe he's just exhausted. He doesn't strain toward the man with his usual desire to sniff pant legs. He just sits nicely and smiles. "Next time you come," the man says, "you work instead of sit. We always need the volunteers."

"Okay," I say. I'm not sure if I mean it. As nice as he seems, I don't know this man, and as much as I love the elephants, being right near their actual selves with their huge, stomping legs and powerful bodies is another matter. I'd have to think that over. For a long time. Maybe such a long time that I'd never come back. Or maybe just long enough that if I did come back, he'd have forgotten he'd mentioned it.

deb caletti

"There's plenty of elephant dung to always shovel," he says, grinning.

"I'm sure."

The elephant keeper locks his car door again, waves a good-bye. I wave back.

I walk Milo out of the zoo parking lot and around the nearby neighborhood. I let him lead, because wherever he goes, there are no red jackets, and no mothers in prom dresses. Finally, it is time to go home. The house is empty, and I reward Milo for that fact with a huge glass mixing bowl of the coldest water. He gulps and slurps happily, making a mess all over the floor. Then he looks up at me with water droplets glistening on his beard. He smiles gratefully, which I guess means that one of us, at least, is satisfied.

CHAPTER FIVE

Male elephants live in a warm, loving family of females until they are
ten to fifteen years old. When the male is of age, he is slowly but
strongly forced out of the herd. He continues to follow the herd at
increasing distances, until he is finally living alone. He lives alone for
the rest of his life, except for siring children. When he is with the
herd, his interactions with family are gentle and courteous, but little
else. Male elephants are viewed by the females as dangerous to their
children, and are not welcome after the baby is born. Their lives are
solitary ones . . .

—Dr. Jerome R. Clade, *The Fundamentals of Animal Behavior*

I go to the movies with Michael and Akello and have a pretty
good time, and then we head over to Smooth Juice and buy a
fruit drink and a pretzel. B-plus fun, but better than pretending the school gym is some tropical paradise with basketball
hoops.

When I get home, Oliver is back from football practice and
is asleep in front of the television, and an exhausted Milo is
curled up with his blankie and doing his dog-dream flinching.
The basement is quiet, but Dad's car is parked on the street, so
he's probably down there. It seems only polite to say hello,
since we haven't seen each other all day, so I tromp down the
stairs and open the door.

"Dad?"

The train set is built on a platform that Dad has put on top of our old dining room table to make it easier for him to reach. Each week, it grows more elaborate. There is a little town with brick streets and tiny plastic people. A general store, a church with a steeple, a train station. A perfect little place. Now, the train is pointing out of town, which is the area of the platform Dad is working on lately. He is building the road out. It aims toward a tunnel that goes up and over a mountain to another place altogether. You can't tell what that place is yet. So far, it's just an empty area that only Dad sees in his imagination.

I don't see Dad at first. He isn't standing by the platform as he usually is, bent over it, painting or gluing or sanding or sawing. But then I realize he's just sitting in the corner in this chair from our old house that we put down here because it didn't go with any of our new furniture. That's what's mostly in the basement—all the stuff that doesn't fit us anymore, from the dining room table and the recliner to a shelf of Dad's college textbooks, and my and Oliver's old clothes that Mom's packed in boxes and labeled with our ages in black marker. There's no decorating, really, except for a framed picture of a castle Dad got on a trip to France he took after he graduated, and a tacky advertisement for Rainier Beer painted on a mirror.

Dad is wearing the gray sweatpants he wore to Oliver's practice, his Mariners sweatshirt. His hands are folded across his chest, his eyes open and just staring. The footstool is up, and his sock-clad feet are resting on it. I surprise him and he jumps when he sees me, sits up suddenly, causing the chair to pop back into upright position, footrest gone as if it had been doing something it shouldn't have.

"Jade," he says.

"What are you doing?"

"Just sitting here. Thinking."

"Are you okay?"

"Sure," he says. "Of course I'm okay. Is your mom home yet?"

"Not yet."

Silence.

"Jade?"

"Yeah?"

"I'm sorry. You know—about that."

"What?"

"You know. Mom. The dance."

"It's all right. It's not your fault."

"Maybe. Maybe not."

We both don't say anything for a while. It's awkward, him saying stuff like that to me. His voice is low and quiet. This isn't the kind of conversation I have with Dad. Mom, maybe, but not Dad. Dad asks how school is. How I did on tests. Dad talks exteriors, Mom talks interiors. He doesn't share the corridors of their relationship like this, or of any relationship. I don't really want to be standing there anymore. It makes me kind of nervous. He's my dad, but I feel some sense of responsibility to keep the conversation going, and have no idea how. *Maybe, maybe not.* I count the syllables on my fingers, May-be-may-be not, but end up on my pinkie the first time, so it's no good. I want to be back in my room, with the elephants and Philomena, but it's one of those times you can't just turn around and leave yet you don't want to stay, either. I pick up this package on the table, a new, tiny house in a bubble of plastic just bought at the train store. I pretend to study it.

"Where's this going to go?" I say finally.

deb caletti

"I don't know yet," he says. He is still just sitting there, looking at his hands. Then he says, "Why don't you put it where you think it should be."

This is a little weird too. See, Dad's train isn't this father-child bonding project, where we get to move the little people around and paint the moss on the rocks. Nope, this is hands-off-Dad's-big-toy-if-you-touch-it-he's-gonna-be-pissed. The whole thing is making me uneasy, and I don't know why. He's not acting like the dad stereotype I know and understand. He's somehow gone from Mr. Black-and-White to something hazier and gray, and right then I prefer the him I'm familiar with to this guy.

"Anywhere you want," Dad says, and I realize then that this is an attempt to reach out to me, to set a tiny bridge across where there are now two separate pieces of land. And I don't want to say no. So I just say, "Okay." I open up the package. I walk around the platform slowly, the little house in my palm. "This is a very serious decision," I say, hoping to lighten the mood. I put it on top of another house. Pretend to contemplate. "No, the neighbors would complain." I put it on top of the train station. "Too noisy," I say.

And then I stop messing around, because I know where it should go. That new blank area outside of town, through the tunnel, where nothing is yet. I set it down there, appraise the situation. It looks funny, this house on this bare piece of undeveloped plywood. Kind of empty, but the start of something new.

"There," I say.

I'm expecting a protest, or a grunt of disapproval, or even a laugh. But he does none of those things.

"That's what I was thinking, too," Dad says.

The next morning, our house has this disheveled, morning-after glow. Mom's wrap is draped over the banister, and her hair clip is on the coffee table, next to a photo of her and Mr. Dutton, our librarian, in a homecoming folder with the date on it embossed in silver. Their hands are clasped and they are standing under a faux sunset. Mr. Dutton looks happier than he ever has in the library. It pisses me off. Actually, it makes me feel kind of sick. A wilted, browning orchid is in the fridge, next to the milk carton.

Mom is bouncing all over the place, yelling cheerfully at everyone to hurry up or we'll be late for Oliver's game. She'd slept in her hairdo, which had barely moved, which meant either she'd gotten in pretty late and barely slept on it, or that the hairdresser had used a shitload of hairspray. I sort of wish she'd walk by an open flame right then, actually. Mom is doing this casual ignoring of me, not mentioning last night, and making the nonverbal point that she isn't bothered in the least about my bad attitude, meaning, of course, that she is bothered enough to be on the edge of really mad.

Oliver is dawdling, which is making Dad tense. At least, that's why I'm guessing he's tense. Oliver can't find his cleats, then his shoulder pads, and then, when we're finally all in the car, he says he's left his water bottle in the house. Passive-aggressive behavior must come down the family line on your mother's side.

I don't always go to Oliver's games, or that's all I'd be doing every weekend. I usually have too much homework, plus it's cold and boring standing out there with all those parents and their big golf umbrellas bought at Costco. But it's his first football game, and I figure he could use the moral support.

deb caletti

Jenna's brother is also on the team, so Jenna and I decide to meet to keep each other company.

Oliver rides with his chin down and his water bottle in his lap, just picking at the threads of his pants. I jostle him with my elbow, but he doesn't respond. He forgets his gym bag in the car when we get there, and I have to run back and get it. I plunk it down with the other bags. Before he runs off to join the others on his team, I tell him not to worry, because I've brought the Flask of Healing.

"Football is so brutal," Jenna says.

"And too cold," I say. "Baseball's sunny at least." I stick my hands in my jacket, jump up and down a bit. It's early-November gray, the sky filled with flat, stubborn clouds. My legs are already getting cold through my jeans. If standing out on a muddy field way too early in the morning isn't enough fun for you, make it cold enough to stop feeling your fingers.

"Baseball games go on forever, though," Jenna says. Her brother plays every sport too. He even *wrestles*. "What's with your mom's hair?" Jenna says.

"Homecoming. Chaperone."

"Oh, that's right. Did you tell her it's *over*?" This is the Jenna I like. We both chuckle at ourselves.

"You're lucky your mom *works*," I say.

We watch our brothers. I don't know anything about football, but, basically, they line up, run two feet, crash into each other, and line up again. The dads on the sidelines are this tribe of jumping, screaming, pacing men, mostly wearing some form of athletic attire and shouting orders to their sons as they parade up and down the chalk marks at the edge of the field. The women talk and pretend to watch the players, except for this hard-core mom that's screaming, "Get in the game! Get in the game!" as she stands there all comfy in her down coat, holding her steaming coffee cup. Every sport of Oliver's is the same—parents who look like they themselves would have a coronary jogging halfway across the grass, yelling at their kid to do it faster, better, harder.

The whistle blows, and no one quite understands why. There's more lining up. Occasionally, our quarterback, the coach's son (the coach's kid *always* gets the best position), breaks out and runs from the pack, throwing the ball in a wide pass, where it lands on the ground and bounces on its nose. The coach shoves his hands in his pockets, looks down, and kicks the ground with the toe of his shoe. You can see the puff of air his sigh makes when it escapes into the cold.

"They're killing us," Jenna says.

"How can you tell?"

"Just look."

She nods her head at our sidelines, toward three scared-looking kids, another who is crying, and one who has just gotten hurt and is holding his arm tight against his chest. The dads crouch over the players, hands on their fatherly knees, giving "pep" talks. I've heard plenty of these, and they are all a version of the same theme: If you really *wanted* to win, you would. It doesn't matter if the other kids are twice your size and look like they're already shaving, it doesn't matter if they are just plain better, or have more players, or have a team that's been playing together since they all were in the womb—it's about *attitude*. Shout the team name, boys, loud enough so the other team hears and is scared out of their already-shaving wits. It all reminds me of animals that eat their young.

deb caletti

My own dad seems to have lost all of his introspection from the night before. He is wearing his nylon training pants with his Seahawks sweatshirt; his hair is combed in rigid perfection. When the game begins again, his jaw is strong and tight as he walks up and down the sidelines, yelling at Oliver, pausing only to turn his head and spit. It's a miracle, I decide then, if team sports don't make a kid hate his father.

"So far, at least, Jason and Oliver are okay," I say.

The words are barely out of my mouth when the whistle screams a fierce *breeeep!* The players stop, look around. One kid is still running forward until the news from his visual cortex catches up to him. Kids huddle around a fallen body, but you can't tell who it is. The assistant coach runs out and clears the kids aside, who all gather to stare like motorists at an accident. That's when I see it is Oliver.

"Oh, shit. It's Oliver," I say.

Dad has stopped pacing and just stands there, then folds his arms as if it's nothing to be concerned about. The mother Mom is talking to points, and Mom stops chatting and sees that Oliver is down. She watches with her hand to her mouth.

Oh, my God, Oliver. He doesn't seem to be moving. Thoughts crash—a broken neck. Oliver in a wheelchair. People's necks got broken playing this stupid sport, didn't they? What if he never walks again? Is he breathing now? I picture an ambulance with lights whizzing, blaring onto the field. He isn't moving at all. The other coach runs out too, and at this, tears start welling up, and my throat shuts. Goddamn it. Oliver didn't want to play. Maybe he knew this would happen. Maybe that's why he didn't want to play—a premonition. Now he is broken.

"He's okay," Jenna says. And it's true. Or else, he's okay

enough. He stands with a coach on either side, limps off the field with their help. The parents clap. Injury always gets applause. His face is streaked with dirt and tears. Some other kid jogs reluctantly out to take his place; they tell him to hurry, and the game goes on.

"I'm going to see if he's all right," I say to Jenna. I head over to Oliver, who's trying hard to stop crying. He isn't having much luck. His chest is heaving up and down. Sobs catch in his throat. "What happened?" I ask. My heart hurts.

"That big guy," he says. His voice is high and tight. "Number forty-six. Jeez, he just bashed his shoulder right into my chest, and when I was on the ground, he steps on my leg with his cleat." He sniffs hard, rubs his nose on his sleeve, doesn't meet my eyes.

"That bastard," I say. "The minute he gets off the field I'm going to kick him in the balls." Oliver laughs a little, his eyes filling up at the same time. "He'll never know what hit him. His balls are gonna go flying, I promise you that. People will wish they brought their catcher's mitts." Oliver half laughs. Dad is there now.

"He's all right. He's fine," Dad says, his usual line whenever Oliver gets hurt. It means: Go away. Don't baby him. Don't show too much compassion. The other dads do this too. It's some kind of group hysteria, based on some fatherly fear that says compassion equals homosexuality. Parents and sports—I've come to the conclusion that it's all about fear— fear that your kid won't come out on top, be a success. Forcing him into these brutal encounters will a) make damn sure he is a success, and b) allow you to see evidence of that success with the added bonus of a cheering crowd. This means that sports

deb caletti

are supported with an almost desperate enthusiasm. The football team gets catered dinners before a game. Honor Society is lucky if it gets a cupcake. Academic success—forget it. That requires too much imagination. There's no scoreboard.

Dad moves in close, hunches over Oliver. I know he's going to say what they all do in this situation. *You're okay, you're okay! Come on, get up! Be a winner! Shake it off!* The kid is bloody and bruised and can't move, but, hey, what's your problem? You've got another leg!

I walk back to Jenna. Mom is sending glances their way, weighing, as she always does, whether or not to interfere. She catches my eye. Gives her head a little shake and rolls her eyes upward to communicate her disgust with the whole masculine display. I nod back in agreement. It makes me miss her a little. Makes me remember that we were usually on the same side. I feel a pinprick in the oversized inflatable beach ball that is my anger. Dad bends down to talk to Oliver. Oliver is looking at the ground.

"Is he okay?" Jenna asks.

"I guess."

"Wow," she sighs.

"I don't see any redeeming value to this stupid game. None."

"Really. The best part for the players is when they get the snack after the game," Jenna says.

"Not even," I say. "Look."

"Oh, man. Granola bars." She points to the box of snacks on someone's foldout chair. Everyone knows there is an aftergame snack hierarchy. It moves from cupcakes and doughnuts at the top, to granola bars and raisin boxes at the very bottom.

My chest is recovering from the feeling that it had been me who'd been hit. Poor Oliver. Poor guy. The "men" line up again. Then their helmets clack together, same as those big-horned sheep doing battle over a mate. The players fall on the ground. Jenna has her eyes closed. I wonder if she is praying or something. Maybe that her brother, Jason, won't get hurt next. Maybe that these fathers would soon find a more evolved way to usher their sons into manhood than this mini battle reenactment. Praying seems like a good idea. I stand in respectful silence. But then Jenna pops her eyes open again.

"Man, I got something on my contact," she says.

Everyone is quiet on the way home. It is the edgy silence of unmet expectations. I can see everyone's reflections in the car windows. Mom, with her hair that has gone from inappropriately frivolous to somehow ashamed; Dad, with his disappointed profile; Oliver, with his faraway face, lost in another place where children fought beasts way bigger than themselves and where potions fixed the worst evils.

It's turning out to be a lousy weekend. Hannah has already left two messages on my phone about homecoming the night before, and my family feels like jigsaw pieces, each from a different puzzle. I have so much homework I'm thinking AP stands for Addicted to Pain. And the red-jacket guy had gone back to his own world, back out to sea, maybe. Gone forever.

That's when I decide that shoveling elephant shit would be better than this.

PART TWO:
Elephants Are Just Like People,
Only More So

Animals will sometimes offer help to others of a different species. In Kenya, an elephant was witnessed attempting to lift and free a baby rhino that was stuck in the mud. Its own mother charged when she saw the elephant, but then went back to eating when the elephant retreated, oblivious to her baby's danger. The elephant waited, then returned and attempted once more to save the stuck baby . . .

—Dr. Jerome R. Clade, *The Fundamentals of Animal Behavior*

I do sometimes shovel elephant shit (which has its own, sunny name: zoo doo), heaving it onto shovels and into wheelbarrows used just for this purpose. After all, each elephant contributes eighty pounds of it a day. Consider yourself informed if the question ever appears on *Jeopardy!* But when I'm at the zoo, I do many different jobs. I spread new hay and slice fruit and fetch Flora's tire whenever she has to be moved, and I set up the microphone for Rick Lindstrom's Saturday elephant talks, featuring the happy-to-oblige Bamboo. I help feed, water, and look after the physical and mental health of the elephants, check their trunks (adequate saliva on the tips means they're drinking enough water), mouths (rosy-pink means no anemia), skin (should be elastic, not dry), pulse (taken below the chin), and prepare their enrichment exercises, which include such things as hiding watermelon in various parts of the habitat so they can hunt for it, and hanging traffic cones from rope.

A little over two months ago, that day after Oliver's football game, my determination to volunteer at the zoo ran out right about the time I got to the elephant keeper's office. I'd followed the directions of Sheila Miller, the zoo's volunteer coordinator, and then, when I got there, I just stood in the hall. I didn't knock. I had nearly convinced myself to go home, when the door opened and startled me.

The keeper let out a little shriek. I guess I'd startled him, too. "Can I help . . ." Then he smiled. "Hey! Elephant girl!"

"Jade DeLuna." I held out my hand. "I'm here to work."

"Damian Rama," he said.

I waited in his office while he gave some direction to Rick Lindstrom, his assistant, a lanky postgrad zoology/animal behavior student with long bangs and a soft voice. I studied Damian Rama's office while he was gone—the window that looked out onto bamboo fields; the sill filled with elephant figures in ceramic, glass, wood, even straw; the messy desk with paper stacks and ring binders. And photos—a picture of him and his wife (he was right—they *were* both chubby), both with wide grins against a background of trees with curving, reaching branches; a family group by a riverbank; a black-and-white image of a bare-footed boy riding an elephant across a band of water; and a large photo of Damian Rama embracing an elephant. He looked so happy, and so did the elephant. I liked him already.

When Damian Rama returned, we discussed the hours I could work and the jobs I would do. It was nuts with all the classes I was taking, but I was committed to coming after school every day if I could. My homework would kill me, but my inner overachiever reminded me it was community service, and my inner psychologist (who had Abe's voice) told me it was

deb caletti

good to get out of my house and that I could handle whatever I chose to.

"I like your photos," I said.

Sometimes a person on first meeting will do something that tells you all you need to know about them. Or at least the most important thing. Damian Rama did not pick up the photo of his wife, or his family. Instead, he lifted the black-and-white image of the barefooted boy on the elephant.

"This one is my elephant, Jum."

"Wow," I said.

"Here, too," he said, and handed me the recent photo of the two of them.

"She's beautiful."

"Indeed. And a good soul." He looked at the picture and smiled. It may as well have been Jum's school pictures, with him the proud parent. "You like her?"

"Very much."

"Oh, we'll get along fine, then, won't we?" He chuckled.

That day, I met the elephants for the first time, in person. This is what the house smells like, I learned—wet concrete, hay, apples, the sweet/sour of crap. There would come a day, Damian warned, when we wouldn't even be able to be with the elephants one-on-one anymore because of the liability risks. Someone might get hurt, someone might sue. Some zoos already had elaborate systems of leading the elephants where they needed to go, caring for them with a barrier between human and animal, between human and lawsuit. But not at his house, Damian said. They need the touch, as we, too, need the touch, he said. As the saying goes, elephants are just like people, only more so.

An elephant is much, much larger when you are standing

beside her than when you are watching her from a distance as you sit on a bench, especially with words like "danger" and "liability risks" in your head, and with your hands full of forms both you and your parents must sign relieving the zoo of responsibility in the event of your injury or death.

Damian brought me to each of them so we could be introduced. First, he buzzed me through the locked gates of the elephants' private quarters, where I met Flora, the smallest of the Asians (only six thousand pounds), with the pink around her ears and trunk, who is never parted from her tire; and Bamboo, the matriarch, with her high arched back and long straight tail. Outside (and for the first time *inside* the enclosure), I said hello to Tombi, the only African elephant, easy to spot with her large ears; sad, old, Onyx; Chai, young mother with the notches in her ears, and baby Hansa.

"Go ahead, touch her," Damian said as I stood before Hansa.

I put my hand out, flinched when she moved her trunk to smell me.

"Oh, my God." I wanted to scream. I almost did.

Damian laughed. "They are not tigers," he said. "Here. Blow in her trunk. It is like saying hello, or shaking hands. Once you do, she will never forget you."

He holds Hansa's trunk out to me, and I blow gently inside. "Oh, my God." My heart was beating so fast, I cannot tell you.

"You must approach them with confidence," he said. "It's essential. Do not show your fear."

I held out my hand, and did as he said. That day, I learned that an elephant feels tough and soft at the same time. Wrinkled, warm. And I learned that you can be brave, if you must.

deb caletti

In the two months that followed, Hannah had four more boyfriends, and Mom had the principal's tea, the holiday bake sale, and the Winter Art Walk. We had Thanksgiving and Christmas, and celebrated my eighteenth birthday. Oliver's football games wrapped up and Dad signed him up for basketball. Michael and I both got letters telling us of our automatic acceptance to Seattle University. I was glad; I knew at least one place wanted me. Seattle University—just a few minutes from home, on a quiet, small campus.

In those two months, I had also gone through two new patron saints when my reoccurring nightmares appeared again— dreams about tsunamis and wings ripping off of airplanes. I hauled out Raphael, my other favorite multipurpose do-gooder, who guards against nightmares, and who also protects young people and joyful lovers and travelers and anyone meeting anyone else. Also, Gratus of Aosta, who is my usual natural-disaster guy (lightning, rains, fire, storms), but who I also discovered protected against animal attacks, which I hoped would give me a little extra protection when I worked with the elephants. In the two months I had also dated Justin Fellowes, this guy in my Spanish class, though after three weeks we decided we should "see other people," which in my case was a joke, but it beat hearing him remark on everything I ate. *I don't know why girls are always on a diet,* he'd say when I ordered a Diet Coke, and *You should watch your starch intake* when I had a muffin. I scarfed a Snicker's bar behind my locker door when I saw him coming once, and that's when I knew his time was up. If I decide to have food issues, they're going to be *my own* food issues, thanks.

You don't think much happens in a couple of months, but, looking back, I guess a lot had. I had many new people in my life now, in addition to Damian Rama. There were lots of volunteers at the zoo—ours were Elaine, a grad student with long black curls tied back in the functional fashion of her cargo pants and boots, who spent almost every day with the elephants; Lee, an older woman with deep wrinkles and a cigarette-husky voice; Evan, an accountant who was apparently recently divorced and expanding his new life. There were others, too, who worked days and whose names I knew only from the work charts or from the few times we gathered as a group. The zoo itself had many volunteers, from gift-shop workers to fundraisers.

And I had Delores from the ticket booth, my favorite of all the volunteers. I should never have worried she'd be suspicious of me that day at the rose garden. Suspicious wasn't a Delores word. Her words were good ones, like "funny," and "kind," and "cozy." The people in the photo at her station were her daughter, son-in-law, and granddaughter who live in San Francisco. Delores drives a Mini Cooper and actually has a wicked sense of humor. She once said she saw Sheila, our volunteer coordinator, by the hippo pen and thought one had escaped—a comment more about Sheila's personality than her body type. Delores used to be a nurse in a cancer ward, and it just got to her one day and she couldn't handle it anymore. She and her husband "cut back," as she put it, and now she just gives her time to the zoo, where there's more living than dying. I've tried to get her to come out of the ticket box and interact with the elephants, but she just wants to stay there, selling tickets and examining passes and doing her seek-and-find puzzle books.

deb caletti

And I know so much more. I now know that it's disrespect-
ful in India to ride an elephant with your shoes on, and that you
should not approach one unless you have a peaceful mind. I
know how to hose down an elephant, which is not something I'd
have ever thought I could do two months ago. They roll on their
side real nicely for you, like Milo wishing for a tummy scratch.
I've learned there are mean-spirited people who shouldn't be let
into zoos, who throw their paper cups and old gum into the
enclosure or yell insults *Hey, stupid! Fat Ass!* to them. And that
there are others, gentle men, grown mothers and daughters, who
come to see the connections, rather than to reassure themselves of
superiority. You get to thinking that maybe the dividing line
shouldn't be *animals* and *people* but *good* and *bad*.

As far as peace of mind goes—I've gone through a lot of
cough drops. But I'm proud of myself. I had this idea, and I did
it, even though it was new and I didn't know what might happen. Especially at first, because I was thinking how elephants
are wild animals, which means they are unpredictable. But I've
learned that animal behavior makes sense. Much more than
human behavior. Also, you look in their eyes and they look in
yours and you see each other. It's not like you see *animal* and
they see *human*, just that you both see your bond. Living being
to living being. No words necessary. It's simple and uncompli-
cated and honest to the point of purity. And besides, I've
learned that Hansa likes the smell of cough drops. She puts her
trunk right up by my cheek, which could really freak you out,
but I love it. Her good intentions make me forget to be freaked.

In those two months, too, I had almost forgotten about the boy
in the red jacket with the baby. Well, maybe I didn't forget

about him, exactly. I just revised him, cut-and-pasted the feelings I had when I first saw him on the computer screen. Momentary sugar high, temporary happy-feeling buzz, boredom looking for a target. Just another good-idea thrill that wasn't so good, like my original intent to study gorillas. File it under Oh, Well.

But there were these moments, I confess, when I lay on my bed, a candle flickering on my dresser, just staring at my framed piece of sky, and thoughts of him would visit, uninvited. When the clouds picked up speed and raced from one place to another as if in a hurry to get somewhere, or when they lazed in one spot, the way you do in your robe on a Sunday morning, that boy would appear with his head tilted back and the first, encompassing feeling I had on seeing him would fill me again, as the elephants (now well-known to me) walked and swayed on my computer screen. I would unwrap the thought of the boy, like you would a treasure kept in folded tissue paper and hidden in your underwear drawer. I would open it carefully, examine it from all angles. It was the kind of memory that had the bittersweet taste of unfinished business.

"You'll never guess what happened this morning," Damian Rama says when I find him in the elephant house. I take my overalls off the hook, step into them.

"I saw," I say. "That tree stump in the center of the field. Who did it?"

"Of course it was Onyx. She dug it up, threw it in the air. Ah, she must have been quite angry."

"Why?" I ask.

"Baby Hansa? Life?"

deb caletti

Damian Rama sighs over Onyx and the tree stump. Onyx had been a growing problem lately; she was becoming less solitary, more aggressive. She had gotten a parasite, and Dr. Brodie, one of the zoo vets, said she had to be separated from the others for a while. This only made her crankier.

"Onyx is angry," Damian says. "Onyx has a right to be angry. You've got to remember, for many elephants, their life is that of a human in a war-torn country. Ravaged homes, killed relatives, separation," Damian says. Here's another thing I've learned over two months—every elephant here has a sad story. Every captive elephant's story is one of loss and separation. Something to remember every time you see happy people getting elephant rides.

Onyx was a cull orphan, which meant, Damian taught me, that she had been taken from her family as a baby. She'd been weaned too soon, stolen from her mother and all of the other, older female caretakers. Even elephants that witness another one being culled, Damian says, can suffer problems like depression and can react to stress with aggression.

"Poor Onyx," I say.

"Well, if you don't feel secure, safe, you'll never feel free. If you're not free, you can't be secure," Damian says. He strokes his beard as he says it, as he always does when he is thinking. I love Damian; we all do. He's easy to love, with his warm eyes, the smile wrinkles embedded into his skin the color of toast. His goodness comes through in the way he handles both the elephants and the people who care for them.

I set two metal buckets of apples on the floor, in preparation to file Tombi's nails. Inspecting the elephants' feet (its cuticles, nails, and pads) and removing any stones from the feet is part of their daily care, but often their nails need to be filed, too. Tombi is already in the house. The pen has a separate door near the floor where the elephants can stick their feet out. My job is to distract Tombi with apples as Damian uses the long, grooved knife to scrape and file her nails. It's important when you do things like this to be aware of just where their trunk is, to avoid being injured. Most of the elephants know to put their trunks against the palm of your hand, for example, when they are being examined. The end of their trunk feels firm but kind of pliable, like the cartilage in the end of your own nose.

Damian lifts the small, square metal gate and latches it. Tombi is so well trained, she just sticks her foot right out. Man, if only Milo were that maturely behaved. I stand by the bars, feed Tombi a piece of apple. Tombi is an African elephant, which means she has two fingerish points on her trunk (Asians have only one), which is how she grabs the apple and brings it to her mouth. An elephant's trunk is pretty awesome— it smells, grabs, breathes, strokes. They suck water up through it and shoot it into their mouth, the same way you get a drink from the garden hose on a hot day. Hansa will shoot you with it, same as Oliver when he's asked to water the front yard.

"I've only known one other elephant to suffer so much. More," Damian says. He sits down on a stool in front of Tombi, puts her huge foot on his lap.

"Who?" Tombi crunches her apple.

"Jumo."

"Your Jum?" I'm surprised. I imagine the pictures on Damian's desk, the happy pair, remember the stories Damian tells me sometimes when we work together. How Jumo would blow in his face to greet him. How sometimes when they traveled,

94   deb caletti

he would sleep with Jumo beside him, Jumo's trunk wrapped around his waist. How Jum would give Damian a push and then run away so he'd chase her.

"Yes."

"You never told me she was unhappy."

"It is a sad thing. Upsetting. She suffered as a baby. She is still suffering."

Damian is quiet. I'm sure his thoughts are there, in India. Damian had been a *phandi mahout* in India, he's told me. *Mahout* means "knower of all knowledge." A mahout is an elephant trainer, or keeper, or sometimes a driver. Damian is from Assam, where being a mahout is looked upon with awe and wonder. In other parts of India, mahouts are lower class, but in Assam, it's a privileged profession, and often passed on from generation to generation. Damian's father wasn't a mahout, but Damian had his own elephant when he was a child, Ol Bala, and he fell in love with elephants because of Ol Bala (and also probably because mahouts got the hot girls). Mahouts actually have their own kind of "university," he's said, where you have to pass certain tests about elephant care and training. You can become a *phandi* after passing these tests, and then a *baro phandi*, which is like a master's degree in elephant behavior. They are held in highest esteem of the other mahouts and the elephant owners, and even the government. That's how Damian knows so much about elephants.

Damian became unhappy in Assam, because elephant management was deteriorating. Younger mahouts, Damian has said, didn't have the traditional initiation into the "art," didn't have the proper knowledge to do the work, or the proper respect for it. They used violence to control the elephants, and

Bhim, the elephant owner Damian worked for, was doing nothing about it. Damian argued with Bhim and almost lost his job, and when Damian was granted a U.S. visa just shortly afterward, he and his wife, Devi, left their home and family and even Jum to set up life here, where Damian got a job first as a keeper, and then as the elephant manager.

"Is Jum okay?"

"The first time I met her, twenty years ago, she was a baby. Still crying. She and her twin were dragged from their mother, kicking and screaming. She'd been crying for days, because just before I came, her twin died during the breaking process."

"What do you mean?"

"The breaking process? It's the first step in training an elephant. They are restrained and beaten."

"Why?"

"So they will listen to the new owner. What they are trying to break . . . It's the elephant's love for his mother."

Damian raises the long file to Tombi's foot, scrapes it rhythmically across her nails as she reaches out to me with her trunk for more apple. I look at Tombi, happy now, and think of poor Jum. Elephants don't just wail their pain—people think their eyes get watery with tears, too, just like us. "That's horrible. I don't get why that's even allowed," I say.

"Thousands of years of tradition. People don't see the humanity that lies in the animals, same as people don't see the animal that is within humans. The first time I saw Jum, she was trying to lift her dead brother up with her trunk. She was trying to get him to stand again. She'd even stuffed grass in his mouth to try to get him to eat."

I don't say anything. I imagine Chai being taken from

deb caletti

Hansa. I imagine Oliver being taken from me.

"And when I left, many years later, she was broken again."

"Because you left? She was brokenhearted?"

"Yes, she was brokenhearted. But she also had to be broken again. *Ketti-azhikkal*. The process where a new mahout takes control over an elephant. They do not easily accept someone new. You see, an elephant is a very cautious animal. She needs to take time to see if something is safe. If you are trying to get her to cross a bridge she's never been across before, she must sniff it and test it, and will only cross if she is convinced of its safety. She will not allow her baby to cross until she has done so. Then she will go back and help her calf over. They are very curious, but very cautious. A new mahout, well . . ." The file *zsh-zshishes* over Tombi's nails.

"It should be a slow process, and he should work with the old mahout to understand the elephant. He should assist with chores so that the elephant will come to trust the new mahout. But in recent years, *ketti-azhikkal* has become violent, and mahouts will use physical force to control a new elephant quickly. One of the elephant's front feet will be chained, one back foot. Then, two or more mahouts agitate the animal, try to get it to chase while it is still chained. The new mahout gives the elephant commands, and the elephant resists. They beat the elephant with the *valiya kol*, the long stick, and *cherukol*, the short stick, until the elephant is exhausted and gives in to the commands."

The vision of this makes my stomach drop. Elephants get angry and show joy and are sad and playful. They are vulnerable, full of tenderness and feelings. Hansa put her trunk around my waist once, just as Jum did to Damian, in a huglike greeting. And then there is Flora, with her tire. Captured in India, she grew up alone in a zoo. She had a tire in that zoo. When she moved here, Damian says, she claimed an old ignored tire in the yard as her own. Like Milo and his blankie, or Oliver and the stuffed Easter chick he's had since he was a baby. When he was little, Oliver wouldn't go anywhere without it, and Mom had to sew the head back on twice. It's so dirty and looks like stuffed-animal roadkill, but he still keeps it on a shelf in his room.

These animals feel. They think. They love. People, one another, beloved old black tires. Chai was moved here because she was chained at her former zoo. She learned to undo the chain, and to fasten it back up when the trainers came. When she figured out how to undo the bolts in her holding area, she was transferred to our more open environment. I know people who aren't that smart. I know people who aren't as sweetly affectionate and loving. I know that feelings should be dealt with gently. Elephants don't have a voice, the power to defend themselves with words, and that only makes them that much more fragile. Four tons of fragility, a funny joke from Mother Nature.

Damian shifts Tombi to her other foot, which she does happily. I give her more apples, and she takes them, twists her trunk to her mouth. "Damian, it makes me sick," I say.

His eyes are sad, and he strokes Tombi's leg. He is very gentle. "My brother. He goes and sees Jum," Damian says. His voice is small. "She stands, rocking herself. For comfort."

"I'm so sorry. I know how much you loved Jum."

"Loved? *Love*. She's my child. I'm her mahout."

I don't know what to say. I can see his pain in the slump of his shoulders. I just keep handing Tombi apples.

"I left her. I fled. And now she is twice broken."

deb caletti

My two hours after school at the elephant house always speeds by, and when I have to leave, I do it reluctantly. Passing Delores in her ticket booth, walking out through the metal gates, always feels like a tough transition, an abrupt transfer between two worlds, like Oliver's Narnia books, where Lucy must pass through the wardrobe, leaving a snowy, magical land to return to the everyday coldness of the empty room in the huge country house where the wardrobe stands. I would walk through the parking lot, where I would often see Jake Gillette riding around on his skateboard with the parachute on the back, flying off homemade ramps and clocking leaps and jumps with a stop watch. Then I would pass Total Vid, where Titus in his pineapple shirt would be sliding *Riding Giants* across the counter to another customer. Sometimes he would look out at me, and I would look down, feeling too embarrassed to acknowledge him. I would count my footsteps on the way home, groups of eight.

I would open my front door and there would be the cooking smells of dinner, the sounds—the siss of something frying or the hum of the oven, a wooden spoon scraping against a pan. Milo would rush over from wherever he was and start barking maniacally (he is very sensitive to all door sounds—sometimes he'll bark when a doorbell rings on television, and other times he'll listen for when a door is not completely shut so that he can nose his way in). He'd turn to and fro and looking for his blankie, a toy, a sock, *something* to bring me; he's generous that way. Dad would be just arriving home, or he and Oliver would be returning from practice, Oliver's skinny legs sticking out from his satiny basketball shorts, his eyes tired and miserable. New invitations for some school function would be spread over the dining room table, and my phone would be flashing its mailbox icon, with the lid opening and closing, opening and closing, with messages from Michael asking for help with proper footnote form, and Hannah asking if she should break up with guy of the moment, and Jenna saying she couldn't do anything on the weekend because she had Bible camp. My mind would be pulled from the animal world into the human one, my hands still smelling like hay. This transition between two worlds—I felt a little like the rocket that burns up on reentry through the atmosphere.

That day, after Damian and I finish with Tombi, I help Elaine hang some hay sheets for enrichment, then change out of my overalls. I head up the path to the viewing area, in my regular clothes now, my backpack stuffed with homework and slung over my shoulder, and that's when I see him. Them. Just like that. Two and a half months later, at five o'clock in the evening—an unexpected time, an unexpected meeting, an unexpected veering in my day, week, life, and oh, my God, oh, my God, there he is, right there, and the little boy in the backpack, too, with his sweet baby cheeks rosy red from the cold.

A rush of adrenaline zaps through me, an all-hands-on-deck, Code Red, physical emergency that basically fixes it so I can't move. I'm stopped in my tracks, like an animal suddenly face-to-face with his predator, only my body is messing me over again, as my mind is saying how happy I am. I am a deer, who can die of a heart attack if it is touched.

The red-jacket boy points. "Look, Bo," he says, and there is his voice, too. Gentle, deep. Soft.

There he is, in front of me, not the object of my imagination but a real person, with a real voice. He stands, a hand around each of his son's legs. Of course it is his son. The baby's hair is bright blond and the boy's is brown, but his touch on that patch of the baby's bare leg, just there between the cuff of the baby's pants and the top of his sock, is too tender to be anything other than a parent's touch.

My legs decide that they can walk again. What I decide to do next, or decide not to do, is to just walk past them, that's all. Just walk past, smiling briefly.

Because I am a cautious animal. And this, too, is a bridge I have never before gone over.

CHAPTER SEVEN

The marmoset father carries his babies wherever he goes for the first two years of their lives . . .

—Dr. Jerome R. Clade, *The Fundamentals of Animal Behavior*

Casual, regular day. No big deal. Casual, regular day. Calculus. Spanish test. Starbucks with friends. Elephants, as usual. Nothing special, I am telling myself the next day after school, before I head to the zoo. Hair pulled back. Nothing sexy, nothing different. I'm going to work with elephants, shoveling crap, among other things. No new sweaters allowed there. Anyway, if I'm going to offer anything to anyone, I'm offering just me, and if he doesn't like it, too bad. But I probably am not going to offer anything, because this is a casual, regular day, so stop thinking anything else! Okay, no new sweater, but a little lip gloss. I'd worn lip gloss to work before, because your lips get dry. Okay, fine. My favorite older sweater. Goddamn, I'm going to ruin this, I just know it, with my own thinking.

There is no time for the perfect patron saint, so I light Raphael, the nightmare guy, so that this doesn't turn out to be one. I light him, blow him out, head downstairs. Mom has made a bowl of peanut butter cookie dough and is eating it off the tip of her finger. Cookie making is never simply cookie making. It is a direct result of an elevated mood, good or bad. It is either joy inspired (see the related French Toast Incident, previously described), or depression inspired—PMS, broken heart, listless boredom, agitation that can only be cured by the near inhalation of fat and sugar. The clues—no baking sheets out yet, the oven still cold—means this is *not* about joy.

"I suppose you'll be home for dinner," she says. Her tone sags. Bingo: depression.

"Five thirty. Or so."

"Don't be late without calling." Finger dip, consume. "Want some?"

"No, thanks."

"Jeez, it seems like I barely see you anymore." Her voice is a ball rolling downhill.

"Busy time," I say.

"You're not going to be around your family forever, you know," she says.

"Well, I could get married and have six kids and we can all live in my room," I say.

"At least we'd still do stuff together. Watch a movie every now and then. Eat cookie dough out of the bowl like we used to. Make valentines."

"Valentine's Day was two weeks ago."

"We used to make valentines together, remember? I'd buy all those paper doilies and the glitter . . ."

"When I was six."

"I loved that," she says.

"I've got to go," I say.

She doesn't answer. I leave the kitchen, close the front door behind me. I have this creepy, gnarled feeling inside. Guilt. God, what'd she want me to do, eat paste and have her tie my shoes for me forever?

The task of the day is to finish the elephant cleaning started by the morning interns. This means Bamboo and Flora, and Flora's tire. I work with Elaine and Evan, who is embroiled in some kind of divorce depression that day and barely talks, except to the animals. I know how it is—sometimes you're sure only they'll understand and/or put up with you. We clean the dirt out from the bottoms of Bamboo's and Flora's feet and give them baths, and when I am done, the legs of my overalls are soaked. Picture washing a four-ton car, only the car is moving.

The task is involving enough that the time goes fast, and I check my cell phone clock only a couple of times, because I am holding one of the hoses. I change out of my overalls about ten to five. My pants are also wet too from the mid-thigh down, so walking around, out toward the viewing area, just before five, after combing my hair and putting on new lip gloss, is also probably a good idea. Not because of anyone, but just so that the air can dry my pants a little. And then back to the elephant house because he isn't there yet, and then out again, and then, oh, shit.

Oh, shit, he's there. He's there, and now I have to breathe, only it's impossible because my lungs are collapsing, folding in on themselves.

I watch him from a bit up the path (stalker!) so that I can catch my breath and until he becomes just the same old him. We practically know each other. Okay, he doesn't have a clue who I am, but I can tell a lot about him already. He is familiar to me now, I remind myself.

Every big happening has a moment of *plunge*, that moment of decision, usually instantaneous even if you've been thinking about it forever. That *now*! Toes at the edge of the pool, looking at the water, one toe in, looking some more, and then, suddenly, you're in, and it's so cold, but nice, too, and you don't even remember where in there you decided to jump.

"Look, Bo, look who's coming. Remember that one? With the tire?" Flora. She's ambling out of the house into the yard with her new manicure. "She sure likes that tire. See, Bo?" The boy points, I can hear the nylon of his jacket swish as he moves his arm, but the baby just squirms in the backpack.

"Dow," the baby says.

"And that one. Remember him, with the really big ears?" Actually, *her* with the really big ears. Tombi. Stomping out with newly bathed cheer.

"Dow," the baby says. "Dow!" The word turns into a half screech.

"Okay, fine." The boy says. He sounds tired. "But no running off."

The boy swings the backpack off his shoulders and around, giving the baby a mini amusement park ride. He holds the baby under the armpits and lifts him out. I still can't tell how old the baby is. A year? A little older? I'm not too experienced with babies—my only real exposure was with our neighbors', the Chens', little girl. They wanted me to babysit when I was about fourteen, but Mom got nervous that something would happen that I couldn't handle, so they had Natalie come over to our house. She was only a couple of months old, and her head was as floppy as my old doll Mrs. Jugs.

The minute the baby's little tennis shoes hit pavement, he takes off running, in this rigid-limbed, forward-leaning way. It seems so unsafe. Like a windup toy headed for the edge of a tabletop. My own feet start moving then, heading to the viewing area where they are. I have this insta-vision—the baby running to me, grabbing my legs. Looking up at me, then smiling. I am going forward, because this is the moment, right now, when the boy and I are going to meet. Two points in need of a line, and now the line is being drawn.

The baby is running in my direction, just like I envisioned. And, yes, when I am in front of him, he stops and looks up. His face freezes in this look of half pleasure/half alarm. I smile. "Hi," I say in a small-children voice. Here is where he is supposed to smile back, big and beaming, the red-jacket boy seeing the connection we already have.

But instead, the baby's mouth twists, contorts. He looks up at me, and his face turns red. And then he begins to cry. Scream, actually. A wail so loud and terrified, even Onyx looks up with concern, and a couple making out by the savannah enclosure stop to watch who might be being kidnapped in case they're interviewed on the news.

"Oh, no," I say. "Oh, I'm sorry." Oh, my God. Horrible. Way to go, Jade! Perfect first impression—his baby screams in fear at you! You make the kid cry, for God's sake! Thanks bunches, Raphael—good job on the nightmare thing!

The boy comes over, lifts his son up in his arms. The baby sobs into his shoulder as if he's been traumatized so terribly he's sure to need therapy far into adulthood. "He's not good with strangers," the boy says over the cries. "Bo, hey. It's okay. Hey, kiddo." He bounces him up and down, pats his back. "She works with the elephants. Right?" he asks.

The baby is still crying, but my shame backs up a step. He'd seen me. He'd been here, when I was here. When I didn't even know it. Sea boy, desert girl.

deb caletti

"Yes," I say. "I help out whenever I can. Almost every day."

"We watched you before," the boy says. "You were hiding pieces of watermelon all over."

"Enrichment. It keeps them interested, working things out."

The baby, Bo, is quieter now. His chin is tucked into his dad's shoulder.

"The little elephant likes you. He sniffed your hair."

I laugh. "Hansa," I say. "She likes smells. You know, my shampoo . . . Hansa's a real handful."

"I know all about that." Bo peeks from the safety of the red jacket.

"I bet. Is this little guy yours?" I ask. I'm bold. I can be. He'd seen me. He'd noticed things about me, as I had noticed things about him.

"Oh, yeah." He smooches Bo on the neck, and Bo wriggles himself further into his dad, into that red jacket, which is right there in front of me. The real red jacket, the real boy, talking. To me. Having a regular old conversation. I am listening to his voice, this real person, this person who is not just an image in my thoughts. "All mine. This is Bo. Say hi, Bo."

Nothing doing.

"Hi, Bo. I'm Jade." I peer back at him.

"Jade?" the boy says. "Wow, that's really pretty."

Heat rises in my cheeks. God, don't blush. Please don't blush. Okay, I'm blushing. I think I'm flaming red. Blushing is so unfair. Might as well wear a sign: WHAT YOU THINK MATTERS TO ME.

He doesn't offer his own name. The conversation stops. Awkward silence. Well, that's it.

"And you?" I have to at least know this. Just this—his name.

"Oh," he says. He seems startled. "Sebastian. Sebastian Wilder."

Awkward silence again.

"Well, I'd better be going," I say.

"Yeah, I better get this guy fed. He's got maybe twenty minutes before he goes ballistic."

"Good luck," I say.

"Maybe we'll see you again," he says.

"That'd be great," I say. "I could show you around."

"Sure," he says, but he doesn't seem sure. Maybe I'd gone too far. Shit, I'd gone too far.

"See you," he says. "Maybe tomorrow." I hadn't gone too far. Okay, I hadn't. I'd done fine.

"Bye," I say. "Bye, Bo."

No response, not that I'm expecting one. I walk away, am almost down the path, when behind me I hear a small voice: "Ba-ba." Bye-bye.

I smile. I refrain from doing what I really feel like doing—leaping and hugging things. Hugging and shouting and doing good deeds for people for the rest of my life. Joy spirals through every part of me, spins and sparkles, lifts up my heart and makes everything look right. Jake Gillette is in the parking lot with his skateboard again, racing over a new ramp, and even his parachute looks bold and majestic.

"Cool skateboard!" I shout, and Jake smiles and does another leap for me. I pass Total Vid. Titus looks out, and this time I wave. He raises his pinkie and thumb in the Hawaiian "hang loose" greeting. The world—it sits in the palm of my hand. It's all mine, if I want it.

Mr. Chen is getting out of his car, coming home from work.

deb caletti

"Hi, Mr. Chen," I say. I hear the singing in my voice.

"Hi, Jade," Mr. Chen says. He sounds surprised. He holds his briefcase and a clump of mail.

"Have a good evening!" I say. The day is one of the most monumental and spectacular in the history of days. I have met the red-jacket boy. And he did not have a wedding ring.

I see the letter on the kitchen counter when I come home, an acceptance to the University of Washington, just a ten-minute drive from home. Mom has already opened it.

"Did you see that, honey?" she shouts from the living room.

"I see it."

"You don't sound too excited. This is wonderful. God, I'm so proud of you."

"I am excited." I am. Everything is working out beautifully. The best school in the state, a red-jacket boy. I'm not sure why I feel this small, grating annoyance. The sense of something being scraped against something else. Maybe I'm just pissed she'd opened my mail. I tell my backstage mind to shut the hell up. I don't want anything to intrude on the happiness I'm feeling. Soaring, red-jacket happiness.

"Well, it's no surprise, though, with your grades. Bring it here so we can read it together."

She has her feet up on the couch, a book open on her knees. She sits up to make room for me and I sit beside her.

"You've got your whole life ahead of you. Wow. God, I'm a greeting card," she says.

"At least not, 'Sorry for your loss.'"

"Really. It's corny, but it's *true*. Can you believe we're looking at this? A letter from college?"

"I know. Freaks me out."

"I'm sure. This is *huge*. Dad hasn't seen it yet," she says. "He's getting changed for dinner. He'll be so pleased."

I hand her the letter, check out the book she is reading. "*The Life and Times of Alexander Hamilton?*"

"It's interesting. Quit with the look. It really is."

"Since when do you read history?"

"I read history," she says. "Mr. Dutton recommended it. It's fascinating. I couldn't put it down. Did you know he was illegitimate?"

"Mr. Dutton?" I say.

"Alexander Hamilton! Not Roger."

Roger?

"Oh. Wow," I say.

"Pretty shocking for those days . . . ," she says.

She's missed my sarcasm. I turn it up a notch. "Now I understand why you're reading a"—I check the back of the book—"682-page book about the guy."

Mom does this thing with her mouth that reminds me of the time Dad took Oliver and me to a trout farm, just after we'd caught the poor targets, pulled them out of the water, and laid them on the dock.

I don't have time to follow this up, because Dad's voice booms from the direction of the kitchen. "Should I be taking this out?" he yells.

"Oh, shit," Mom says. "Dinner. I forgot." She tosses aside my acceptance letter and leaps up. I follow her into the kitchen. Dad is wearing an oven mitt with smiling vegetables on it, and he's holding a pan. The vegetables are the only things smiling. There's a small dark item the size of my fist in the center of the pan.

I crack up. "Was that a roast? Toasted roast. Toasted *miniroast*."

"I didn't even smell it burning," Mom says. "It's supposed to cook slowly, but probably not for . . ." Mom checks her watch. "Oh, my God. Three and a half hours. " She chuckles and so do I.

Dad sets the pan down on the stove with a clatter. He seems pissed. Big deal, so she forgot. You know, give her a break, for God's sake. In the last ten minutes, I've been annoyed at her for opening my mail, and at him for being mean. When Oliver comes downstairs to help me set the table, I'm so glad to see him, I sock his arm. It's one of those times where you look for someone to like just so you don't hate everyone.

At dinner, Oliver chews his roast dramatically. It's pretty impossible—a piece of tire that had self-destructed on the free-way would have been easier. "Okay, all right," Mom says. She is half grinning, too, because, really, it's pretty funny. But Dad actually spits an attempted chunk of beef into his napkin and then shoves his plate away. He's being a real ass, if you ask me.

"I guess reading comes before dinner," he says.

Mom ignores him. She scoots her rice around with the edge of her fork. She doesn't apologize (good), acts as if no one has spoken. She puts a mouthful of rice in, then looks up and meets his eyes. She's daring him to say more—her eyebrows are raised in a silent statement of *Anything else you care to say?* They stare at each other for a moment, saying a thousand unsaids. Oliver has gotten very still. I'm not sure he's even breathing. The silence crawls around into the corners of the room, scary-movie-music style, something-bad-about-to-happen. I count the syllables in *Reading comes before dinner* and end up on my pinkie on the second try. Finally, the silence is more than I can take.

"Oh, my God, I forgot," I say. My voice seems loud. It's better than the silence, though, better than them staring like animals about to fight. "Coach Bardon called yesterday. He cancelled practice tomorrow. Good thing I remembered! Work or something." Mom's head pops up. She looks at me. Her eyes ask the question, and my eyes answer. She rubs the bridge of her nose, hides her smirk behind her hand. She's pissed enough at Dad to go along.

"I don't understand why he took the position if he's never going to show," Dad says.

"Well, don't say anything to him about it," Mom says quickly. "He's a *volunteer*. They're never appreciated as it is. Boy, don't I know."

"I never said I was going to say anything to him. I'm not *going* to say anything to him. I just don't think he should volunteer if he's never going to show. It's a lousy lesson to teach the team. That's his third cancellation."

Oliver kicks me under the table.

"He's obviously a busy man," Mom says. "Who also has a *life* besides *sports practice*."

"We're all busy people," Dad says. "If this continues, I'm talking to the league, volunteer or not."

Oliver kicks me again. After dinner, Mom mouths *You're good!* as we get up from the table. I snag a piece of Oliver's sweatshirt. "Let's get out of here."

"Okay," he whispers.

"I'm starving. Dairy Queen? Something with butter-scotch."

deb caletti

"Ice cream like Mrs. Cartarett's hair," he says. Mrs. Cartarett was his kindergarten teacher. She did have that hair—tall, with a curl on top.

We take Milo, too. He hates the feel of the leather seats of Mom's car, so he gathers himself up and perches on the carpeted mound of the side armrest, tail up, butt against the window and mooning every car we pass. Every time we turn a corner, he balances against the curve like some surfer in *Riding Giants*. Gnarly hot doggin', Milo. Bitchin'.

A few moments later, Oliver and I are happily clutching our pink plastic spoons.

"Don't ever say I don't take care of you," I say.

That night, I lie on my bed and look out my window, into the darkness. It's supposed to be sunny and clear tomorrow, one of those rare February tastes of spring, and so the stars are out, getting ready. I replay my conversation with Sebastian— *Sebastian!*—a thousand times. I watch the white and red lights of an airplane move across the sky. I am soaring, too, like that plane, so full of hope that for once I don't think of the weight of its metal, hanging improbably in midair, the impossibility of that. No, instead I wonder about the people up there. I wonder who is reading a magazine, who is fishing around in their purse for a stick of cinnamon gum, who is quieting a baby. I wonder where they are all heading. I think not of wings falling from the sky, but of wheels touching down, just as they should. The airplane landing. One piece, whole. I think of the doors opening, revealing a new place—a place so bright and welcoming it would make you blink.

CHAPTER EIGHT

Animals who are bored in captivity will think of ingenious ways to amuse themselves. A chimpanzee will pretend to get his arm stuck in the bars of his cage, or will hang by his teeth from a piece of string he's found and spin around. One lion realized that if he urinated at a certain angle, he could spray his visitors and make them shriek . . .

—Dr. Jerome R. Clade, *The Fundamentals of Animal Behavior*

American Government is group anesthesia. It's so mind numbingly dull that I stoop to counting the ceiling panels and the floor tiles. After that, I watch Jason Olsen flick pieces of pencil lead, trying to hit the bottom of Alicia Watanabe's shoe. He actually succeeds once, and I have to refrain from clapping. Of course, Mr. Arron isn't teaching us the fascinating, page-turning, and dinner-burning excitement of Alexander Hamilton's illegitimacy, so who can blame me.

I bolt out of there, but so does everyone else, and we jam up the doorway like cattle moving toward the slaughterhouse. Or Calculus, rather—same thing. After that, Jenna drives me and Hannah and this other new friend of Hannah's, Kayla Swenson, to McDonald's for lunch, and even that model of fast-food frenzy seems slower than a stationary bike on a freeway. I am so looking forward to getting to the zoo later that time has turned slow and oozing.

"I really liked the rest of the campus, and then the tour's

almost over and I have to go to the bathroom," Jenna tells us. "I go in there, and I'm washing my hands, and I see this sticker on the tampon dispenser. It says something like, 'The apostle Paul says to let the love of Jesus Christ guide your every action.'"

"*Every* action?" Hannah says.

"That's just it," Jenna says.

"On the tampon display?" Kayla says. "That's just twisted." The weatherman was right about the day's weather—it is crisp and blue but still February cold, which doesn't stop Kayla from wearing this tiny skirt that barely covers her ass, thanks for sharing. Kayla is a cheerleader, so ass showing is part of her regular daily routine, same as some people brush their teeth.

"I'm just thinking that maybe the student population there isn't as serious as they should be," Jenna says. She crumples up her fries bag, wipes the table with napkins even though we haven't spilled anything.

"Isn't that a good thing?" Hannah says.

"Yeah, you know, I don't see how you're going to have any fun at a Christian school," Kayla says.

"Depends on what kind of fun. There are lots of different kinds of fun," Jenna says.

"*Fun* fun," Kayla says. Her Coke straw has lipstick on it. "Guy fun. Party fun. Drinking fun."

I'm staying out of this. It's the whole culture of all-consuming nowness I try to avoid. Ever present and screaming its message in the halls, on television, on everyone's personal web pages. Do me, I'm yours. I'm part of the counterculture who actually thinks about the future. Subversive activities are always best kept a secret, so I keep my mouth shut. I take the lid off my milk shake, watch the blob of ice cream come sliding down the cup, heading for a collision with my face.

"You guys just don't get it," Jenna says.

"Isn't it time to go?" Kayla says. "I don't have a watch."

I open wide, slide in the ice cream, aim the lid back on the cup, and get up. "Yeah, we better get back."

Jenna is silent on the ride back, but it doesn't matter, because Hannah and Kayla don't shut up the whole way.

It goes something like this:

Kayla: I'm just about to go into the dressing room, and I turn and there's Chad, and I just about have a heart attack because I haven't seen him since all that, and I just freeze, and of course he still looks so hot, and then I say to Melanie, 'Let's get the fuck out of here,' and I just get in line with what I've got because it looked great on the hanger and if I put it back and come back later I know it's gonna be gone, so I buy it and now I've got this pink shirt and it's got this elastic right here . . .

Hannah: Ugh.

Kayla: I know it. But, shit—*Chad*.

Hannah: I'm a sucker for guys with sexy eyes. And Chad . . .

Kayla and Hannah: Has sexy eyes! (laughter)

The whole time, Jenna is breathing out her nose like a cartoon bull about to charge. I'm biting my tongue, because I'm trying not to remind Hannah that she's not a sucker for guys with sexy eyes, she's a sucker for guys with any eyes at all.

I am starting to get that vaguely irritated feeling again, that sense of fingernails scraping down my internal chalkboard. We are friends, it seems, simply because we've always *been* friends. Like Milo and his blankie, Flora and her tire. My friends are a habit, same as the way I always put my socks on before I put on my pants.

"Great, Abe. Everything's terrific." I'm hoping to make this quick. My weekly appointment and I can't cancel without my parents finding out and it being a big deal. If I hurry out of there, I'll still have an hour or so with the elephants, and a chance to see Sebastian.

Abe taps his pencil, just waits. I know he does it so I'll fill in the blank space between us with words. I know it, but, shit, it always works.

"Terrific, really. You know, except for my parents' having a long-distance relationship even though they live in the same house."

"You think they might be growing through some changes?"

Another Abe-ism. "Are you a vegetarian, Abe?"

"No. I've tried. But I can only go about three days before I'm craving some huge juicy cheeseburger." He lets out a little groan of carnivorous pleasure.

"When you say things like 'growing through some changes' you sound like a vegetarian. I don't think they're growing so much as about to kill each other."

"I didn't say growth doesn't hurt." Another thing he says often. So often, in fact, he has a poster on one wall: ALL NEUROTIC PAIN IS CAUSED BY THE AVOIDANCE OF REAL PAIN—JUNG.

"Can you kill with silence?"

"Oh, yeah. Absolutely," Abe says. "How do you feel about that silence?"

"Makes me nuts. All the unsaids are like a heavy-metal band playing at some higher vibration only me and dogs can hear."

"And you manage the stress how?"

"I get out of the house. The volunteering's been great." No way am I going to tell him more right then. I look up at the clock in his office.

"Attacks?" he asks.

"Just an almost-once, but I'd had a cup of coffee, which was stupid." Coffee is not my friend. It gets me feeling agitated and looking around for a reason why.

"Are you late for your plane?"

"What?"

"You keep looking at the clock."

"Oh. No. It's just . . . I'm going to meet a friend."

Abe smiles. Taps the damn pencil.

"I'm kind of . . . looking forward to it."

"Jade?" Abe says.

"Yeah?"

"Go. Get out of here."

I have my mom's car, which is great, because I basically have this traveling freshening-up station. Don't get me wrong—I'd never put on makeup while I'm driving or anything like that, because I could just see me running over some bicyclist and killing him because I had a mascara wand stuck in my eye. No way in hell. Just the idea of it makes me want to unwrap a cough drop, quick. But as soon as I park, I swipe on the travel-size deodorant I keep in my backpack and put on a little make-up. I want him to accept me as I am, but I want to look good too.

I change into my overalls, and notice that Onyx isn't in the elephant house. I go around out front, look for her saggy old self in the enclosure. No Onyx. Maybe she's just out of range,

deb caletti

but I get this little seed of worry. I find Damian in his office.

"Good afternoon," he says.

"Hi," I say. "Where's Onyx?"

"You didn't hear."

"Oh, no." I have a sick feeling. My stomach rolls up, sinks in sadness preparation.

"Chai charged her. She's being treated. She's all right."

Relief. *All right.* All right meant *not dead*. It hit me then with tidal-wave, lightning, hurricane force—how much I cared for them. The devastation I'd feel if something happened to one of them. What we risk when we invest in one another.

"What happened?"

"Baby Hansa. Onyx was being aggressive with her. Butting her, shoving. Mama Chai was furious. It was a dangerous situation for Elaine, who was there. And Hansa. I was just on the phone with Point Defiance. She'll have to be moved if this continues." Point Defiance—the zoo in Tacoma. "They'll take her, but Onyx is suffering. More rejection—is that the answer? I think not. But I have to think of Hansa and our humans, too."

"I feel so bad for her," I say.

"Every elephant you see in captivity who was not born there, each is a witness to violence, abused, abandoned. Broken animals. Sometimes I do not feel like an elephant keeper. I feel like a social service worker."

"At least they have you, Damian."

"They have me. And I'm glad for that. But I can't help thinking of my Jum. Jum has no one."

My task of the day is to take over Lee's place in watching Hansa after Lee goes home. Hansa had been eating sand over the past few days, and there is worry that she might fatally clog up her stomach. Victor Iverly, the zoo director, thought that maybe Hansa's diet was deficient, but Dr. Brodie disagreed. Damian personally oversees all diets, and he had another answer. Every time anyone turned their head, Hansa would dart across the yard to a patch of dirt and start shoveling it in her mouth, causing whoever was nearby to hurry over to her in a panic, yelling, "Hansa, no!" This was what she was after, Damian said. She just loves the attention she gets, all the shouting and running. So now we have to watch her, and if she does it, just very calmly and with no fuss redirect her trunk from the dirt with the bullhook.

I love Onyx, but I am kind of glad she is out of the yard when I get there. I think about Elaine and the morning's incident—Elaine with her functional cargo pants and firm demeanor would have handled it, no problem—but a charging Chai would have freaked me out. It makes me remember that release I had to sign, about my death or injury. My mother started trying to talk me out of the whole thing when she saw it, until my dad told her to hand it over, bearing down hard on the pen as he signed. If I didn't take risks, he'd said, I'd end up being one of those people who live limited lives, too afraid to take airplanes and swim in the sea and ride on boats. People whose fear of death becomes fear of life. Still, there are risks, and then there are RISKS, and Onyx, beloved as she is, is a bit like this kid in my fourth-grade class—usually quiet and sweet, but once frustrated enough that he picked up his desk and threw it across the room. I think they sent that kid to Point Defiance too, and I'm only half kidding about that.

Anyway, the dirt-eating Hansa doesn't make me nervous.

deb caletti

She's just a really large toddler. So I babysit her for a long while, and I don't mind just standing there, because even though it is February, the sun is toasty enough and everything looks bright and the tang of elephant shit warmed by the sun smells kind of good. It's a positive smell, somehow, like when you drive past a farm with your windows rolled down and it's the kind of day where your tank top makes your arms feel free and brown and healthy and the backs of your legs stick a little to the vinyl car seat. That grassy, cow-crap-and-livestock smell that means it's been a day of open windows. Life is good babysitting this elephant, and Hansa is behaving, too, except that I can tell she is watching me out of the corners of her eyes. Finally, sure enough, I turn my head, and off she jets to the patch of dirt.

I'm probably not the best person to be safeguarding Hansa's digestive health, because the reason I turn my head is that I see Sebastian coming down the path, his jacket over one arm. Once I see him, I really don't want to turn away. I'm sorry, Hansa, if you ate extra dirt because of me. But I see Sebastian and my heart lifts and I just want to watch him, same as I used to when he was on the computer screen. I want to see him walk toward me and know that there will not be a world between us this time. Someone walking toward you is such a simple, happy-to-be-alive thing.

Bo is with him, asleep in the backpack. Bo's cheek rests against Sebastian's back. Sebastian waves when he sees me and I wave back, then go to retrieve Hansa from her dirt feast.

"Is she digging holes?" Sebastian asks.

"Worse. Eating sand."

"Oh, man, Bo used to do that. Out on the beach. Once, he

was rolling something around in his mouth and I stuck my finger in and fished around, and he was sucking on a rock." Sebastian laughs.

"Yum," I say.

"You'd think I never fed him, the way he was going at it."

"Maybe they're tastier than we think. Do you live near the water? You said 'the beach.'"

Our back-and-forth stops. He pauses. "Well, I did . . . I . . . Not now."

I've said something wrong, hit a tender place. Awkwardness butts in; it's a rude person shoving to the front of a line. Maybe he'd had an upsetting divorce. Maybe his wife left him. Maybe a thousand things. Maybe I am too eager to get information. Maybe I am pushy.

A couple appears with a small child and a baby in a stroller. The man, in a baseball cap, says the usual. *See the elephant, Jakey? See? Say Hi. Say hi, elephant.* Jakey ignores Dad, picks a leaf off of a tree. Mom rattles the ice in a drink she's carrying. *Let's go see the monkeys,* she says. *They're not so boring.*

"That's what their neighbors say about them," I say to Sebastian.

"This one guy threw an empty Fritos bag in there once. I wanted to kick his ass."

"Or dump garbage on his lawn."

"Really." The uneasiness is gone again.

"Bo's just sleeping away today," I say.

"He's been a monster. He's just resting up for more, I'm sure."

"This one too," I say, nodding my chin in the direction of Hansa. "See her looking at me?" I ask. "She's watching me."

"She sure is," he says.

deb caletti

"The minute I turn my head, she'll go cruising over there." I keep my head straight, watching Hansa. It's easier that way. Sebastian is so close to me that my heart is going nuts—not in the usual, full-anxiety mode, but in this new, soaring, zipping, full way, same as those planes at air shows. The fence is between us (always something between us), but I am near enough to smell his breath, and I think he's just eaten a mint. Little poofs of freshness bounce in my direction.

"Bo does the same thing with the telephone. And the remote control. Or my grandma's record albums. Or just about anything."

"It must be exhausting."

"Oh, man."

"Your grandma helps you?"

"Yeah. She lives with us. She watches Bo while I'm at work. She saved us, she really did." He looks away, rubs his jaw line with his hand.

The question sits between us, large and unspoken, just like, well, an *elephant* in the room. The question about her, the mother, the one who had given Bo that white-blond hair so unlike Sebastian's brown curls. I want to ask. I want to *know*. I'd lived with the mystery of him for months now. But I don't want to go to the tender places when we barely know each other. Maybe he needs to cross bridges carefully too. He is here, I am here, both of us in front of the camera, and that's all that matters for now.

Hansa has lost interest in the sand. She wanders away. Damian was right—our calm reactions take away all the fun. "She's going off to think up more trouble," I say. Sebastian smiles. He has the perfect smile, meaning slightly imperfect, just a little off. There's something about exact, white, ordered teeth that seems insincere.

"I should let you get going," he says. "You're busy."

"I'm about done," I say. "I'm heading home." I can't tell him what I am heading home to—AP American Government, Calculus, AP English. Schoolwork. Maybe a phone call from Hannah so she can tell me about some shoes she bought, or an IM from Michael asking about what pages we're supposed to read. Dinner with Mom and Dad. My life seems so far from what his must be. My life seems so *young*.

"Have you worked here long?" Sebastian asks.

"Just a few months," I say. "Do you come here a lot?" *As if you don't know, Jade.*

"I used to come every day, or, you know, when I could. I'd bring Bo after work. Or just myself." *At night sometimes. You'd climb the fence. You'd watch the stars. You'd tilt back your head and look at the sky. You'd think it over, whatever it was.*

"Just to see these guys?" I say. "Or all the animals?"

"These guys," he says. "I read a book that hooked me. This man studied elephant troupes and then ended up raising an abandoned calf. So good, it made me want to see them in person."

"Sounds great."

"I could lend it to you," he says.

"I'd love that."

"I'll bring it next time," he says.

"Thanks," I say. We hit the sudden conversational roadblock, that place where you're talking along just fine with plenty of road and ideas before you, when, all at once, bam. The silence of the end of the line. Your brain races away like mad, trying to think of what to say next, but all the possibilities are fading

deb caletti

fast, same as trying to remember a dream after you've woken up. No, too late.

"I'll leave you to your visit," I say.

"Okay. Well, bye."

"Bye."

"Jade?" he says. "Good to see you again."

"You too," I say. Casually, though my insides feel anything but. I wave, walk to the elephant house. I hang up my overalls and dissect the conversation, and I remember how I asked too many personal questions and how he had seemed uncomfortable, and then there was that awkward silence when no one said anything about Bo's mother.

I go to the bathroom to wash my hands, and then I see that I have a very noticeable set of brown mascara spider tracks under each eye, and I just about die. Shit, I'd sneezed when I was in the dusty pen, and should have checked then. I convinced myself I've completely screwed up because a) I'm a conversational imbecile, and b) I looked awful and had been acting like I looked great. He probably won't even come back. God, I'm an idiot. I unwrap a cough drop partly out of habit and partly because I'm suddenly feeling this steel ball in my chest.

And then I remember all the good things. He'd been glad to see me again. He was going to lend me his book. And that mint. A breath mint. A breath mint means you care.

I say good-bye to Damian, to Delores in her little ticket box. The sun is just in those beginning stages of going down, when it spreads magic light on everything. An orangey glow warms the trees and sidewalks and even makes the garbage-can lids look beautiful. Jake Gillette's parachute, too, is golden and glowy, and gives me that bittersweet sense that time is passing. The "76" ball at the gas station glints in its slow twirl. I don't see Titus in his pineapple shirt, but I do see Mr. Chen coming home from work. The fountain is on in the center of our building complex, and the grass is yellowed with twilight.

"Beautiful day," I say to him.

"Ah, yes," he says, as he hauls his laptop from the backseat. "In spite of being rag-dolled at the office." Rag-dolled—to be drilled, rolled, and tumbled by a wave. He'd seen *Riding Giants*, too.

I hurry through an average, nonburnt dinner. Dad goes downstairs to work on his train, Mom leaves to call volunteers for the Winter Art Walk, and Oliver heads to his room to read *The Ultimate Narnia Fan Handbook*. I'm anxious to get through my homework, and I ignore the message from Jenna, who wants to talk about Kayla and what a bitch she is. I think she actually said "witch" in the voicemail, but if that's what she means, I don't see what difference the vocabulary makes.

I finish my homework by about ten fifteen, and it could have taken me longer, but I want to have some time to think, so I rush. After I pack everything away in my backpack, I clear my dresser of all the patron saints except for St. Raphael. I give him front-and-center billing.

Raphael flickers, and I sprawl on my bed and look through my lava-lamp frame, at the stars glittering, at the wisp of a cloud drawing across the sky like the tip of a paintbrush. I hold up the moments with Sebastian, gaze at them again with a gentle eye, with careful hope. I do the necessary work of falling in love, that time spent alone with your imagination. I close my eyes, remember the smell of mint, the baby's cheek against his back, his smile, not quite perfect.

The scent of a blown-out match, melting wax, fills my room. St. Raphael, patron saint of meetings, of young lovers. Patron saint of joy.

CHAPTER NINE

During a sparring match between chimpanzees, female chimpanzees will stand on the sidelines, wave their arms, jump up and down, and screech their encouragement. In other words, chimps have cheerleaders . . .
    —Dr. Jerome R. Clade, *The Fundamentals of Animal Behavior*

"Didn't you have a friend with a car?" Kayla asks. She's going home with Hannah, and we are climbing the stairs of the bus. I see Michael and Akello, and I walk down the aisle and sit down in the seat behind them.

"She got a job after school," Hannah says. They take the seat across the aisle from me. The three of us never would have fit in one, because Kayla has brought her pom-poms, which she holds on her lap and clutches like an old lady with her purse.

"I haven't ridden a school bus since we had a field trip to Pioneer Village in the eighth grade," Kayla says. She bounces on the seat a little, making her pom-poms *chsh-chsh*. "I never get why these things don't have seat belts."

"I never got that either," I say.

"Where'd Jenna get a job?" Akello asks. "I need a job."

"Her church," I say.

"That's out," Akello says.

"If I had a job, I'd never keep up my grades," Michael says. The bus rumbles to a start, lurches forward in takeoff.

"I always thought it'd be funny, you know, when we have to job-shadow? To do a priest or something," Kayla says. Actually, it's mildly funny for once.

"The pope," Hannah says. They both crack up.

"Pope for a day," Hannah says. She's on a roll.

"It could be the prize on some radio station. Be the seventy-seventh caller and you could win," Kayla says.

"Call in when you hear . . ." Hannah says.

"'Jive Talkin'" by the Bee Gees," Akello says. Michael and I laugh. Hannah and Kayla stare.

"Do you guys want to go to the movies with us tomorrow night?" Akello says.

"Saturday?" Kayla asks.

"Yeah, that'd be right, since today is Friday," Akello says. Michael whacks him on the arm. "What?" he says. I like that about Akello. He doesn't get the social rules—*Don't insult the intelligence of a cheerleader, no matter how tempting*—or else he just doesn't care.

"Par-tee," Kayla says. "We're busy." Kayla is in "the popular group," obviously, since she is a cheerleader. "Popular group" is a phrase that's slightly embarrassing to use. If you use it, you aren't in it. I always think it's kind of weird how everyone knows who this group is and who it isn't. How does it form, anyway? It's not like there's some sign-up sheet. But you know and they know. I never can figure out what the separating factor is. It isn't just pom-poms or looks. Take Hailey Nelson, for example, with her orange hair and plain face, who is as popular as they come; and Renee Desiradi, who is gorgeous and shy and who no one pays attention to. Someday she's going to be famous and they'll show her yearbook picture on television and none of us will even remember her. No, what I think it comes down to is who asserts a sense of dominance, just like baboons. It isn't necessarily the strongest and biggest and best-looking baboon that'll be the leader, but the cockiest and most self-assured, the one who assumes he'll win any fight. I guess we tend to believe people's high opinion of themselves, whether it is earned or not. And don't go buying into that psychology BS that says overly confident people only act that way because they don't feel good about themselves inside. They feel *great* about themselves. They can be stupid, irresponsible, a smart-ass, with failing grades or a sex-will-save-me pout, and will still walk around with the self-esteem a Nobel Prize winner should have but probably doesn't.

I'm thinking we ought to rethink the whole self-esteem thing. It should almost be a dirty word. I mean, look at Kayla. She has the intelligence of a tree stump, and its sense of humor. She's less about real attractiveness than she is about advertising, like those cereals with zingy boxes and toys inside and that make the milk turn chocolate but taste disgusting. The weather had turned rainy again, and she's still wearing this tiny T-shirt and this tiny skirt with rhinestones on the back pocket, like she's Western Barbie. Humiliating, only she'll never realize it. She's the kind of girl who shows how hot she is because she has nothing else to offer, who doesn't realize that hotness has an expiration date. Yet, I'm still a little nervous talking to her, like she's holding a lottery ticket she just might or might not decide to hand over to me. It is nuts, if you stop to think about it. I give her this power, and it's kind of like voting some idiot into office. But, hey, we're good at that, too.

"Sorry we can't go to the movies," Hannah says. Now that

they'd become friends, Hannah is hooked to Kayla like life support.

"I mean, you guys can *come*," Kayla says. "To the party. If you."

"Sure," Michael says.

"It's at Alex Orlando's," Kayla says. "You know where he lives."

"Oh, yeah," Michael says. He has no idea, I am positive. He'll have to MapQuest it. This seems particularly humiliating, Michael sitting at his computer, typing in Alex Orlando's address that he'd found in the phone book. "You'll come, Jade."

"I don't know. Probably," I say. This I know: It's easier to say yes and cancel later then to say no when people are right there. Lying on the spot is an acquired skill. Already, I am feeling the heavy ball forming in my chest, this weighted hand pressing down. It's new-situation anxiety, this time, rather than about-to-die anxiety. Mom would love it, me going, but, hey, my skirt with the rhinestones is at the cleaners.

My inner turmoil isn't noticed. In fact, everyone has already moved on. Akello has pulled out his Twain reading for English, and Michael is writing something down on his calendar that I can only imagine—ALEX'S PARTY—in stubby pencil. Hannah and Kayla are talking without saying anything. Their conversation goes like this:

Hannah: Uh-huh.

Kayla: It was like, ugh!

Hannah: I know.

Kayla: *Shit.* Come on!

Hannah: Well, you know, whatever.

Kayla: I guess, but still.

Hannah: Yeah.

Kayla: You know?

Hannah: Yeah.

The bus arrives at Hannah's stop and they both get up. Kayla adjusts her clothing, tugs on her hem, then twists her skirt so the zipper is centered.

"Aren't you freezing?" Akello asks her. Michael whacks him again. "Whaat?" he says.

"You would have loved it, Sis," Oliver says. "They had this camera, hidden in a pile of crap. Or this stuff that looked like a pile of crap."

"Cool," I say.

"It was. They followed the herd that way. They even showed a baby elephant being born. All the elephants gathered around to help it stand up. And then the male came, and they all circled around the baby to protect it."

Oliver is telling me about the video they'd seen in science that day. I pour myself a glass of cranberry juice, which is supposed to be full of antioxidants to keep you healthier. It is going to compensate for the brownie I am going to eat before I go over to the zoo. I have to be careful. The way I eat, my arteries are going to clog and I'm going to have a heart attack at thirty-five, like those type-A businessmen.

"Imagine the camera guy who has to hide it there." I take a swig of my drink.

"No, seriously," he says. "It was great." I can tell I am frustrating him a little, which makes the sicko part of me want to do it more. "It was awesome."

"I still want to know if it was real crap or manufactured crap. That'd make a difference."

"Sis," he says.

"You know, smell versus no smell," I say.

"Quit it," he says. His voice is so full of disappointment that I feel bad.

"Okay, I'm sorry. Tell me about it quickly, 'cause I've got to get out of here or I'll be late."

"Never mind."

"Come on," I say.

"I'll tell you later."

"O-kay."

"You would have really liked it," he says sadly.

My conscience would be guiltier if I weren't in such a hurry, and if I weren't so looking forward to getting to the zoo. I finish my snack, brush my teeth, zip through the dining room. I don't know where Mom is, but there's a stack of books on the dining room table. *The Jefferson Connection; The Forefathers at Home. Washington and Delaware.* Okay, it seems strange. But I figure I don't have to worry until she starts wearing a three-cornered hat and hanging old pistols above the fireplace. Then again, just because I worry about everything, doesn't mean I worry about the right things.

"Elaine and I can do it," I say to Damian. Bamboo and Flora need to be washed.

"Elaine is babysitting Hansa. And besides, washing them is one of my favorite things," Damian says. "It's so satisfying. Damn the administrative work."

"It's my favorite too," I say.

"Prepare to be drenched, then."

"All right," I say. I'm glad I won't be in the same place as yesterday if Sebastian comes, sitting there like I'm waiting for him. Okay, I *am* waiting for him, but I don't want to seem like it. Plus, Damian is right—washing the elephants is satisfying. It is like washing your car, as I've said before, but it makes the car happy too.

The elephants have a bathing area outside in their enclosure, but it's so important to keep them clean that we try to give them a daily bath as well. Baths are a big part of their lifestyle in the wild, and baths protect them from disease and insect bites and from getting too dried out. It also relaxes them, just like us with our bath beads and scented candles. The best time to bathe them is in the morning, but sometimes there isn't enough time for everyone. The one thing you've got to watch out for is that the elephant hasn't just done a bunch of exercise, or the sudden change in temperature can make them sick—like if you jumped into a cold shower after running a marathon.

We bring Flora and her tire in first. Flora lies down so I can squirt her with the hose. I have to be careful not to aim at any of her tender areas—inside her ears, near her eyes, her genitals, the tip of her trunk. Damian does the actual washing, because he can do it safely and quickly. In India, they bathe the elephants in the river, he's told me. He washes Flora's face and tusk, her stomach, and hind legs, scrubbing with a pumice stone. We wash her tire, too. All the while, Flora is making these little squeaks of happiness. The elephants love the water, but maybe it's just baths of any kind they love, because they take mud baths, too.

We work hard with Flora and then Bamboo, and then we let them out into the enclosure. Bamboo strides off (probably to cover herself in dust, same as Milo rolls in the grass after a bath), and Damian and I watch her, like a couple of proud parents. Damian chuckles.

"What?" I say.

"I was thinking about how scared you were when you first came," Damian says.

"Real funny," I say.

"It was funny, all right," he says, chuckling away.

"Well, you know, they're kind of *large*."

"You are progressing," Damian says. I look over at him and he grins at me. He nods. "Yes, indeed."

We admire Flora next, as she ambles over to the others. I know it is about time for Sebastian to come, and I keep checking and watching until I finally see him. Suddenly, he's there, and my heart just rises up again. Part of it is happiness, and part relief. I guess I halfway expected him to just not show, to disappear, taking this new joy with him. But no. He's there and he sees me and waves, and I wave back.

"Ah," Damian says.

"What?"

"Hmmm," he raises his eyebrows up and down.

"Quit," I say.

"You are progressing more than I even realized."

"You're embarrassing me."

"He has a baby on his back."

"I know. He's not married, but . . . Is it a bad thing? He's got . . . a different life."

"He's a responsible young man. Look, do you see? He has given the child a graham cracker even if it means the crumbs are sure to be in his hair. And you are a young woman. You are not an animal in an enclosure. And he has waved at you and you are still standing here."

"Damian? Thanks."

"I'll see you tomorrow."

I run back to the elephant house, take off my wet overalls, wash my hands. I hurry out to the viewing area—*Don't leave, don't leave, don't leave*—and hope I don't look as awful as I probably do.

Sebastian smiles when he sees me approaching. Bo ignores me, intent on his graham cracker, and Damian was right about the soggy pieces of brown that have dropped from Bo's hands and landed on the side of Sebastian's head. It's the third time we've seen each other, and something about this is significant. I can feel the change between us. The third time means the start of familiarity.

"Hi, guys," I say. "I'm a mess, and I'm embarrassed to see you." It's that trick prosecuting attorneys use, right? Where they bring up all of the flaws in their case first, before the other guy does?

"No, you look great," he says. Which I'm sure I hear wrong. What he says is, *You're muddy and wet and smelly.* What he says is, *You've got mascara there, under your eye.*

"I was washing Bamboo and Flora. Flora—there, the small one with the pink around her ears? And Bamboo—the big one. She's the matriarch."

"You think they all look the same at first. But then you realize," Sebastian says.

"I know. And their personalities are so different."

"I brought you that book," Sebastian says. "But I left it in the car. I can't believe I forgot it. I can go get it. . . ."

deb caletti

"I'm heading out," I say. "I can walk with you when you guys are ready."

"We're ready. We only came by for a minute. I like to take Bo out for a while when I come home. It gives him and Tess a break from each other."

"Tess? Your grandmother?"

"Yeah."

"Do you guys live around here?" We start walking. It's nice walking beside Sebastian. There's a coziness to it. The easy normality of heading in the same direction.

"You know where the houseboats are? By the Fremont Bridge? We live in one of those."

"Wow. That must be great." Seattle has a couple of houseboat "neighborhoods." Floating houses moored in rows along docks. They range from narrow and grand to quirky shingled shacks, a mixed-up combination of bobbing lives all packed close.

"Not the easiest with a little guy who just wants to *go*. Not much room to run around. And he's in this fearless stage, where he bolts and doesn't think. And all I do is see danger everywhere—him falling in the water, him escaping and us not realizing. Every other word out of my mouth is 'no.'"

I understand that, seeing danger everywhere. We leave through the entry gate, pass Delores in her little box. She pops her head up, raises one eyebrow at me. Man, I can't get away with anything in this place.

"That water all around would make you a wreck," I say.

"Exactly. I want to put him in a life jacket every time we walk to the car. Maybe I can just keep him in a life jacket the rest of his life. Here we are."

He has a really old Volvo, one of the square, boxy ones, with a car seat in the back, along with assorted children's books and toys and bottles and crumbs. It's the same way Mrs. Chen's car looks, while Mr. Chen's is vacuumed and ordered and spotless.

Sebastian swings the backpack off his shoulders, sets it down, and then lifts Bo out. "God, Bo, look at you." Bo has made a smeary mess with the graham cracker. He has it around his face, his hands, and down the front of his shirt. "How much of that got in your mouth?" Sebastian says.

"You had fun with that, didn't you," I say to him.

"I've got to warn you, he hates the car seat." Sebastian holds the crackery Bo away from himself, aims Bo's rear end toward the seat, and backs him in. Sure enough, as soon as Bo is ducked into the car, he straightens himself and stiffens. He starts to shriek. "Come on, Bo," Sebastian pleads. They wrestle a bit, until finally Sebastian is able to get the strap over Bo's head and buckle him in. He clicks the belt shut, closes the car door. Bo's face is red and devastated, still screaming behind the glass.

"Whew," Sebastian says.

"Whew," I say.

"All right," Sebastian says.

"I hate to even mention it, but the book?"

"Oh, God, I forgot." Sebastian opens the driver's side door, letting a few of Bo's protests escape. "Come on, Bo," he says. "Relax, man." Sebastian takes off his coat. He roots around in the front seat, plucks the book from the passenger seat, and shuts the door again. His face is flushed, and he stands there in his curls and a navy blue cotton shirt, and, God, he looks good. His shoulders are broad and strong.

"Here," he says. I laugh. He's just gone through a lot of effort to say that word.

deb caletti

"Thank you," I say. I pretend to read the back, but the text just floats meaninglessly past. "You look so good," I say, and shit! Oh, God, that's not what I meant. Shit! "It looks good. The book." I feel the blush coming, stampeding in. I curse my backstage mind. I can't believe it. Oh, my God.

"Jade, I . . ." Shit, what? Am I right? He's hesitating, struggling with something. I am such an idiot! But, wait a sec. I'm not sure he's flushed from wrestling Bo. It's not really a flush. It's more . . . Is *he* blushing? "I've got this child," he says.

I wait.

"And I know we don't even know each other, but it's been great, you know, just talking a little to someone who's not either under two or over sixty." He laughs.

"I'm glad," I say.

"Since we moved here . . . I mean, I don't have a lot of time to go out, you know, with Bo. But I work at this bookstore, and there's a coffee place there, and I was wondering if maybe you might want to come by tomorrow night, because I'm working. I mean, I'll be working, but I could take some time . . ."

"I'd really like that." I would love that. I would so love that.

"I know this isn't the usual thing, guy with kid, not the kind of *date* you're used to . . ."

I shoot past humiliation, roller coaster to relief again. I'm feeling so light, there's the possibility I might take off right there, lift up, like those dreams you have where you suddenly realize you can fly.

"That would be great."

"The store—you know Armchair Books?"

"No."

"Greenlake?"

"I can find it."

"Right by the place where they rent bikes."

"I can find that," I say.

"Eight-ish?"

"That's great."

"All right." He claps his hands together.

I look at him, and do something I would have never done if I'd had time to think. I raise my hand, take a chunk of graham cracker from his hair. He reaches for my fingers, turns them to see what I had retrieved. "Oh, no," he says, and brushes my hand clean. Then he holds my fingers for a moment, just a moment, and looks at them as if he'd just discovered something.

I, too, discover something right then, as he holds my fingers. I look up, and realize that I had stepped onto the bridge, that now I am on the other side. I am on the other side, and there is Sebastian next to me, looking at my hand, both of us, it seems, wondering how we'd gotten there.

CHAPTER TEN

Beavers make specific mate choices. They may completely ignore members of the opposite sex until they see "the one." Then the pair will go off, play, mate, build a home. They stay bonded though life, though if a partner dies, the beaver may eventually "remarry" . . .

—Dr. Jerome R. Clade, *The Fundamentals of Animal Behavior*

"He's pretty cute," Delores says on Saturday when I come for work.

"You noticed," I say.

"I noticed he had a baby, too. Is it his?" Delores circles a word in her seek-and-find book.

"Yes."

"Where's the mother?"

"I'm not sure yet," I say.

"I'd make that a priority to find out," she says.

"Okay."

"It could be complicated."

"I know," I say. I did know.

"You're young, and a child . . . whew."

"Okay."

"He's young. And a child . . . You know?"

"I know."

"But he sure is cute," Delores says.

The early morning jobs at the elephant house are cleaning stalls, laying new hay, washing elephants, and feeding them. On weekends we try to do this before the zoo opens, since we get the most visitors then, and it's best to have the animals out where people can see them. Enrichment tasks, like hiding fruit and adding new toys, are best done in the afternoon, so zoo goers can watch. That morning, I find Damian (who only takes Sundays off and is on call even then) scrubbing Onyx.

"Damian, I think you must spend half your life soaking wet," I say.

"Oh, I don't mind. I could give this job to one of you, but then I'd be miserable."

"Hey, Onyx," I say. "You big old girl. You old softie." Onyx is smiling, her lips curled up.

"Washing these beasts, it relaxes me. You, too, right, Onyx?" He pats her side. "Thinking time. I remember my home, the river, and my Jum and family."

"Your poor hands. Permanently wrinkled."

He stops, looks at his hands. Onyx lifts her big head and nudges him, same as Milo when you're done petting him. "Maybe so. And what of you? I'm surprised you are here today. I thought you would be on a date with that responsible boy."

"Tonight."

"Ah. Falling in love is such a magical time."

"We just met, Damian. I'm not in love."

Damian laughs. "I am going to have you clean the stables today, since you are already so full of shit."

"Great," I say. "Thanks a lot."

"Every job will be a pleasure today," Damian promises.

deb caletti

When I get home, I tell Mom I am going to a party at Alex Orlando's house. She knows who Alex Orlando is, of course. She looks so excited, I worry for a minute she'll want to come along. Suddenly, she's overly interested in my clothes, and she's suggesting this really short skirt I bought when I was in one of those stores with the loud, pumping music—the kind of store that makes you think you're brave enough to wear anything, until the music is no longer and reality hits. It's weird she's acting this way, because this is the woman who's been telling me for years that a guy should appreciate who you are, not what you look like; that you demean yourself if you advertise that you're just someone for them to have sex with. She's never really been one of those mothers who'll let you wear anything if it helps your popularity. But then again, I've never been invited to Alex Orlando's house. She hands me the too-tight sweater bought with the above-mentioned skirt. If she knew I would wear what she suggested to meet a guy of an undefined age who I had just met, who has a *baby*, she would have strangled me with her new leather belt she's just also offered to lend me. But to Alex Orlando's house, no problem. Alex Orlando, who ran for ASB president with posters showing him with his shirt off. Who won on the campaign slogan, "Vote for Alex. He'll make you feel gooood." Mom has lost all sanity with such riches at our fingertips—she's suddenly turned into a popularity pimp.

I decide on a pair of jeans and a nice sweater instead, and Mom gives up with a sigh. I'm not Barbie, and Sebastian's not Ken. Mom has a talk with me as I hunt around for the car keys, which I'm sure I've lost, meaning Mom will have to drive me in Dad's car to Alex's, or something else that will result in me missing this night. Her lecture goes something like this:

Mom: If there is any drinking at this party, I want you to come home immediately. If the environment gets destructive or out of hand, it's okay to leave. You know that, right? We have to look out for ourselves in situations like that, no matter what people may think. And if you do anything stupid like actually drink if there is alcohol there, I'll be very disappointed, but I'll still love you, and the important thing is to *call* and I'll come get you no matter what time it is. I don't care what time it is, because I'd rather get up and be inconvenienced than have to sit by your hospital bed. And speaking of the hour, I want you to come home by midnight, because all of the drunks are out on the roads after midnight, and remember that you need to say no to boys in a way that they understand you mean *no*.

Me: Have you seen the keys?

Anyway, by the time I get out the door, I almost forget where I'm actually going. I've been so convincing about going to Alex's party that I have to stop for a minute and realize I'm not really going there.

I wait until I'm out of the driveway and around the corner before I start shifting gears and thinking about seeing Sebastian. I have this ever-so-slight backstage-mind thought that Mom will pick up on my guilt somehow, my lying vibes. As I head for the bookstore, though, I have a huge natural-disaster wave of nerves. Are my jeans too casual after all? I don't want to seem like that's all I wear. Or too schoolgirl. He'd maybe been married, and I had barely kissed anyone on a date to the movies. In terms of our life experience, we really were from two different worlds. I start to get that foolish feeling, where you're embarrassed at yourself and haven't even done anything too stupid yet. Anticipatory humiliation. And I was going saintless—I'd left without even lighting Raphael or anyone else.

Seattle has two lakes right inside the city—one, Lake Union, where Sebastian lives, and the other, Greenlake, where Armchair Books is. Greenlake is small, about three miles around, and people go there to jog, walk, swim, lounge on the grass, and walk their dogs. Cozy businesses dot one end of the lake; peaked-roof houses in various shapes surround it. If you keep driving south, you'll eventually hit the zoo. Armchair Books is tucked between a bakery and a place that rents bikes. It's small and narrow, and an armchair is painted on the front window. I can see a fireplace inside, a couch and two plump chairs in front of it, and a large braided rug on the floor.

The store hours are listed on the door, and I have a plunge of disappointment when I see them. The store closes at nine, and it's eight already. It's going to be a short date. But what did I expect, anyway? He probably needs to get home to Bo. He has just a few more demands on his time than an upcoming history test.

I push open the door, and the bells on the handle jangle. It's quiet in there, only the voice of some old jazz singer softly playing in the background. There's just one customer that I can see, a man with a backpack who doesn't look up from the book he's perusing when I come in. The fire is lit, and there is the nice, warm smell of coffee and cinnamon and bread, probably from next door. The ceiling is high, and books rise up along the walls, reached by rolling library ladders, and where there aren't books there are posters, pictures of authors, I guess—I recognize

Hemingway in his big beard and wooly sweater—and scenes of Paris bookstalls and quotes about the pleasures of reading. The building is long and thin, with a winding staircase that leads to a second level. A set of doors to one side opens to the bakery, dark now, but which I can see has a few tables and chairs, and a large glass cabinet.

I pretend to look at books in that slow, meandering way that bookstores require, all the while looking casually around for Sebastian. I consider going in and out the front door again to make the bells jangle some more, and would have if the man with the backpack hadn't been there.

I wander; I tuck myself between two rows not far from the register. I am staring with Academy Award–winning interest at a shelf of books when I hear my name.

"Jade?"

And there he is, Sebastian, with his dark curls and dark eyes, in a nubby brown sweater and jeans. Comfy, happily worn student clothes. "Hi," I say. "This is a really nice place."

"We've got many fine gardening books," Sebastian says.

I look at him, puzzled, and he gestures toward the books I'm staring at: *Tips for Northwest Gardeners. Terrace Gardening. How to Garden at Night*—okay, that one wasn't there, but you get the idea.

"I may be a little nervous," I say.

"Okay, I'm really glad you said that, because I just went to the back room to put on more deodorant," Sebastian says. He flaps his arms a bit. "I probably shouldn't even have told you that. Those aren't the things you're supposed to admit."

"No, I'm glad," I say. I *am* glad too. I thought of my own car-freshening, and this makes me happy. If nothing else, we have sneak deodorant swiping in common. His nervousness calms me.

The bells on the door ring again, and Sebastian takes my elbow. "I'm sorry—do you mind? I've got another hour, and then it's just us. I've got to do some restocking, but we won't have customers." I get a shot of happy, a direct injection to my veins.

"It's all good. I don't mind at all. Do what you need to," I say. I try not to grin like an idiot. "I've got all these gardening books to get through."

I like the way Sebastian looks behind the counter, the way the big lady with the canvas book bag who just walked in asks him questions that he seems to have the answers to. I like the way he rings up the man-with-the-backpack's purchase, and talks to him about the weather. I like that when an old man with a shiny bald head comes in, he knows Sebastian's name, and Sebastian knows his. More than anything, I like just being there while he works, doing what he knows to do, in his own place. A place that I now know is his own place. I like the way he looks my way and rolls his eyes or twirls a pen between his fingers to make me smile. I could have gone home right then, and it would have been the best date I ever had.

A little after nine, Sebastian takes a ring of keys to the door and locks it. The jazz singer is still singing over the speakers, but it feels suddenly quiet. Sebastian turns the sign to CLOSED, looks out onto the empty street.

"I like this time of night," he says. I can see his reflection in the glass. It is the red-jacket boy that I remember, the one who has big thoughts to think, decisions to make. It is the same red-jacket boy who comes to the zoo at night, who I now know works in a bookstore with posters of Paris on the walls and too many gardening books, with customers who call him by name.

"Okay, now for the fun part of the date," he says. "This is pathetic, because now I have to restock." Sebastian runs his hand over his forehead and through his hair.

"Let me help," I say.

"You want to?"

"Sure."

"All right," he says. "I'll be back in a sec." He disappears through a doorway in the rear of the store. Suddenly, the music changes. It's cranked up. The kind of rock that's all guitars and energy and lyrics with a message. "God, that jazz puts me to sleep," he says. We work together. Sebastian shows me how to check the computer for sales, how to fill the empty spots where the books are leaning lazily against each other. The music keeps us moving fast. When we are done, Sebastian looks around.

"Man, we did that in record time," he says. "Thanks to you."

"It was fun," I say.

"You're kidding, right? You, who gets to work with amazing, fantastic creatures?"

"No, I really liked it."

Sebastian looks at his watch. "It's early, still," he says. "I'm not expected back until eleven thirty or so. It's my late night. Can you stay? This is the time I was hoping for."

"Sure," I say.

"Okay. Great. All right. Come here," he says. He takes my arm, leads me to the reading area by the fireplace. "Have a seat. I'm going to get us something."

I sit down on the couch, all old soft leather, and it's like sinking into an oversize baseball mitt. The fire is in front of me, still blazing, and I notice for the first time that it's electric, which explains the lack of firewood and the ever-glowing flame. Sebastian trots to the back room again, changes the music. A woman singing, quieter, the voice of creamy liquid poured over ice. Then he heads through the doors to the dark bakery. He disappears from sight, and I look out the window. The street is quiet and it is beginning to rain. Drops patter against the glass, making me feel warm and tucked inside. I can hear dishes clattering from the bakery, and then the crashing sound of metal falling.

"Shit," Sebastian says.

"Are you all right?" I call.

"Aside from the broken foot," he yells back, but his voice is cheerful.

He appears a moment later, carrying a tray. He sets it down on the table in front of the couch. Two mugs, filled high with whipped cream, a plate with a pastry—a strawberry tart of some kind—and two forks.

"Wow," I say. "What's this?"

"Something for hanging out with me at work on a Saturday night when you could be at a party, or something," he says. I remember, suddenly, that I actually am supposed to be at a party. I feel sorry for the people there. That life seems far away, and the memory of it annoys me. It intrudes, same as the phone ringing during a really good movie.

"I don't really like parties," I say. "Actually."

Sebastian hands me a cup. Hot chocolate with whipped cream, or, rather, whipped cream with a little hot chocolate. It seems another good reason to be falling in love with

Sebastian. He knows how to get the balance right.

"I don't really like them either," he says. "All that phoniness. Pretending you're not uncomfortable. I can *do* it, I just don't *like* it. And drunks never look good to anyone except other drunks. You've got to have a bite of this. It's my favorite thing over there." He taps the plate with his fork.

He's right, it's incredible. Buttery, and the bright sweetsour of strawberry, and thick vanilla custard. "Oh, yum," I say.

"Isn't it?"

"The best." I put my fork down. Maybe it's the faux fire and the rain and the sinking couch, I don't know. Or maybe it's his soft clothes and warm eyes, but I'm just comfortable there with Sebastian. Some guys give you the edgy feeling of dogs behind chain-link fences, and some give you the nervousness of high heels you're not used to. But Sebastian—he makes me feel like I just buried my nose in warm laundry. It gives me a casual bravery—not how I'd be with anyone at school. With Sebastian, I am new.

"Okay," I say. "Here's what I know about you. Your name. That you work in a nice place and know a lot about books. That you have a son; that you appreciate elephants and live in a houseboat with your grandmother that you call by her first name."

"Tess isn't the type you call 'grandmother,'" he laughs.

"She sounds unusual."

"That's one way to put it. She raised my mother and my aunt by herself, used to have a community theater . . . But she's always been an activist. Give her a cause, she's happy. Old-growth forest—great. Picketing the NRA—no problem."

"Wow," I say.

"Tess is one to get carried away. She once led this secret uprising to switch the voice boxes of Barbies and G.I. Joes. When they hit the shelves, G.I. Joe said, 'Let's go shopping!' and Barbie said, 'The enemy must be overtaken.'"

I laugh. "No way."

"Yes way. Sex-role stereotyping in children's toys, all that. She calmed down for a while when she hooked up with Max. Weaver. You ever heard of him by chance?" I shook my head. "He used to run the Iditarod. He was an early climber of Everest, too. Great man. She was peaceful with him. But he died last year. Lung cancer. He didn't even smoke."

"I'm sorry."

"Me too. I think Bo gives her a distraction from her grief."

"I'm sure." We sit quiet for a moment. "So, what else is there to know about you?" I ask.

He sips his chocolate. He has cream on his upper lip. "That's a big question," he says. "Although maybe not so big. I wish I had more to say. Mostly, I'm all about Bo right now. I'm Bo's father. It freaks me out to say it sometimes. I'm someone's father. God. It shouldn't be allowed. But you have a baby and they take over your world. One little person and . . ." He put his palms down, gestured a spreading, a widening. "Your whole life."

"Was he planned?"

"Oh, shit, no," Sebastian says. He half laughs, runs his hand through his curls again. "When I found out . . . I thought my life was ruined. I was pissed, scared . . . Man, so scared, I cannot tell you. I was ready to start college . . ."

"Did you ever consider other . . ." I looked around for the right word. "Options?"

"I would have, absolutely, only I didn't know she was pregnant until too late. She hid it from me. Everyone. Herself." *She*. Bo's *mother*. I wonder where she is. Who she is. "Now that Bo's here, I can't imagine him not here. The first time I saw him, man, that was it. Something happens to you I can't explain. But then, I was ready to start college . . ."

"You were just out of high school?"

"Just finishing. I wasn't even eighteen."

Quick math calculations. Sebastian is somewhere around twenty. We have a two-year difference, no big deal. Not to me. But with me still being in high school and him with a child, we are a lifetime apart.

I decide to let him know, get it over with. "That's where I am," I say. "It's hard to imagine dealing with that now."

"Oh, yeah?" Sebastian says. "I thought you were older." So that's that, I think. I consider taking a last swig of chocolate and heading out. What was I thinking? He had a baby. I had a locker.

But Sebastian seems to have moved on from our age difference just fine. "You seem older," he says. "Maybe it's the way you care for the elephants."

"I graduate in June," I say. Might as well hammer a few nails into the coffin lid.

Sebastian holds his mug between his hands. His elbows rest on his knees. "Are you going away to college?"

"Probably not. Probably here. Is college out for you now?"

"I hope not. I wanted to study architecture. *Want*. When Bo gets a little older . . . I can't burden Tess too much. It wouldn't be right."

I sip my chocolate. The mother question is there again—I

can almost feel it. It is the rain on the windows, though, the music, the feeling of being in a cocoon, that makes me slip off my shoes and tuck my feet under me and ask. There is nothing like safety to make you feel bold, I was learning. "What about Bo's mom? Can she help you?"

"She's . . ." It almost seems as if he has to think about this. "Dead. Died."

He gets up from the couch. Walks to the window. Folds his arms around himself.

"Oh, my God," I whisper. Oh, my God, oh, my God. He hadn't wanted to talk about it, and now I know why. Shit, that explains things. And I had to go and open my big mouth. I could be so stupid. I could be so bad at reading signs. My instinct spoke in a foreign language.

"Yeah," he says.

"What happened?" I whisper. This—it requires soft voices. I feel sick with horror. He doesn't speak for a while.

"She died. . . . Childbirth," he says finally.

"Oh, my God," I say.

"Yeah."

Childbirth. Oh, God, how awful. How traumatic. How rare was that? And what guilt he must have. I can't take it in. I can't picture his life. It's like seeing some disaster on TV. The words go in, even the pictures, but there's no way to grasp it and make it real. Real tragedy, not the kind of my imagination.

"I'm so sorry," I say.

"Can we . . . talk about something else?" Sebastian says to the window. "You know . . ."

"I am so sorry," I say.

"It's . . . what happened." He stares into the street. "I just want to say one more thing," he says at last. A gust of wind blows the trees outside, and splats of rain hit the window. I picture people under umbrellas on the grounds of a cemetery. "This thing that happened between Tiffany and me . . ."

Tiffany. A real girl. With white-blond hair . . .

"Getting pregnant and all . . ." Sebastian crosses his arms, looks up at the ceiling for a moment. "I didn't go around doing that, you know, having sex with people. Tiffany . . . She was someone I loved since I was like, eleven. Her parents were really overbearing. They put all this pressure on her. She would cry and tell me about it and I would just break in half. This sad, beautiful little person I wanted to watch over. She said when she was with me was the only time her life was *true*. When we finally got together, I mean really got more serious . . ."

"It's all right," I say. I don't know what is all right. Nothing, really.

"We don't know each other, but I don't want you to get the wrong idea about me because of Bo. Me having Bo. 'Getting a girl pregnant'—I mean, it sounds like someone who's this . . . I didn't even go on *dates*."

"I appreciate your telling me. I didn't think that, anyway. . . ."

"You—you're like the only other one I've even *noticed*."

I don't say anything, mostly because my insides are tangled. Sad, happy, heavy, dancing. I want to cry. I want to smile.

"When that baby elephant put his trunk up to your hair, and you kind of pulled back, surprised . . . And then you rubbed his trunk. *Her* trunk. It was really . . ."

"I *was* surprised. . . ."

"Caring," he says.

154   deb caletti

"You can't *not* love them," I say.

"Oh, I'm sure some people could manage," he says. "Most people, it seems like they've only got one part of the equation down. Caring for themselves, or caring for someone else. And I've learned how important it is to have both. I don't know. . . . Look, I'm sorry about all the deep talk for one night. I feel like a fuck-up. First date, and I make you work in the store and then we discuss these things, and I don't even take you to the movies or something. And I don't even know your last name. . . ."

"DeLuna," I say.

"Jade DeLuna. God, that's pretty," he says. "It fits you. I'm so glad to know, because it's been bugging me. One of those things you're embarrassed to ask after too much time passes. Something I should have found out a while back."

"Like how old Bo is," I say.

"Fifteen months," he says. "Tess tells me we stop counting his age in months after a year and a half. If not, he'll be five and we'll still be saying he's sixty months."

"Yeah, that might embarrass him."

"That's supposed to be part of the job, right? I'm looking forward to that."

"My mother was great at it," I say. "She brought me my lunch once, when I forgot. I was a sophomore. She came to my math class."

"Ouch," Sebastian laughs, and then we are off, talking and laughing, and things are easy and there are no sudden roadblocks. We are in front of a blazing faux fire, surrounded by books, the reflection of the streetlights showing on the wet pavement outside. Later, he reaches for my stockinged feet, puts them in his lap.

And that hand on my foot—just that, is one of those uncommon moments, those times when you don't wish for something else, for even one thing to be different; when you have no other needs and no worries, where your insides are calm, and everything you were ever restless about, anything that had ever given you angst, is quieted to stillness. No steel ball in your chest, no breathless fear. No blue numbness of nearly passing out, no nagging doubts of the backstage mind. All of that, forgotten. It is just rightness, so rare.

We say good night outside the store, hug briefly. He'll be coming by the zoo soon, he says. I head to my car. The fir tree I parked under is decorated with raindrops. They glisten white and magical under the streetlight, cling to the needles of the tree, and then slide off. I tilt my chin to the sky, to that treetop. I take in the night, Sebastian-style. I let the drops dot my face. I feel that hand on my stockinged foot again. I breathe the night air. I drink in its cold, wet happiness.

CHAPTER ELEVEN

A rhesus monkey mother will sometimes do a "double-hold." She will grab her own baby, along with the baby of a high-status monkey, when its mother is not looking. She will hold them both together in her arms, thereby encouraging a bond between her child and the high-status offspring . . .

—Dr. Jerome R. Clade, *The Fundamentals of Animal Behavior*

When I get home that night, I see that Mom's been waiting up, reading. I tell her I'm too tired to talk, that the party had been great. She's obviously pleased. She tightens the tie around her robe, puts her arm around my shoulders, and kisses my cheek.

The next morning before breakfast, I switch on the elephant cam and watch for a while. I won't be going in to work—I've got so much homework, I'll need a shovel and one of those hats with the lights that miners wear just to get out from under it— so I want to see how everyone is. Watching the elephants also makes me feel closer to Sebastian. I replay our night in my head—restocking the books, drinking hot chocolate, hearing about Tess and Bo's mother.

It was such a perfect night, but when I play it back, my brain keeps snagging on something. Maybe it's a sabotaging snag. Maybe it's an important listen-to-me-now snag. How can you tell the difference? My body sometimes told me I was in mortal danger when I was taking a calculus test, so, you know, how can you trust your instinct? I want to tell my thoughts to shut the hell up, but I still keep going over what Sebastian had said about Tiffany. Dying in childbirth. The way he'd told me she was dead. The way it had almost sounded like it was a surprise to him, too.

It's stupid, I know, to think like I'm thinking, because what did I know about any of this? I couldn't have any idea how someone might feel or act if something so awful had happened. Maybe you'd feel distanced from it. And he did seem a little distanced. He had sounded sad about his grandmother's friend, Max Weaver, dying. When I'd said I was sorry, he'd said that he was sorry too. But not so with Tiffany. Had he said "I'm sorry too" about her? I didn't think so, but maybe I was remembering wrong. Maybe this was more of the psycho revisionist editing my brain was so fond of. Maybe he just couldn't bear to think about it because the pain was too much. Maybe he didn't want to overwhelm me. Maybe my backstage mind just likes to screw things up whenever something feels okay. Whenever something feels great.

I am watching Chai and Bamboo hanging out near the water when an instant message pops up.

YOU MISSED OUT, Michael types in these huge letters.

So sad, I write back.

More booze than a liquor store convention

I smile. Tap the keys. **You drink?**

Had half a beer and I could barely talk

Moron

No answer yet. I wait. **Felt like one of those foreign films where the soundtrack doesn't match the moving lips**

Lost all respect for you. Not that I ever had any

Stupid party. Should've done homework. Alex's dad came home early and . . .

My door opens. Shit, my door opens, and Mom stands there in her robe.

"Hi, honey," she says.

No knock, nothing. My heart pummels my insides, fueled by this panicked surge of guilt, and I reach around for the mouse to click off Michael's messages. Getting that little arrow into that little X is tough to do with shaking hands, suddenly as tricky as those pathetic vending machines where you have to pick up a stuffed toy with a mechanical claw.

"What was that?" she asks.

"What was what?" God, I'm guilty. I sound so guilty. I'm so guilty, my hands are trembling with double-shot espresso shakes. Man, I'd make the worst criminal.

"Up on the screen."

"Just Michael, messing around." She saw. I knew it. She saw, Goddamn it.

"It says, 'You missed out.'"

"Oh, yeah. He went with Akello to a party for Akello's dad."

"I thought you said he was going to Alex Orlando's last night."

"I did say that. But he changed his mind at the last minute. Akello's dad had this thing and his parents made him go and he was just begging Michael to go, so, you know, he wouldn't be the only one under forty, and so, you know, Michael went, because that's the kind of guy he is. . . ."

"So how was the party?"

"Michael said it was boring. His dad had a lot of alcohol there and the adults got embarrassing."

"No, your party. Alex's."

"Oh, it was great. Yeah. I had a really great time."

"What'd you do?" She sits on my bed. Crosses her feet at the ankles. Folds the flap of her robe closed so I don't see unshaven legs. She's all comfy. I feel an ungenerous, inward groan. Sometimes living with Mom is like trying to walk in those new shoes you buy at the drugstore, the ones connected by plastic string.

"Oh, you know—talked, listened to music, ate. Some people danced."

"What did you eat?"

If you want any further evidence that my brain is a vicious and cruel traitor, then here you go. Eat? My thoughts zip crazily. What did we eat? I rack my mind, try to come up with some food, and for some reason, the question feels like something off of *Jeopardy!* Food, food! All that's coming to me is this vision of Titus from Total Vid. Why Titus? Why right then? I have no idea, but that's what's there. Titus, giving me the "hang loose" sign.

"Pineapple," I say.

"Pineapple?"

Oh, my God. Oh, for God's sake! Who had pineapple at a party? Pineapple? Jesus!

"It was Hawaiian themed," I say. "Pineapple. And pork."

"Pork."

"Yeah. You know, that barbequed kind they have in Hawaii."

She thinks about this. "Oh."

"Tiki lamps outside." Shit!

"Wow. Were there costumes? Were you supposed to wear a costume? If we would have known . . ."

"Yeah, I could've worn my coconut bra if I hadn't grown out of it. No! There weren't any costumes . . ."

"I'm sorry. How am I supposed to know?"

"Alex in a hula skirt. Whoa."

"So, do you think it went well? I mean, do you think you'll get asked again?"

I want her off my bed, then. With that question, I just want her *away*. This anger boils up inside, spills over in sarcasm. "Well, you could slip him a couple of twenties to invite me next time."

"Jade! Come on."

"Or maybe you can try out for cheerleader. Then you could be invited to the parties yourself."

Mom's face falls. "That is so mean. Jeez, Jade. I was only wondering if you had a good time. If you'd be going again." Her mouth turns down. She looks like she might cry.

"Okay. I'm sorry." Mom stares down at her hands. Studies her fingernails. Shit. I shouldn't have said what I did. "Yeah, I'll be going again. Maybe next weekend."

"God, Jade. After everything I do for you. You didn't have to say those things."

Guilt creeps around, plucks at my insides. I feel like I have stolen something. Maybe her dignity.

"I'm sorry. I'm just . . . tired. It was a late night and I didn't sleep well, and now I've got all this homework . . ."

Mom smoothes her robe against her knees.

"I didn't mean to be mean," I say, even though I did.

She is quiet, and then finally she says, "Okay." And then:

"I'm still glad you had a good time. I think it's important to try new things, mix with new people."

I think of all the beaches she won't go to and boats she won't ride and trips she won't take, and I keep my mouth shut. Blue ribbon in self-control.

"I'm going to get dressed," she says.

I remember, then, something Damian had told me. About an elephant that had been part of a circus for fifteen years, who had suddenly broken loose and gored one of the trainers. I don't know why I think about it right then. All I know is that I do. This thought, it makes me sad. I feel like a traitor, but more than that, I just feel the weighty, fullness of loss. For the times we used to talk. For that time we were in the bathroom at the mall, and she was being silly, thinking we were the only ones there. *Shouldn't have had that Slurpee. Get it? Slur-PEE? Ah! Ah! Ah!* She fake-laughed, real loud. It was only after we'd washed our hands that we saw a pair of clogs underneath the far stall, causing us to laugh our heads off for a good ten minutes as soon as the door closed behind us.

I go downstairs to have some breakfast. Milo appears, sits at my feet, and looks up with pleading hope. "You, with the fur. Quit staring," I say. I pour the last bit of Cheerios in my bowl.

"Eyuw," I say to Oliver, who has come downstairs wearing the pajamas that make him look like a husband in a fifties TV show.

"What?"

I show him the bowl.

"Cereal dust," he says.

"I'm not eating it. Don't tell." I empty my bowl into the garbage.

Oliver checks the freezer. "Waffles," he suggests.

"Okay."

Oliver reaches into the waffle box and pulls out a couple that had seen better days. If we had an ice pick and a few hours, we could probably chip away and eventually find them.

"'Always winter and never Christmas,'" Oliver says.

"Think if Aslan comes, he'll bring some Eggos?"

"Sis, if you're wishing, you can wish for anything. Not just waffles. How about a whole breakfast? Bacon and pancakes with strawberries and whipped cream."

"I'm always too practical in my wishing," I say. I use my inhuman strength to break off a waffle. I put it in the toaster and push the lever down, and that's when we hear this shout.

Dad. Yelling. Man, is he angry.

"Tell me!" he says.

Then Mom's voice. Too quiet to hear.

"Why hide it? Huh? What are you trying to hide?"

His voice shoots down the stairs, bounces and crashes against all the regular parts of our kitchen—the coffeepot and the fridge, the pot holder hanging by its loop on the stove. Oliver looks at me with wide eyes. See, our parents never fight. Well, they fight, but *disagreement* is the word that comes more to mind. Someone would say something a bit sharply and the other would stare off or leave the room. And then the issue would just fade away, like invisible ink after the lemon juice has dried. No one ever *yelled*.

Oliver and I just stand really still, looking at each other. Milo is still too, but he's just waiting for a waffle.

I gesture for Oliver to follow me. We tiptoe over to the stairwell, like a couple of burglars. Listen.

"Since when are you so interested in this stuff? That's what I'd really like to know."

"You're making a big deal out of nothing," Mom says. "Roger just thought I'd like these. He's trying to be helpful. I *am* interested. . . ."

Roger. Mr. Dutton? Dad was jealous of my *librarian*? Giving Mom *books*?

"And they're under the bed—why?"

Nothing.

"Goddamn it, Nancy, answer me."

Silence.

Answer, I plead. Books, for God's sake. Big deal! Answer!

"Well, that tells me what I need to know. Fuck, this is great." Oliver practically gasps. *Fuck* is not part of Dad's usual vocabulary, at least that we know. It was the kind of thing he'd say when he was fixing the kitchen sink, or as part of a joke to the car mechanic when they both looked under the hood of Dad's car—*Carburetor is French for* Don't fuck with me, *is what I believe*. But it was nothing he would say to Mom. Nothing he'd yell at her in anger.

"No!" Mom says. "Stop it! I don't know why I hid them . . . There's no real reason to hide them . . ."

"And what about our household, huh? It's a mess. There's no food in the house. The laundry—"

"I never get to the laundry. Okay? I'm a criminal."

"It's overflowing. There's no coffee. The kitchen's a mess. . . ."

He might have been a little right.

"I noticed that too," Oliver whispers.

"You don't even care about this house anymore!" Dad shouts. "Us. Me."

"That's all I do. Care about everyone else. Do everything for everyone else! You are all capable people who can clean the kitchen and do your own laundry. Who does my laundry? Who cares for me?"

"I don't even know you anymore," Dad says.

Mom starts to cry. Shit, she starts to cry. I hear her voice break down. A lump starts in my own throat.

Oliver whispers, "Are they going to get a divorce?"

The word is huge, catastrophic. A word like *earthquake*, or *tidal wave*, or *plane crash*.

"Of course not," I tell him. "Not in a million years."

We listen to Mom cry. Then I feel Oliver's hand slip into mine. We sit like that for a while. Oliver seems small in his husband pajamas. I can't take it anymore. My heart hurts. First, Mom in my room; now this. I feel all hollow with grief.

"Come on," I say.

"What?"

"Get dressed as fast as you can and meet me downstairs."

I step to my room quietly, knock three times softly. I throw on some clothes and pull a few bills from the wad of money I have in my sock drawer. Every time Mom or Dad gives me any, or I get a birthday card with money tucked inside from one of my relatives, I stash it. I'm not much of a spender. I prefer the comfort of those bills in a fat lump to anything I might think I want for a moment.

I feed Milo some of his food, which looks like a brown version of Capn' Crunch with Crunch Berries. Oliver hunts in the closet for his shoes. The waffle has popped up, and I know how it will taste anyway, that stale, frozen taste of things in one place too long. I leave it there. It will be a waffle statement. I grab Mom's keys from the kitchen counter and we leave out the front door.

"Where we going, Sis? Are we coming back?"

"Of course we're coming back." I swat his leg. "Okay—clue. 'If you're wishing, you can wish for anything.'"

He still hasn't guessed by the time we turn into Yvonne's House of Pancakes parking lot (or YHOP, for the acronym minded). Yvonne's had been there forever, or at least from the seventies. Big, ugly brass flower sculptures decorate one wall. The menus have thirty years' worth of stickiness, and the waitress still has a crush on Tony Danza, but the pancakes are big and buttery. Strawberry pancakes, bacon. Large orange juice with pulp clinging to the empty glass. We go from starving to stuffed in twenty minutes.

Then I suggest we go to Total Vid. "I don't want to see the surfing movie again," Oliver says, but that's not what I have in mind. Titus in his pineapple shirt apparently has the day off, but this other girl wearing pigtails and a leopard-print shirt helps us find the nature videos. They don't have the spycam-in-crap one that Oliver wanted me to see, but we get another one about elephants. Back at home, there are only the usual sounds. Dad is downstairs; I can hear him hammering. Mom has the television on in her room. I guess the fight is over, but it seems like Oliver and I are still recovering. Something feels bruised.

I have so much homework that I'm bound to be up all night for the next few days, but this is more important. Oliver puts in the movie and we sit on the couch together. We watch a herd, followed over several years. We watch babies being born, elder members dying. We watch as the family struggles through a drought, through a flood, through a long voyage in search for food. We watch as they stay together, through mourning, through celebration, through all things. Depending on each other for their very survival. Family, always.

I find Damian in his office the next time I go to the elephant house. He is leaning back in his chair, his hands folded across his stomach.

"You look sad," I say.

"Jade," he says. "Good afternoon. I've posted a new list of jobs this morning."

"Are you okay?"

"Oh, yes."

"But why do you look like that? No smile." Damian never looks this serious.

He sighs. "It's Onyx. They want to transfer her."

"They've said it before," I say. "They can't get rid of her." I love Onyx. Onyx is troubled and sometimes mean, but she looks like she knows things, the way people who've seen pain know things.

"No, this time Victor Iverly is preparing. I need a plan," Damian says.

"What?"

"I don't know. But I don't have much time. Victor has given her three weeks. He's making her travel arrangements. He's worried about 'public safety.'"

"I'm sorry, Damian."

"I'm not giving up yet. There's got to be something that will help. An idea that will work without banishing her. I don't think she can take another move, another break."

"You're like a father to them."

"Some fathers aren't driven from the herd, I guess. Some stay."

I work with Elaine on enrichment, hanging up the big chain wrapped in a fire hose, which gets put up after January so that tires and barrels and treats can be strung from it. We also help drag over a huge pine tree that had formerly been with the Siberian tigers, and we dump it in the fields. The elephants love anything with a new, strong scent, and before we even get out of there, tails are up and ears, too, and the elephants start vocalizing and Tombi and Bamboo sway on over. It makes you happy to give them something new and interesting to check out, same as giving Milo a new rawhide.

Sebastian comes alone that day, right as I am finishing up. I'd been trying not to obsess over the would/wouldn't, and I am rewarded, because there he is—an appearance that is expected and unexpected at the same time.

"They sure are excited over that tree," Sebastian says.

It's true. In the time it took for me to change and come out to see Sebastian, Tombi and Chai are already throwing it around. You should have heard the noise. Like thunder and happy elephants.

"And they're getting great exercise," I say. "But I wouldn't be surprised if that tree lights up like Christmas." It looks as if it's about to get tossed, in the direction of the electric fence.

"Will they get hurt?"

I'd asked Elaine the same thing. "Nah. They'll just pick it up and throw it again. In a day or two, they'll get bored and we'll have to haul it out."

"Like Bo with a new truck. He's so into trucks right now, I'm worried he's going to end up with a CB radio and a girl-friend named Wanda who works at a diner."

I smile. See, these are not the kind of conversations you'd have with an Alex Orlando. Sebastian thought about things, filtered them through his own sea-boy lens.

"I'm glad to see you," I say. And I am. My insides are all cheery again. He's erased all the ugly feelings about Dad being angry, about Mom and her sudden, nutty interest in history books. "Where is Bo?"

"At home. I've got a weird schedule this week, because Derek, the owner, is on vacation. So I probably won't be here in the next few days. I wanted to tell you that."

"Oh," I say.

In a second, my backstage mind has already opened up the door. Thoughts fill in the crack of his hesitation. He does think I'm too young. And maybe I was the only one who'd been having a good time the other night. I was stupid to ask about Bo's mother and all. I'd moved too fast. I should have lit Raphael, at least.

"So that's why I came by."

"Well, thanks."

Sebastian runs his hand through his curls. "Jade, I . . . I'd really like to see you again, you know? I just feel kind of bad to ask, with Bo and all. . . ."

"I had a great time, Sebastian. I really did. It was my kind of night."

"No way."

"Really."

"Tiffany's so into parties and all that . . . I'm just surprised. It was my kind of night, too."

"It was cozy. I like cozy."

"Well, then, I'm going to go ahead and ask you for dinner. At the houseboat this week, if you can. I've got the night off, Wednesday, and Tess has got a new group she meets with. But, it'd be the three of us. Bo . . ."

"Sebastian, it's fine. I'd really like that."

"This is new for me. Dating with a kid . . . It's really bizarre."

"I'd love to come."

"Sevenish? Macaroni and cheese?"

"I'll bring the hot dogs."

He laughs. "That's great. That's terrific."

I ignore the mind-snag, the realization that he used Tiffany's name in the present tense. I mean, she isn't going to parties anymore, is she? I banish the thought. Grief has got to play all kinds of tricks on you. Maybe it's hard for him to imagine she's really gone. I let it go; instead, I just let the Sebastian-happy fill me. The relief of not messing up after all. It practically lifts me from my shoes. I am flying when I go home. Sure as Jake Gillette's skateboard parachute.

CHAPTER TWELVE

Animal kin sometimes appear to feel each other's pain. An entire pod of whales will beach itself so as not to abandon a beached clan member, and chimpanzees will touch, pat, and groom a family member who has been a victim of aggression. A grandmother lemur once attacked the mother of her grandchild, after the mother ignored and rejected the injured infant . . .

—Dr. Jerome R. Clade, *The Fundamentals of Animal Behavior*

"A barbeque? But it's raining."

Why'd I say barbeque? Why not just dinner? Why did lying make you so stupid? It's like there's some eerie morality department of your brain that just tries to trip you up and teach you a lesson.

"Well, you know, Alex's dad will probably just jet in and out with the food."

"Kind of strange to have it midweek," Mom says.

"It was a spur-of-the-moment thing. No big deal."

"I just wish you felt you could have your friends here sometimes."

"I do. I will. I would. They just have this big house, I guess, so people go there."

"Oh."

"One of those places with a living room no one goes in. You know, like it should have a red velvet rope across the doorway and a plaque telling about the furniture."

Mom is quiet.

"I can never understand having a room no one uses. A whole room just to look at but that you still have to dust."

This seems to make her feel a little better. "I know it," she says.

"It's stupid. What a waste."

She's still quiet, though. Like she's tried to file away sad, but can't quite close the drawer. "Alex told me he thinks you're cool," I say. It's shameless, and my insides fold up with guilt, but I know this is the big parental prize, something that makes them inexplicably happy.

"Really?" she asks.

"Who knows why," I say.

She socks my arm. "Well, just make sure the meat's cooked all the way," she says.

It's raining really hard when I get outside, and I duck into Mom's car and then see we're out of gas. I stop by the 76 station. The old guy at the counter whose nametag reads ROGER greets me with a Yooit Wahine, (Greetings, Female Surfer) as he rings up my gas and the package of hot dogs I've just remembered that I said I'd bring.

I wind my way toward the water of Lake Union, peer in between the banks of trees to find the right dock. I park in a strip of gravel, swing open a gate, walk through a gnat cloud and down the ramp. For anyone who's never seen a houseboat, they really aren't boats at all. They are houses built on floating logs or cement, and they don't move from their location like a boat would. They stay put, if you don't count the ups and downs of moving with the sways of the water. It's getting dark, and tiny Christmas-like lights in yellow and red are draped overhead, running the length of the dock. Most of the houses are snug cottages, shingled or painted bright colors and adorned with hanging flower baskets and pots. There are several two-story houses with modern angles, though, too, and all of the houseboats are separated by thin bits of water strewn with sailboats and kayaks. For a neighborhood with no ground, there are a lot of gardens—climbing vines and roses and hanging baskets of fuchsia.

I look for Sebastian's house, Number Three, as a cat winds its way around my ankles and another plunks himself in my path. A dog hears my footsteps and appears in a window to bark. Someone calls his name— "Sumatra!"—tells him to quiet down. I can see the end of the dock up ahead, and the sprinkle of white city lights on the other side of the water.

I find Number Three. It's a combination of styles, a narrow two-story house, but old looking. Painted red with blue trim, a small, crow's-nest deck on top. Pots of plants decorate the platform the house floats on—there's a palm tree, some ferns and marigolds. A cement Buddha sits in one leafy pot, a bullfrog in another. An ancient, half-rusted watering can with a whirligig on a rod sticking from it is propped in one corner.

I step onto the float, and feel it dip with my weight. There's a set of rubber yellow gardening clogs by the front door, and a tiny set of rubber rain boots painted with dragonflies and insects. A grass welcome mat sports a sunflower. After I knock, I realize something: I have tapped three times on the doorframe, just like at home.

At the sound of the knock, I hear little running steps, and Bo's shout, "Da!" Then bigger steps, and the door opens and there is Sebastian in this new place, this homey and wonderful new place. Bo grasps him around the knees again.

"You made it," he says. "It's okay, Bo. It's Jade." He picks Bo up so that he can peek at me from the comfort of Sebastian's T-shirt.

"Hi, Bo," I say. "He said 'dad,'"

"I know it. It blows me away. First, that lately he's got these words for things. Second, that I'm his *dad*. Come on in." He steps aside. "A dad is the guy that does the taxes, you know? Not me."

"This is such a cool house," I say. A denim couch and a rocking chair are crowded in with a table and Bo's toy chest. Big windows look out onto a wide canal of water that eventually opens into the lake. Colorful, plump pillows are strewn on the couch, and there's a tall bookshelf that follows the staircase to the second level. Black-and-white photos in every shape and size cover another wall. There's a woodstove, and a viney plant that's making its way up and around a side window.

"It's my great aunt's place. Tess's sister. Mattie and her partner came into some money and bought a bunch of little houses all over. They're living in Santa Fe now."

"I love Santa Fe," I say. "At least by the pictures. I've never been." I think of my college application, my Abe homework. University of New Mexico, the one I had chosen to apply to. A piece of me that is actually there, right at this moment.

"They love it too. Mattie's taking some time off. . . . They've got this amazing adobe house there. Anyway, let me show you around. The grand tour takes about thirty seconds."

The house is small. It makes you want to take careful steps and sideways moves, but it also feels sturdy from years of love

deb caletti

and use. "Ta-da, the kitchen . . ." Painted in green and yellow, with cups of all colors hanging over the counter. There's also an Indian rug on the floor, and horseshoes along the tops of the walls. The lamp is made out of an old gas can—MOBIL is still painted on the side, along with a red, winged horse. The windows are steamy, and a pot with a lid boils on the stove.

"Mac 'n' cheese?" I ask.

"Well, no. I actually cooked. This is the one thing I know how to make. Maybe I shouldn't admit ability in case it's awful. Chili?"

"Yum. Oh, and I brought hot dogs."

"You'll be Bo's friend for life, now. Bo—gogos!"

"Gogos?" Bo seems worried he heard wrong.

I take them out of the bag and show him. He reaches out, and I hand them over.

"Maybe we can put those in the fridge. Okay, Bo? You do it." He sets Bo down, opens the rounded door of the old refrigerator. He pats one of the shelves. "Right here, bud. Then we'll have them for dinner." Bo places them on the shelf. "'Atta way, bud." Bo runs off to the living room, the plastic of his diaper *chsh-chshing* as he moves. "That's a victory lap," Sebastian says. "Did you notice how nothing is on the bottom shelves?" He opens the door again to show me. "He can open this. One day, Tess found his trucks in there and the apples all over the floor. We figure he's got about a minute and a half alone, max, before he gets into trouble. He's doing this climbing thing too. If you can hear him, it's okay, but if he's quiet . . ."

"Oh, man," I say.

"Exactly. I found him sitting in the middle of the kitchen table once."

Sebastian continues the tour. "Dining room." A wood kitchen table with three chairs and a high chair, all looking out onto the kayaks in the water outside, and a pair of fishing poles on the dock. "Bathroom." I poke my head in. A tiny wood-wrapped room with a small claw-foot tub and a porthole for a window. "Study." He gestures to the wall of books and I smile. "Now, upstairs."

We pass Bo, who is fishing through his toy box, taking out all the toys one by one. "I just picked up all those, of course," Sebastian says. We walk up the narrow stairs. Through one arched doorway is a tiny bedroom that is all quilt-wrapped bed and view, and another small bedroom, obviously Bo's, with a crib and toys and a bright, woven wall hanging. "He's almost getting too big for his crib," Sebastian says. "And here's my room." It's not a room, exactly, but a bunk. A doorway and three laddered stairs to reach a bed on a platform. A shelf above the surrounding windows holds photographs and train cars and metal sculptures of animals. "Mattie's decorating, but I don't mind," he says.

"What a view," I say.

"You get used to the motion. Sometimes it's a surprise to see that everything out there is rocking up and down."

"I bet."

"Up those steps?" He points to a wall ladder. "There's a deck. But if Bo hears them creak, he'll want up, and he'll have to be wrestled down."

"That's okay," I say. "Another time."

"Oh, shit—dinner," Sebastian says. He jogs down the stairs and I follow. He trots to the kitchen and lifts the lid and stirs. Yanks open the oven door and takes out a pan of cornbread with a towel, warm, sweet smells following.

"You made that? He cooks, too?"

"Tess's friend, Max? He taught me how, but I didn't pay attention. This is 'add water and stir.'"

"Can I help?" I love it here. The cups above the counter, the wicker chairs at the table, the old California license plate hanging over the stove. Sebastian cutting hotdogs into small, Bo-size pieces.

"Nah. I got it covered."

I wander back out to the living room, examine the wall of pictures. "Hey, Sebastian, is this you?" I call. Curly-haired little boy. Overalls. Standing in a sprinkler fully dressed. Mini-Sebastian eyes.

He pokes his head out of the kitchen. "Which one? I'm in a lot of them."

"Sprinkler."

"Oh, yeah."

He appears next to me. "And there. That's Tess and me and my sister, Hillary, fishing at Tess's old place where we used to live, Ruby Harbor. That's Tess on her motorcycle."

"Oh, my God." Tess, a gray-haired, strong-looking woman wearing jeans and a bright orange shirt, atop a Suzuki.

"Mom got it for Dad, but he thought he was too old for it, so Tess bought it off them." He points to a separate grouping of pictures, on the space next to the window. "That was my great-grandmother, Lettie. And Mattie and her partner, Lou. Tess and her daughters—Mom and Aunt Julia. Mom painting." Sebastian's mom has brown hair pulled into a ponytail. She is pretty, with a kind face and a paintbrush clenched playfully in her teeth. These pictures, mothers and daughters and sisters— they make me think of elephant clans.

"She's an artist?"

"Mostly for fun. She's sold a few." He points to the main wall again. "There's my dad." Standing next to a swimming pool and wearing a funny long bathing suit, hoisting a water wing like a barbell.

"They all look so nice."

"You know, they are nice. That's my Aunt Julia again, Mom's sister, and her husband, Tex Ivy, and their twins." A really beautiful, long-legged woman in cutoffs. Her husband, an outdoorsy guy who looks a little like Abe, with his long hair and bristled cheeks. One girl and one boy, about four or five, both beautiful like their mom but with their father's hair. "The twins are monsters. Good thing they're so cute."

"And look at you there," I say. It is one of the typical high school dance pictures, the kind Mom has plenty of, with Sebastian looking kind of goofy, actually, in a tux, his arm around a girl with straight blond hair.

"Don't look. God, I look stupid."

"Not your most relaxed. Is that Tiffany?"

"Yeah."

"Jeez, Sebastian, she's gorgeous." She is, too. Perfect nose, the kind of cheekbones you see in magazines. Tall but thin. This smile that's Tampax-ad happy, free. It's weird to see her. That was her, alive. Now she's dead. Bo's mother. Sebastian's lost love.

"She used to do a lot of competing—you know, beauty pageants. Her parents made her at first. She *hated* it. I felt so sorry for her. I was like, eleven, and I wanted to save her. Hide her in my room, or something. She was so . . . *fragile* to me. She seemed like glass." He cups his hands in front of him, holding something delicate. "Later, she just gave up and got into it. It was sad. She wasn't the same person who just wanted out, to live like a normal girl instead of on some perpetual stage. She got to liking all that stuff. From this really sweet uncertainty . . . She changed. It took me a long time to see it."

"Wow." It leaves me speechless. I mean, I've been told I'm pretty, but no one would put me in an evening gown and a tiara. "She really is gorgeous."

"Jade? You know what? I think you're the beautiful one."

It's not a beautiful-one, high-self-esteem thing to do, but I actually laugh.

"I mean it. Tiffany was so focused on her looks. It got . . . ugly. *She* got ugly, to me."

It seems kind of mean. To say all this about this girl, now dead. I try not to look at the picture too hard, but I want to. Same as I used to look at those pictures of my great-grandmother's sister, who died of pneumonia all those years ago. See, Tiffany didn't know when she was standing there that she wouldn't be for very much longer. That she'd get pregnant and die. I'm looking at her when I know the end of the story but she doesn't.

"Bo sure does look like her."

"I know." I watch Sebastian for signs of sadness, but he seems okay. He seems happy, really. "I think we're ready for dinner," he says. "Come on, Bo!" Bo has taken all of his trucks from his toy box and has lined them up on the carpet.

"No," Bo says.

"Dinner. Gogos."

"No."

"Power tripper," Sebastian says. "He knows about eight or ten words, but that's his favorite. Close your ears, Jade." He swoops Bo up and Bo screams. He zooms Bo to his high chair and plunks him in. Tosses the hot dog bits on his tray in a flash, and Bo suddenly stops screeching.

"You have that down," I say.

"Man's got to be quick."

I move around in the tiny kitchen, help carry out the bowls he's laid out, and the silverware. I sit in one of the wicker chairs, and Sebastian brings in the rest of the dinner.

"Cheers to our first meal together," he says. We clink our soda cans.

Bo munches on his hot dogs, which he smashes up toward his face. Sebastian gives him pieces of cheese, some crackers. A sippy cup of something that smells sweet and sticky, apple juice maybe.

"You have this handled so well," I say. "You just think, *Young father* . . . You know, that you'd be tearing out your hair."

"Oh, I do that," he laughs. "I do a lot of that. This is a show of togetherness to impress you."

"But you know what to *do*. How do you know what to do?"

Sebastian sprinkles some cheese on his chili. I have a bite of mine. It is way too salty, but who cares. "I don't always. I mean, I have a lot of help. My family." He gestures at the wall. "Without them, forget it. Even then, when Sebastian was first born? They gave him to me, you know, at the hospital. When it was time to go home. I almost handed him back. It felt so wrong. Like they shouldn't give him to me to take anywhere because I might wreck him. Or break him or hurt him. Later, I was so tired. I'd never been so tired in my life. It's not like you have an all-nighter and can sleep the next day. It goes on and on. . . . I'd feed him in bed with a bottle and we'd fall asleep there, and I'd jump up in this panic that I'd rolled over him and suffocated him."

"Scary."

"I was so crazy about him. This love just . . . overtakes. But, shit. Suddenly your whole life is dominated by this one thing. I can't even explain the adjustment. Like someone just hung a bowling ball around your neck and you've got to go on like you used to. That's not quite right, because the bowling ball's got to be kept alive. Needs to eat every few hours, cries and spits up and needs to eat again. Gets a cold and can't breathe . . . You've got to handle any need of his right then, not when you feel like it. There's this little demanding human and he is yours every day, every minute, and sometimes I'd have to step outside of the house and shut the door. Just, I was so fucking exhausted. I didn't think I could do it."

"What happened?"

"Well, we were with my mom and dad then, and they helped. Took over if things got too crazy. And just, day by day, I guess. You get to know what you're doing. I got used to the demands, and then the demands changed. Now it's demanding in a whole new way. Honestly? Sometimes I want to strangle him. But, look." We watch Bo munch his hot dog. His shiny hair. His rows of tiny, white teeth. He tries to scoop up some cut bananas with a spoon, with maybe 20 percent accuracy. "I go to work and I miss him. I go out without him and I feel like I've forgotten something. I think, *Wallet? Jacket?*" He laughs.

"It's strange, because here you are, just two years older than me, and every guy my age seems like he's still thinking about his video games or sex or football."

"Na-nas!" Bo says, holding his spoon in the air.

"Don't get the wrong idea. I used to love video games. I can't wait until Bo's old enough—man, that'll be a kick. I just don't have time. That all feels like a lifetime ago. Sometimes I feel like I'm fifty. Sometimes I feel like I was just seventeen and had this experience where someone hypnotized the real me and took over my life and, shit, look what they've done."

"I'm impressed, though."

"Don't be. It's not heroic. Someday you'll see Tess tell me to pick up my socks like I'm seven. Or hear me yell at Bo, and then feel like he'd have been better off adopted. But, talk to me about you. I'm not kid obsessed, really. Maybe a little. But tell me more about you. Your family—start there."

So I do. I tell him about Mom and her prom dresses and her parents in Florida, and about my dad and his sports obsession and Oliver and Milo and my dad's family. I tell him how Dad once tried to teach us all to ski and how Mom had the television on all day every day after 9/11, and how she even bought masks for us in case of chemical warfare, and how I accidentally knocked out Oliver's first tooth and how my mother used to sometimes cry and stay in her room with the door closed before we had to go over to my dad's parents' house.

Bo has basically smooshed or examined everything on his tray, which now is all half swimming in what is definitely apple juice. Then he wants "Dow!" and off he runs, and Sebastian tries to clean his face with a wet paper towel, which Bo distinctly hates.

"Want to get your jams on?" Sebastian says, which cues Bo to fling off his socks and begin a frustrating attempt to take off his own clothes. Sebastian finishes the job, and Bo has a glorious minute of naked freedom, running around like a cupid.

"Hey, Turbo," Sebastian says. "I'm gonna getcha!" Sebastian catches him and they wrestle Bo's pajamas on. "He can take off most of his clothes, but no way can he get them on yet," Sebastian shouts over the noise, and I carry our plates to the kitchen.

The phone rings and a newly p.j.'d Bo dashes to it, beating Sebastian easily.

"'Lo?" Bo says, then drops the phone where it is. You can still hear a voice coming out from where it lies on the floor.

Sebastian retrieves it. "Hi. Yeah. My secretary. Hey, can I call you later?" He pauses. "No, like tomorrow." He rolls his eyes toward the ceiling for my benefit. "She's supposed to be back late. FFECR meeting." He pauses again, listens. "Say it fast and it sounds like a word we don't want Bo to learn. Mmhmm. Okay. Tomorrow. Promise—jeez! Bye.

"My mom," he says.

"Hey, I should let you get going. Get Bo to bed."

"Let me just get him his toothbrush. He thinks he's brushing, but basically he sucks on it. He loves it, though, so it'll give me a chance to say good-bye."

"Ba," Bo says, and blows me a kiss. "Mwah!" he says, movie-actress style.

"Not yet," Sebastian says. "Hey, man, she's still here."

He finds Bo's toothbrush, and he is right, of course. Bo sits right down on his diapered bottom and sucks that toothbrush like a Popsicle. Sebastian walks me to the door.

"I really enjoyed this," I say.

"Go home and take a couple Tylenol," Sebastian says.

"No. Come on, he was great. This place . . . I had a terrific time."

"Me too," he says. He gathers my hair behind my back, lets it fall. We are close enough that I can feel his warm breath on my face. He leans down, and sets his lips not quite on mine. Just to the edge of my mouth. A light brush, oh, God, and then I perfect his aim.

We kiss for a while, not long enough. His mouth is chili-warm. We pull apart. Sebastian, my red-jacket boy, looks at me for a while. He puts his hand behind my neck, pulls me to him and kisses my forehead.

"Good night," he says.

"Bye," I say.

"Bah," Bo says from the living room. "Mwah!"

Wow lifts me up, plunks me outside into the cold, misty-wet night air. The lights that are strung along the dock reflect in the water of the lake. Ripple, dance. I head past the flowerpots, am just about to step off the dock, when I almost bump into a figure coming on. I barely see her, in her dark coat with the hood up against the rain. The hood comes down and out pops a fluff of gray hair, eyes direct and blue as the color of the china some old ladies have.

"Well, you don't look like a burglar," she says.

"I'm Jade. DeLuna. A friend of Sebastian's."

"Uh-huh."

She just stands there, drilling me into the ground with her eyes. This is Tess, I know, the one with the smile and the fishing pole in the pictures, the one with her arm around the big, bearded man, the one sitting with her sister on a rock wall somewhere that looked over the sea. Somehow, though, it doesn't seem like a good idea that I know who she is. That knowledge makes me too close, and she is already shoving me back with her gaze. I decide to fake ignorance. For a small woman, she seems capable of lifting me up in her fist and throwing me into the water. She seems too fierce for yellow gardening clogs.

"And you are . . . ?" I say.

"Early, it appears."

My insides gather up in some kind of shame, huddle together against her bad feeling of me. "Excuse me," I say. "Good night." I walk past her, feel her eyes follow me down the dock. The wind picks up and the houses rock up and down, their moorings creaking. I have gone from happy to humiliated in less than a minute, and as I walk to the car, I start getting that creepy, alone in the dark/someone about to jump out/victim of violent crime/check your backseat feeling. My chest starts growing dark and heavy, my palms sweat a little. I have a flash of fear that I won't be able to catch my breath, and so I get in the car in a hurry, lock all the doors and sit for a minute with my hands cupped over my mouth and nose. Breathe. In. Out. It's okay. I can. Handle this. Nothing is wrong. Only my body. Giving me. The wrong signals. Breathe. In. Out. From the diaphragm. See? There is no danger. Only the sense that I suddenly have something important to lose.

CHAPTER THIRTEEN

Some animals are emotionally invested in the help they give others. Rescue dogs, for example, become depressed if instead of saving lives they only encounter corpse after corpse. After the Oklahoma City bombing, the search dogs became morose, wouldn't eat, had to be dragged to work. No amount of treats or rewards could alter their sense of hopelessness. Only after a live "victim" was placed where the dogs could find him alive did their joy in their work resume . . .

—Dr. Jerome R. Clade, *The Fundamentals of Animal Behavior*

"So, Abe, how do you know what to listen to inside?"

"What do you mean?" Abe sips his tea. He'd stolen another one of Dr. Kaninski's coffee cups. GET A GRIP! it reads, with a cartoon guy holding a club in a half-swing. Probably what Dr. Kaninski felt about his patients, too.

"Well, how do you know if something is a good thing for you or a bad thing?"

"For example."

"For example, you meet someone. And they're great. Really great. But there are these other parts of it that people would generally think of as not good. Maybe your insides think those things are okay, even nice, but you have some other worry you can't put your finger on. How do you know? When to trust your inner voice?" Sebastian—God, he's warm and funny and smart and caring. But something is still nagging me about

Tiffany. His reaction to her, the loss of her. Then again, maybe everything is getting wrapped up in his grandmother's reaction to me. I felt like I had been caught stealing and wasn't sure if I could go in that store again.

"Why are these questions important to you now?" Abe says. "Tell me about the person you've met."

"Don't get all psychologist on me, please? I just want to know how you know what to listen to. Person to person. Your human being knowledge."

"Shit." Abe sighs. "That's a big question. You're looking at instinct like it's a foolproof system. Like it's a global positioning device."

"I thought that's why we have it. That's why animals have it. To protect."

"Sure, but it's a tool. Not THE tool, one tool. More like an old-fashioned map, not a GPS. You know, it's great to have a map, but there's the chance you can hold it upside down, read it wrong. Sometimes you just have to see where the road leads."

"But instinct should be *right*."

"It's mostly right. Think about it. You're descended from the very first person or creature that existed. Think what they had to do for you to be here in this time and place. All of your ancestors came from someone before, and you're the end product. You have Australopithecus ancestors."

"Who?"

"The guys with the big jaws, small brains."

"Are you insulting my father?"

"Ha. But think about it. Even before that. I love this stuff! You have ancestors that made fire and fought saber-toothed tigers and explored new territory and traveled oceans and went to war and survived the Great Depression." Abe gets up. His shirt is coming untucked. He refills his teacup with hot water, bobs a tea bag up and down.

"I never really thought about that."

"Well, look. They have. Your *ancestors*. You didn't just, poof, appear. You have the pieces of every person that came before you, from the dawn of time. You've *lasted*. That's what you're made up of. You've done pretty well, huh? Made of strong stuff."

"Me? Always afraid? They'd laugh."

"Think what a huge force fear must have been. Imagine being out in the dark, alone in the elements. Fear, great enough to change the formation of all living things—eyes on the side, eyes in the front, protective coverings, spikes, and venom. Other protections, too—shyness and anxiety and superstitions—all remnants of fear. Rituals and rain dances, gods and mythology. Living in groups . . . It goes on and on. Fear causes the greatest changes, when you think about it. Fear is a monumental force."

"Maybe my ancestors left behind too much of it. My instinct sucks."

"Sometimes it can get drowned out by other things. Maybe it gets tweaked by people in your life. Urged in one direction. Sometimes that's just the way you come."

"Or it gets broken . . ." I think about Onyx and the other elephants. How they will become afraid to the point of harming people after they've been hurt, even people who try to help them.

"Nothing about you is broken, Jade."

"I'm not talking about me. Just . . . in general."

"Sure, okay." He rocks a bit in his chair. "Instinct's an awesome thing, but we don't have to be a prisoner to it." He scratches his whiskers. "So. Anyway. What's happening now that's brought all this to mind?"

"I met someone. Not just someone, but *someone*."

"You're in love." He grins.

"Quit it." I glare at him. I look away, stare at his bookshelf and his photo of Tibetan prayer flags, waving yellow, red, blue, green in the wind.

"Your instinct is there and in fine working order, okay? You've just got your fear turned up a little loud. Like your stereo with too much bass. Makes it hard to hear the lyrics."

"I don't want to get hurt."

"How does a person stay safe, always? Lock yourself away? You're looking for a guarantee and there are no guarantees. If you love, you'll feel loss. You can't 'careful' yourself into avoiding loss. You're trying to get day without night."

"All the marshmallows without the cereal," I say.

"Summer vacation without the school."

"We can stop now," I say.

Abe sighs. "I was just getting going."

"I've got a new plan for Onyx," Damian says to me when I arrive at the elephant house. "It's brilliant, if I do say so myself." Damian is checking health charts when I find him. His warm, brown face is soft and pleased with himself, his eyes bright. "I could barely sleep last night, I was so excited. It's so simple."

"What?"

"What Onyx needs. A mother. Her own, full-time mother. Consistency. Unconditional love."

"Okay . . ." I wait for more.

Damian faces me, clasps his hands together. "Delores!" he says.

"Delores?"

"She's perfect. The solution has been right here all along."

"Delores? Are you sure?"

"Of course I am sure. She is a caregiver. She is a mother with a loving heart. Do you see those pictures of her children?"

"Yes, but have you asked her to do this?"

"Well, that is my one small problem. She says no."

"That seems like more than a small problem." I step into my overalls, zip them up.

But Damian's eyes are still all gleaming and dancing. "That's where you come in!"

"Me?"

"She likes you. You will coax her out of that little box she hides in."

"Damian! I barely know her."

"You are young and you make her smile, I've seen it. And she is missing her daughter. Get her to come out of her box and just *see*."

"If she doesn't want to, what can I do?"

"Try," Damian says. "And try quickly. Onyx is running out of time."

I work a little cleaning stalls, and then hang a traffic cone on the chain for enrichment. Hansa is the first one over. She saunters right over to it and sniffs to examine it. She sets her trunk to my head as if to get me to play too.

I pat her, rub her trunk. I love its roughness under my hand,

and her funny little face. The fluff of hair. "Sweet one, you are," I say to her. "Funny girl."

As it gets closer to leaving time, I watch for Sebastian. After Tess and her reaction to me, I don't know if he'll even come.

And I am right. It's a nice day, and there are several visitors in the viewing area. *See the elephants! Say hi to the elephants!* But there is no Sebastian and no Bo.

I pass Delores as I leave the front gate. She is in her booth, doing word searches and drinking a can of Diet 7 Up.

"Wow, you look down," she says. Her voice is small and echoey from behind her window.

"I do?"

"Written all over your face. That boy?"

I nod.

"Complicated," she says. She picks up her purse from the shelf near her feet, fishes around inside. She pulls out a pack of cinnamon gum and offers me a stick through the half-circle hole in the glass. "Here. I just got to give you *something*," she says.

She's a person with a loving heart, just like Damian said. "I'm supposed to talk to you about Onyx," I start.

"I don't want to hear any more about it," she says. She unwraps a piece of gum for herself, folds it into her mouth.

"Delores, you'd love it."

"I'd get attached, I'd get all involved, I'd never leave. . . ."

"That's the idea."

"I had that in my old job, remember? That's why I left. No more. This is perfect for me."

"You're missing out," I say.

"So, I'm missing out." She chews her gum, smacks it all juicily.

"Hansa would love that gum. The smell," I say. "She'd put her trunk right up to your cheek."

"Go," Delores says.

"I'll be back," I say.

I walk the long way home, through the rose garden, hoping Sebastian will still show. The garden is mostly green sticks, an improvement over the brown sticks they were a month ago. Green stick bushes and hedges, a pavilion at one end. In the summer it will be beautiful there, but now it is harsh and prickly. Jake Gillete isn't in the parking lot, and Titus is too focused on his work to wave. Through the window of Total Vid, I can see Mrs. Porter, our mail lady, perusing the display of *Riding Giants* as Titus heads her way, determined as a salesman in the Nordstrom shoe department.

When I open the door of my house, I can hear my mother talking on the phone in the kitchen, laughing. I shut the door loudly, to let her know I am there. I don't know why this feels necessary, except that her voice has something different about it. A lightness that erases the mother parts of her. That makes her seem like a girl. Her voice—it's like ice cubes tinkling in a glass.

"I have to go," she says. I hear the phone clunk to its cradle. "Jade?" she calls.

"It's me."

"How was your day?"

"Fine."

"I've got to pick Oliver up from basketball. Oh, and can you start dinner? Hamburgers? 'Cause I've got a meeting at seven."

"Okay."

I take everything from my patron saint box, look at each candle carefully. Saint Dymphna is the best choice. I know it

deb caletti

sounds like a growth that should be surgically removed, but really she's this young woman with a handkerchief over her head and an understanding look. In her picture she holds something that looks like a box of chocolates, but I don't have a clue what it really is. Maybe some kind of cure, some magic released when the lid is off, like in one of Oliver's Narnia books. She is the patron saint of family happiness, of possessed people, of therapists and nervous disorders and runaways. I figure she'll do the trick for Tess and Sebastian, close enough, and I feel qualified on the nervous disorders end. Even Abe will be watched over, and I figure it's the least I can do, considering all he does for me.

I have a ton of homework, but I don't care about reading twenty-five pages of biology right then. I'm too worried about Sebastian, about that angry white-haired lady with the blue eyes that he cares so much about. Instead, I lie on my bed and look out the lava-lamp window. I watch the white clouds make shapes against the sky, drifting, but with purpose. As if they know just where they are going.

After dinner, Mom leaves for her meeting, and instead of helping with the dishes, I am bouncing Oliver's basketball around in the kitchen.

"Jade, you better help," Oliver says.

"If you think we're doing your plate, just know you'll be seeing it at breakfast," Dad says.

"Go out for a pass," I say. I bounce the ball Dad's way. He ignores me and it crashes into the oven door.

"Something's going to get broken," he says.

"I'm giving you another chance," I say. I dribble around the kitchen table. Scoot beautifully around a blocking chair. It doesn't have a chance. If I were this good in PE, those people never would have laughed. I give the ball a single bounce toward Dad. He turns in a flash, drops his kitchen towel, and neatly catches the ball.

"Now you're in trouble," he says.

And I am. See, as I've said, Dad's a really good athlete. Even in his dress slacks and shirt, his tie slightly loosened, he moves around the kitchen as if he's on some gym floor with his tennis shoes going *sweek-sweek* and the crowds going wild. He stops, dodges, and advances. Already, he is over by the refrigerator. I approach, but he is gone again. Just dribbling, oh, so full of himself, back by the stove now.

"Help me, Oliver," I say.

We pounce, and Milo starts barking like crazy and Oliver lets out a tribal war whoop. Dad dances and jets around and we keep reaching out, grabbing at nothing.

"I-I'm whip-ping your bu-utts," Dad sings.

"Get him!" Oliver screams. I'm not sure whose team Milo is on, but he should be kicked off for unsportsmanlike behavior.

Oliver has his hip right against Dad's. Then he moves ever so slightly in front of him, neatly snatching the ball. Suddenly, Oliver is over by Milo's water bowl, dribbling with that same smug look Dad had.

"Yes!" I screech. I jump up and down. "Victory is ours!"

"Well, look at that," Dad says.

"I learned it from Coach Bronson," Oliver says.

"Game over. Let's have a beer," I say.

Dad shoots me a look.

"Kidding!" I say.

We finish up the dishes, and then follow Dad downstairs to see the train. "Wow," I say.

The new part of his town has been filled out—there are patches of nubby green trees and serene rolling hills, a small lake, all surrounding the house I had set there. Off a bit from the house is a very small town, one store, with its own tiny gas pumps, and a truck beside them getting filled. There's only a small corner of board left.

"You're almost done," I say.

"What do you guys think?"

"I like it there," Oliver says, pointing to where the new house is. It's true—it's the prettiest part of the board, away from his old center of town with the streets and people and miniature trucks and stores and factories.

"Me too," I say. "What are you going to do with the corner that's left?"

"Don't laugh," he says.

"What?"

"An ocean."

"Cool," Oliver says.

"I've never seen a set with an ocean before," he says. "I'm still trying to figure out how I can craft it."

"Then you'll be done," I say. "And then what?"

"I don't know," he says. He takes his tie off, tosses it on the chair.

"The train goes on its first trip," Oliver says.

"I guess you're probably right," Dad says.

We leave Dad downstairs.

"Jade?" Oliver says. He's been thinking about something.

"What?"

"I still don't like basketball."

"That's okay," I say. "More than okay."

I knock on my doorframe. I settle in front of my computer for homework, try to concentrate on things I don't care about instead of obsessing about where Sebastian might be. I flip over to the elephants, hoping for even red-jacket cyber contact. Anything. I would have called him if I weren't scared to death of his white-haired grandmother. I watch Tombi swaying, moving her feet in that restless way. I know how she feels. I do more homework, pop on the web, and try to look up FFECR. Maybe it would help me understand something about Tess. I stop looking for it after three pages of French phrases and medical conditions, nothing I'm guessing Tess would be at a meeting for.

I clomp back downstairs to feed my misery. I have a couple of chocolate chip cookies left in the bag from about six months ago, which are lifeless and stale. Milo appears with his blankie, and I give him a big new rawhide to brighten his evening. It cheers me up to make him so happy. He takes it from me, gently, politely, and then trots to the living room with it sticking sideways out of his mouth. I watch him. He paces, hunts around for just the right spot to bury it.

"Chew on it, don't hide it," I advise.

He ignores me. Continues his quest with the focused, got-to-find-it obsession of someone in a long checkout line hunting for that last nickel. He tries out one place, under the couch, decides against it. No good. He walks to the potted fern and sniffs, but no. Under the armoire with the television in it? Maybe. He sets it down, looks, decides it is not quite right. He finally sets it next to the basket of magazines. He pushes his

deb caletti

nose against the carpet over and over, burying it with imagined dirt. It sits there on the rug in plain sight, and Milo looks at it as if it weren't there. It's kind of embarrassing. But you can tell even he knows he's kidding himself.

Milo stares up at me with his deep brown eyes. He seems like he's at a loss at what to do, and this makes me sad for him. "You did a great job," I say. "Awesome. I don't see a thing."

I pat his soft head. Talk about broken instinct.

It's one of those life rules that when you don't care about guys noticing you, they most often do. The next day at school, with my thoughts on Sebastian, I catch Ben Nelson checking me out, and in Spanish, I have an unexpected encounter with Jacob Leeland, manic pothead. Another rule of life is that if you are a decent and hardworking student, you will pay for it by always getting placed by your teachers next to some hyperactive headline-of-the-future. Your reward for your responsible and respectful behavior is to be "a role model"—basically, babysitting junior borderline criminals. You will have the honor of putting up with them rolling pencils at you, cheating off your tests, throwing paper clips, borrowing your pens (which they never give back), and sitting in a reeking cloud of marijuana or cigarette smell, the haze of which drifts around their jackets like fog in a field on a cold morning.

Jacob Leeland is one of those. Señora Kingslet always pairs us up, primarily so Jacob can at least get a decent grade on the stuff we do in class, and we are supposed to be developing a dialogue that would take place in a restaurant. Our conversation goes something like this:

Me: So, you're the waiter, and you say: *¿Qué usted tiene gusto de ordenar, Señorita?* (What would you like to order, Miss?)

Jacob: Do you find me attractive?

Me: Huh?

Jacob: Do you? I think you're hot.

Me: (Pause) So, anyway, then I can say something like: *Quisiera los pescados, por favor.* (I'd like the fish, please.)

Jacob: You didn't answer my question. We'd be a cute couple (scoots closer).

Me: (Scoots away) Then you say: *Cualquier cosa?* (Anything else?)

Jacob: Does that mean, no, you don't find me attractive?

Me: You're a nice person, Jacob, but . . .

Jacob: Sure. (Sulks.) So where'd you get that shirt? My girlfriend would like it.

At lunch, we stay at school for once, sit on the benches outside since no one feels like going anywhere and Akello and Michael are broke. Jenna bows her head over her tuna sandwich. Hannah and Kayla squeal over their shared Cheetos bag, and Michael and Akello and I study for our AP Government test and eat Michael's Corn Nuts. I look up and watch the crowds, who remind me of cows—if one lies down, they all do. If one is standing, they all are standing. I have this ache inside. My insides pulling with a desire for too-salty chili in a bowl and a rocking houseboat and my feet in someone's lap. I belong there, and suddenly this bench in its plot of grass is the place I don't know, somewhere I've never been, and these people are the ones that seem like strangers.

"Come on, Delores."

"I told you, no."

"I'm not saying you have to do anything. Just come with

deb caletti

me. Come out. I promise you, you're not making some kind of decision. You're just *looking*. See? Beverly is here to sell tickets. She can spare you for a sec."

Delores pretends to study her seek-and-find word book. Then she smacks her pencil down on the page. "Just to look."

"Okay, great! That's so great."

"Don't sound so excited. I'm only doing this to shut you up." Delores leans for her purse, then turns the handle inside her booth. I never realized there was a handle. It's the first time, actually, that I've ever seen her out of the booth. She steps out, shuts the door. She's a little shorter than I am, has those jeans with the huge back pockets that cover a wide, flat rear end. She wears tennis shoes and an orange sweatshirt and her big ASK ME zoo button. She carries her purse in her left hand, the one that sports one of those watches that have circles of various, removable colors. I notice gold hoop earrings peeking from her short, white-blond hair. She's a real person with a real life, and that seems like a surprise. I wonder what she does when she's not here. If she watches sports on TV or likes to cook. It reminds me of the time some little kid in the viewing area asked me if I lived at the zoo.

"Look at you," I say.

"What?" Delores says.

"You're out."

"Make it snappy," she says.

"I'm going to take you into the house first," I say. "But, warning—it smells kind of strong in there."

"I used to work in a hospital," she reminds me.

Delores's walk is efficient. I have to work to keep up with her. We go around the back, where Damian's office is, and the staff quarters. Then I bring her through to the stalls. Rick Lindstrom and Damian are washing Chai, who lolls on one side and rolls and sneezes like Milo on the lawn. Damian grins at Delores.

"I'm looking," she says to Damian. "That's all."

"Just look, then."

"Let's go out to the yard," I say.

I can see Tombi and Onyx out by the water, and Hansa near the viewing area. When she sees me, she ambles over. "Ambles" is not quite right for Hansa—she's actually quite fast. Hansa and I are special pals.

"They're rather . . . large." Delores says.

"Don't be nervous," I say. "The trick is to be the boss. Hey, I'm the most worried person in the world, and I handled it. It's a little intimidating at first, but trust me, if I can do it, you can. Come here, you," I say to Hansa.

Hansa stops near us and sniffs around to see if I've brought her any fruit or treats. "Sorry, girl," I say. I rub her side, and reach my palm for her to snuffle her trunk in. "Put your hand out," I tell Delores.

"Forget it."

"Honestly, it's okay."

"Oh, my God," Delores says.

"See?" I say. "I was so scared at first."

"Oh, shit," she says. She squeals a little when Hansa smells her palm.

"We should have brought some watermelon," I say.

"She's really cute, though," Delores says.

"Everybody loves her, except Onyx. There's Onyx. Over there. Not her best side." We're looking at Onyx's huge, saggy ass and her tiny tail, twitching from side to side. Funny thing is, I can almost picture Onyx in those same wide-pocket jeans Delores is wearing.

"She's really huge." Hansa is sniffing Delores's sweatshirt.

"But she's sad. Her anger is just too much sadness with nowhere to go."

Hansa's trunk is everywhere. In my hair, on Delores's shoulder. "You're a pest," I say.

Delores pats Hansa's side, like I do. "It's softer than I thought," she says.

"I know it. Like rough leather." I see that Damian has appeared in the enclosure to watch us. "Let's meet Onyx," I say.

"All right."

Delores follows me through the yard, looking over her shoulder as if she's in a rough neighborhood. We approach Onyx from the front. Onyx can still make me a little nervous, and I'm glad Damian is nearby. Still, it's so important not to let the elephants feel your uncertainty that I force myself to shake off any fear.

"Onyx, you big softie. Meet Delores."

"Hello," Delores says formally.

"Now you must blow in her trunk, like this." I show her. "It's a handshake. An official greeting. Once you do, she'll never forget you."

I hold Onyx's trunk out to Delores, and she blows inside. Delores looks at Onyx and Onyx looks at Delores. "It's a pleasure," Delores says after a while. Here's what passes between them: the look of a couple of older women who have seen things in their day.

"Let me think about this," Delores says as we head back. "Don't go taking that as an encouraging response. I'm only thinking."

"You won't regret it," I say.

"You did a wonderful job," Damian says to me afterward. He is outside with Onyx and Flora. "It is like the car salesman trick, you see? Once you drive the car, you will want to buy it."

"You think?"

"I know. An elephant is impossible to resist. Look at that face," he says to Onyx. "What are they saying, those eyes?"

"They are saying, 'I want to be with Delores,' right, Onyx?"

Damian chuckles. "Those eyes know things."

I haven't even changed into my overalls yet, so I head back to the elephant house to do that. When I hang up my coat, I hear my phone ringing in the pocket. By the time I fumble around and get it out, I miss the call. But the words on the screen make my heart lift. ARMCHAIR BO the screen says. I press the call button, trying to wrestle my backstage mind, which is barreling in with thoughts and what-ifs. Tombi is making a happy racket in the house, so I go outside, lean my back against the building.

"Armchair Books."

"Sebastian? It's Jade. I just missed your call."

"Hi," he says.

"Hi."

"I'm so glad to hear you." The tension that had risen in me like one of the waves in *Riding Giants* crashes and breaks into relief.

"Me too."

"I was calling . . . I wanted to apologize for Tess. Can you hang on a minute?"

"Sure."

The phone clunks onto the counter and I hear Sebastian's voice far away, speaking to another man. Then he's back.

deb caletti

"That was so weird," he says softly. "This guy, he looked like an escaped con and wanted a book on puppetry."

"Do you have one of those buzzers on the floor, like they do at the bank in case of robbery?"

"I wish. Anyway, Tess . . . I know she saw you. I hadn't told her about you yet, and I know she overreacted. . . ."

"She just made it clear where she stood." A peanut shell is in the dirt on the ground, and I send it into a figure eight with the toe of my shoe.

"You always know where you stand with Tess. She's a good person, really, she's just worried about me. We got in an argument. She's repenting. Told me to ask you over here to dinner so she could meet you."

"Is that what you want?" I was wondering if it might be easier to roll around in some raw hamburger and visit the Bengal tiger, but, hey.

"I do. I mean, I'd really like you to know each other. I guess, actually, it's important to me. If it's okay with you. Is this . . . too much, too fast?"

"No. I don't think so."

"Well, great. Next Saturday? Are you free? Six? I'm not working."

"No, that's great. Great."

"Great," he says. "That was a lot of greats."

"It sure was."

"You should see who's standing in your gardening section now. Pierced lip, tattoo going up his arm. Some kind of dagger. Very Seattle. Oops, gotta go."

"Next Saturday."

"Bye."

"Bye."

We hang up, and I'm filled with excitement/loss. The happiness at his company, the sadness that his company is gone. But the sadness turns out to be unnecessary. A few hours later, after Armchair Books has closed, my phone rings again.

"I just thought you might want to know that I wasn't robbed after all," Sebastian says.

Glee is such an old-fashioned word. A corny one, but that's what my heart feels—the equivalent of every corny, ridiculous, gleeful scene. I'm the living embodiment of those musicals where people break into song at monumental moments, of square dancers twirling in bright, ruffled skirts, of glittery snow on Christmas cards.

"I'm so glad," I say.

"And the pierced guy bought *All About Bulbs*."

We talk into the night. After that, he calls every night of the week before our Saturday date. When Mom asks, I tell her it's Michael with girl problems. Poor Michael's got a lot of girl problems lately, and poor me, I have to sit there and listen. When Sebastian calls, I get comfy, cross-legged on the floor, keep my voice low to keep from disturbing anyone—okay, to keep from anyone knowing how late we actually talk. Sebastian calls when he's stocking books. I picture him with the phone crooked between his shoulder and his ear, working in that cozy room with the faux flame in the fireplace. Occasionally, he drops me when he reaches a high shelf. There's a huge crashing clunk and then Sebastian's voice, far away—"Jade! God, just a sec! I'm here! Don't go anywhere!" And then he returns, his voice loud again. "Are you all right? Are you still in one piece?"

We talk about his customers and my school day, books

deb caletti

we've read, some movie, a dog he used to have—small stuff. Then about God and the universe and why we're here—the biggest. One night, it becomes so late that we reach the hour where the rules and bindings drop away, where it's just the raw, feral pieces under all the rational ones. Sebastian confesses that he's always been afraid of things with wings—bats and birds and cicadas. I confess that I've been afraid of everything. I tell this to the darkness of my room, instead of to the boy on the other end of the phone. Abe says not to be ashamed, we all have anxiety to some degree, but sometimes I still am ashamed.

Sebastian asks questions—gentle, past-midnight questions. He has some knowledge of anxiety, from a friend of his. He tells me it's okay, that everyone has something to struggle with. *Okay*—that's all that really matters.

It is a few nights after that, just before our scheduled dinner date with Tess, that I see Sebastian on the webcam in the elephant viewing area. We'd just hung up—he was heading home, he'd said. It is late, so he has snuck in again. It feels wrong to be watching him now that we know each other, but I do it anyway. I lie on my bed, my head propped on my hand, as he sits on the bench, his legs crossed in front of him. His own hands are folded under his chin, and he is still there after a long time. And then he bends his head down, forehead on his hands, and I realize what he is doing. He is praying.

This is not a place he has invited me to. I turn off the screen. I sit back down on my bed, watch the green light of the computer glow. In my mind, I take Sebastian's hand, hold his head against my chest and comfort him.

CHAPTER FOURTEEN

Animals can form kinship relationships with species not their own. In a Thailand zoo, a dog has raised three tiger cubs, and now resides with her "children"—three full-grown tigers and her own pup. Should the tigers be returned to their "own kind," however, their own kind would likely be viewed as some strange, alien, other. It is the dogs that are family . . .

—Dr. Jerome R. Clade, *The Fundamentals of Animal Behavior*

"I was hoping you'd be home tonight," Mom says. "I've hardly seen you lately."

"I thought you *wanted* me to get more involved in the social stuff," I say. Mom is unloading groceries. I get the happy what's-in-the-bag excitement that comes when someone's just gone shopping, especially since she hadn't been in so long. I peek in, hunt around for something worth the enthusiasm and only find plastic bags of broccoli and bananas and lettuce. Diet food—what a letdown.

"But what about us?" She turns to face me, a carton of yogurt in her hand.

"You got your hair cut," I say.

"Do you like it?"

"And highlights."

"Too much?"

"No, it looks nice." And it does. It's sort of flippy and fresh.

The PTA women all look alike—hair that tries to look young but still seems like it has a list of things it needed to accomplish. Politician-wife hair. But this style is looser. Free. Oh, my God, that's not what it is. It's sexy.

"I just needed a change."

"Well, great. Anyway, I don't want to miss this thing at Alex's. I won't be late—you won't have to worry about me driving."

"All right." She sighs. But as I turn to leave, I catch her looking at her reflection in the dark glass of the microwave door. She angles her head to the side, raises her chin. Then she's back to the grocery bag, taking out a loaf of brown bread. I rush out of there. I get this weird feeling, like I'd seen parts of her that weren't my business. Like those times when you watch your parents at a party with their friends, or find some pills of theirs in the bathroom, or when you see too much as they're coming out of the bathroom—soft abdomens, an uncovered chest. That glance made me remember that there were pieces of her life that were only hers, that she had thoughts that had nothing to do with my report card.

I drive out of Hawthorne Square, wave to old Mrs. Simpson, one of the neighbors, who is clutching her sweater closed for warmth and walking toward Total Vid with a copy of *Riding Giants* to return. I can see her wrinkly fingers wrapped around the surfing guy on the front of the box. I am getting a tightness in my chest, the cinching. There is too little air outside, it seems, for everything that needs it. My heart sits right against the surface of my skin, and I try to breathe deeply. You can handle it, Abe would say. I count this on my fingers. *You-can-han-dle-it. You-can-han-dle-it.*

the nature of jade   207

I decide to count coffee shops to take my mind off of the fact that I am going to dinner at Sebastian's and am about to be devoured by a grandmother. One espresso stand near the 76 station, two coffee houses by the zoo, a Starbucks on the main drag, another across the street. Another espresso stand by the bank, count the one inside the Laundromat, two more on the street by Lake Union. Another Starbucks, then Seattle's Best, a Java Jive, and I am at the lake.

It is still light, and late-March cold and gray. The trees are uninspired, and the lake steely and determined. The city sprawls across the water, with the Space Needle dominating the sky with its white, spidery legs and alien-ship top. I shut my mouth tight against the gnat conference that is apparently ongoing there at the start of the dock, creak down the planks, step over another cat, and notice things I hadn't before—flags on sailboats whipping, their rings clanging against metal masts. The sound of wind chimes and seagulls. Ducks cruising around between the houses, stained-glass windows, door knockers in the shape of sailboats and whales.

I walk up the ramp of Number 3, and am struck again at how snug it feels there. The plants have just been watered—the earth in the pots is dark and wet and smells freshly upturned, and the dock wood is still drying. Spicy odors, something with tomatoes, drift from the house, and I can hear Bo inside making a racket. A pair of tennis shoes have joined the gardening clogs on the step.

Before I ring the doorbell, Sebastian opens the door. He is wearing jeans and a sweatshirt and looks tousled and relaxed; he's barefoot. He is the visual equivalent of a Sunday morning.

"I felt you step on," he says. And to my baffled expression: "The house tips when someone walks on the float."

"I just realized I never asked you what I should bring. I even forgot the book you lent me."

He took my arm, squeezes. "No worries. We've got everything. Come on in."

"I promised I'd behave," Tess shouts from the kitchen. Tomatoes, all right. Garlic. Bo driving trucks on the floor, some music in the background. Lit candles on the higher windowsills.

Sebastian guides me to the kitchen. "Proper meeting. Jade, Tess. Tess, Jade."

"Pleasure," Tess says. I think of Delores, saying the same thing to Onyx. Tess is wearing a sweatshirt too, but hers has the solar system on it and a little arrow and the words: YOU ARE HERE. She wears jeans, and a pair of wooly socks, and her eyes are as blue and direct as I remembered. You get the sense that with one look, she'd opened all your file drawers and read the contents.

"It smells great," I say.

"Shrimp Creole. Hope you're okay with shrimp." She clatters the lid back on the pot, wipes her hands on a kitchen towel. "So."

"Tess is restraining herself from asking you a ton of questions. She's probably going to ask for your résumé."

"I am not," she says.

Conversational roadblock, and oh, shit, so soon. Everyone's quiet. We all look at Bo, watch him drive his trucks around the floor. He is oblivious to the three pairs of eyes boring into him in social desperation.

"Hey, buddy," Sebastian says to him lamely.

Somewhere in my mind I must have something I can say to

her. "Sebastian tells me you're an activist," I say finally.

"Well, I get *involved* in what I feel needs attention."

"That's great."

Silence. Just more silence and more staring at Bo.

Sebastian claps his hands. "Shall we get ready to eat?" he says.

"Oh, for God's sake, Sebastian, relax," Tess says. "She's too cute to bite."

"Not too tasty, either," I say.

"Well, Sebastian should probably be the judge of that," she says.

"Tess," Sebastian says.

"What? It's the truth. Do you fish?" she asks me. Those blue eyes again.

"Well," I say. I think. There was that one time at the trout farm. I remember dropping our lines in and pulling up a fish, easy as spearing a maraschino cherry with a toothpick in a glass of Coke. "Not much."

"Not much?"

"Once or twice."

"So, let's go," she says.

"Now?" Sebastian says.

"Why not?" She is already heading out of the room. "You need a jacket?" she calls.

"I'll be okay," I say.

"Now?" Sebastian says again. "We've got dinner, and Bo . . ." He looks at me, and I shrug my shoulders.

"Bo's fine," Tess says from the other room. "He loves the boat. Bring some crackers."

Tess appears again, wearing a zip-up jacket. She tosses me

a blue wool coat. "You're skinny. You'll get cold."

"Ba?" Bo asks.

"Yep, I guess so," Sebastian says. He rolls his eyes at me, takes Bo's fleece jacket off a hook by the door, and then his own red one.

A few moments later, we are sitting across from each other, knees to knees in Tess's small motorboat. She is at the helm, manning the rudder, and Bo is on Sebastian's lap, his orange life jacket up around his neck same as those people who have to wear a white collar after a car accident. Fishing poles and a tackle box are in the back, and my own life jacket is snug around me. I'm having one of those moments where you don't feel like it's you in your own body. I'd gone from this warm house with garlic smells to a boat with a roaring motor, wearing Tess's wool coat, my hair flying around my face and catching in my mouth.

Tess kneels at the helm with her back to us, showing us the bottom of one rubber boot. Her nylon coat whips back and forth, and her white hair springs around with its own contentment. The sun slides out and the water twinkles, and we pass the rows of houseboats and head into the channel that connects Lake Union to Lake Washington. The water gets a bit choppy and we hit a wave with a big, jouncy thud, and I say a small prayer, *oh, shit,* that Tess knows what she is doing, and she must, because she pushes the boat's levered handle and slows the speed, until we are jostling gently forward.

I relax—we're obviously in good hands. Sebastian smiles at me, and I smile back. Cold air blows in my face and fills me with joyful wake-up. Bo could care less about the plastic bag of goldfish crackers Sebastian holds out to him. His blond hair is snapping around and he sits stone-still on his dad's legs, watching the waves, the houses, the big underneath side of a bridge we pass beneath. My heart is in-love happy, with this boy across from me, this boat, this ride, that baby, even that grandmother, who's shouting things in the wind she thinks we can hear but don't. Finally, she turns and we do hear.

"Marvelous, yes?"

I nod and smile. The wind, the ride, the bumping. The *outside*, so present, close enough to breathe in. The smell of gasoline on water, the sun-glints and the sky with drapey colors—it is binding. You take a boat ride like that with people and you're as close to them as if you've spent a hundred lunches together across tables in crowded restaurants.

She slows the boat to idling now. We are slopping around, and Tess has me hand her a pole, already hooked, and the tackle box, with its jars packed with bait—red eggs, yellow and pink marshmallows—and its shiny, odd lures and rolls of line, a container more varied and fascinating than any jewelry box.

"Sebastian watches Bo, I cast, and you hold the pole," Tess says. *Ssszink*, the line is in the water and she hands it to me. Tess tugs at the line. "Feel that? If you feel that, pull back hard to set the hook, then reel. Got it?"

"I think so," I say.

"Yes, you do. You're a fisherman from way back, I can tell," Tess says.

"Tess met Max fishing," Sebastian says. "Sort of."

"I found his old wedding ring, in a trout."

"You're kidding," I say.

"I am not. That's what happened. I saw his name engraved

deb caletti

inside the ring, and I knew the man lived nearby. I returned it to him. And, basically, I never left."

"It was just his cooking," Sebastian says.

"It was just his everything," Tess says. Her voice wobbles a little. She clears her throat. "Yes, well," she says.

I feel my own eyes fill, and my throat tightens. Sebastian leans forward and takes my hand. I squeeze. I want to cry. See, she is a woman in love, and I suddenly feel the magnitude of that. I am one, too.

The sun is setting when Tess docks the boat by the house again, and we step up and out, handing each other the poles and the tackle box and life jackets, and Bo, who passes through the air with his legs dangling. Tess knows what she is doing, all right. By the time we all get out, we are working as a team, and Tess rests her hand briefly on the back of my coat. "Fine fishing," she says.

"I didn't catch you anything," I say.

"Fishing is about the expectation of good things," she says. "Not about the fish."

Inside, it feels warmer than ever after coming in from the cold. We shed our jackets. I'm starving. We set the table, put Bo in his seat, and I give him some spiral pasta and bits of ham and bananas. We eat hot, spicy Creole shrimp and bread, wash it down with sparkling lemonade. Tess sips a glass of wine, which makes her cheeks red. Sebastian has his hand on my knee under the table. Tess brings out a small album of Mattie's. She points to pictures of her and Mattie with locked arms (*My sis*, she says), of Sebastian's parents' wedding (*They were too young, but it worked out all right*), of Sebastian and his sister Hillary, standing in front of the tea-cup ride at Disneyland (*Puke fest*, Tess says. *This was the* before *picture*). We talk about my family and Tess tells stories about Sebastian when he was little, and we laugh and Tess pours another bit of wine.

"This has been so fun," I say. And it has. Further proof that when you are positive something's going to be great, it isn't always, but when you don't expect great, it just might be. We are all in that drowsyish contentment that fresh air plus good food brings. Bo has been snapped into his pajamas and is watching Elmo singing on a video.

"You can come back and we'll take the boat out," Tess says.

"Now that Jade knows you're a nice little old lady," Sebastian teases.

"Smartass. Ha. I'm younger than you in ways," she says. "I was *worried*, all right? No one could blame me. You getting involved. When you've got so much to handle. When your life is . . ."

"A mess?" he suggests.

"In flux. You know, after we left, after Tiffany's car accident and all, Sebastian was a wreck—"

"Childbirth," Sebastian says.

"Childbirth?" Tess says.

"Childbirth is what you meant." Everything is quiet. All you can hear is Elmo singing in the next room. What the hell is going on? Tess leans forward on her elbows. Sebastian runs his hand over his forehead. "Shit," he says.

"Childbirth?" Tess says. She shakes her head. "God, Sebastian. No one dies of childbirth anymore."

"What?" I say. The word is barely there. I don't understand

deb caletti

what is happening here, but I know it's big, huge. I'm suddenly at the edge of a cliff, my toes hanging over. I feel the long drop down in my chest.

"She's got to know," Sebastian says.

"Car accident, Sebastian," Tess says. "For Christ's sake."

"I want her to know, Tess."

He has gone from the sweet, solid Sebastian I know to someone with pleading and desperate eyes. "What's going on," I say. "Please." I'm falling off that cliff, that's what it feels like. Free-falling, with nothing to grasp onto. I'm holding my breath. I'm waiting for the crash.

"This is the royal fuck-up I was afraid of," Tess says. She pushes her plate away from herself, as if she wants it all, everything, away.

"She needs to know. I hate this lie. Please, Jade. I want you to understand. Tiffany," Sebastian says to me. "She's not dead." His words are whispers too.

"What?" I don't understand. "What?" I say again. I picture Tiffany, her long, shiny hair, the beautiful face I'd made tragic. The face I'd seen in my mind a thousand times, imagining her unaware of her own fate, feeling real sorrow for her unrealized future. She's alive somewhere? Right now, she's somewhere, eating dinner, watching television, wearing sweats, or brushing her teeth? My mind attempts to make the mental shift, stalls in the bringing her back to life. I feel cheated somehow—the lie and my belief in it, all that misdirected compassion. I feel like a fool. I feel like I'm making the long drop down that cliff, with the ground rushing at me.

"Jade," Sebastian pleads. "See . . . I did something really stupid." He looks up at me, then down again, puts his head in his hands. "I'm sorry I lied. Bo . . . God, how do I say this? I've never said this out loud. I left with him."

"You took him?" Away from her? His mother?

"This is not simple . . ." Tess says.

"Tiffany—she didn't want Bo. Never wanted him. She wanted to give him away. We knew too late to change things, and she was so angry about that, like her refusal to face it was *my* fault." He is talking fast now. "She'd have these moments of guilt, you know? And she'd deal with it by shoving it all away. Calling the baby *It*. I guess I can understand that. I can. I just don't think I can *forgive* that."

"Bo is not an *it*," Tess says.

"She would cry. She cried *a lot*, but it was always about what was happening to *her*. Her body, her life. She was devastated by what happened, but it was never about the baby, or me, or my family, or anyone else. I thought she loved me. I thought we loved each other. But all she could see was how this would ruin her. Her parents . . . Everything they'd worked for with those stupid pageants . . ."

"God, those people . . ." Tess says.

"I saw Bo, and I couldn't give him up. None of us could. My mother, she just . . . no one could let him go."

"He's part of our family," Tess says. "We raise our own, Sebastian. This is not about a mistake. . . ."

"We had him for almost a year. Tiffany never saw him, Jade. Not once after she left the hospital. Not *once*. It, *he*, was done and gone for her. I didn't even know her then. She wasn't someone I ever even knew. Her parents came by once and gave him this cup, this silver cup with some prayer engraved on it. We all sat in the living room, my folks, them, me. Tiffany's

deb caletti

mother held Bo and talked to him, and it just made me sick. Every minute she held him, I was just dying. She held him like this." He cradles his arms out, away from himself. "As if she couldn't even touch him."

I don't say anything. Part of me wants out of there. Part of me wants away from something way bigger than my normal life. Delores had been right. *Complicated*—she had no idea.

"I raised him, my family did. *Every day*. I didn't bail. I was the one who was there. Tiffany would ask how he was, but that was it. Little guilty questions, but all in all, more relief than guilt. She kept talking about what he'd done to her body. We met once, and I'll never forget this—she lifted her shirt and showed me the white lines on her stomach. Stretch marks. She said she felt branded by what happened. Talked about how depressed she was. How she was trying so hard to *move on*. She kept going on about school—college." His voice catches.

Tess puts her hand on his arm. Her hand, veiny and road-mapped. Highways and paths of her life in relief on her skin. My heart hurts for him.

"So then, a couple of months ago—four months, four and a half—she calls me. After I hadn't talked with her forever. She starts crying. Saying she fucked up. That her parents were putting all this pressure on her to have Bo in her life now. She was confused. . . . That they got a lawyer . . ."

Elmo stops singing in the other room. "Da!" Bo shouts.

"Come here, buddy," Sebastian yells back. His voice is full of tears.

"Da!"

"Here!"

Bo appears, the plastic feet of his pajamas *skush-skushing* along the floor. Sebastian lifts him, cradles him against his chest and rubs his back. Bo watches us, then gives up and sets his head against Sebastian's shoulder. Pops his thumb in his mouth.

"They got a lawyer. They were going to file for custody. And that's when I made the mistake. I took off. I told my parents I had to go, and I ran. Stayed with him in a motel for three days. I didn't know what to do. I didn't want to be around to get served any papers. And then, the fourth day, Tess shows up. She tells me that if I'm running, I'm not going to go through it alone. If I'm going to hide from those papers, I was going to do it right."

"I'm an idiot," Tess says.

"She saved my butt. Made a plan. We came here. The plan is, *was*, don't tell anyone who we are. Tess was pissed I told you my real name. Got involved . . ."

"No one can know where we are," Tess says.

"I understand." I don't know if I do. I think I do. Sebastian reaches for my hand. He looks at me, deep in my eyes, asking for my forgiveness. And then I'm not falling anymore. I've grabbed ahold of a branch, and I'm not going to hit the ground. See, it's still just Sebastian. I see him in his eyes as he looks at me, my sea boy.

"I'm not kidding myself," Sebastian says. "I can't run forever. I know that. I just believe that if she has to work at this too hard, she'll give up. I *know* her. I've known her since she was in elementary school."

"But it's her child," I say.

"It's not about him, for her. It's about herself. The looking, the waiting—she'll get bored. She'll lose interest. Too much *effort*. I *know* her."

"It's the parents I'm worried about," Tess says.

"Maybe it was a mistake to run. Though, I tell you, it doesn't feel like a mistake. The courts are going to think otherwise, but . . . Look at him. I'm all he's ever known. She's a stranger."

"I thought you were grieving," I say.

"I *am* grieving. If Bo . . . If I ever had to give him up, even part-time, to those people . . . I don't know. I just don't know." He kisses the back of Bo's neck, keeps his mouth there for a long time. Tess stands, begins to clear the dishes.

I want to cry for him. I guess now I am grieving too. "You could have told me," I say.

"I'm sorry. I wanted to. I'm a crappy liar, anyway. I hope you can understand. If anyone found out, someone who didn't get this, those papers would be on my doorstep within a couple of hours."

"I'm going to lay him down," Sebastian says. Bo is zonked. His thumb has fallen out, but his mouth is still sucking a little, as if the thumb were still there. His cheeks are rosy and his hair slick from the warmth of Sebastian's sweatshirt. Sebastian looks so young holding that baby.

I carry some dishes into the kitchen. Tess wipes the inside of a glass with a soapy sponge.

I just stand there. I don't know what to say, honestly.

"He trusts you," she says. "And I do too." She rinses the glass, sets it upside down in the rack, and dries her hands. "I'm sure this isn't quite what you were picturing."

"I care about him," I say.

"I can see that," she says.

Sebastian appears. "Can I walk you out?"

The wood planks creak under our weight. At the end of the dock, he takes my hands in his. "I can understand if this changes things," he says.

His eyes hold my own. I understand he's not guilty of anything except maybe loving too much. This boy, he is just . . . mine.

"No."

"I really want you in my life, Jade."

He kisses me then. And we are there outside, arms in each other's jackets, for a long time, and I stand with my ear against his chest, just listening to his heart.

PART THREE:
Tsunamis, Hurricanes, and Doors
Flying Off Airplanes

Chimpanzees will thrust their tongues in each other's mouths. In other words, chimpanzees French kiss . . .

—Dr. Jerome R. Clade, *The Fundamentals of Animal Behavior*

"This is Onyx," Damian says. "Onyx, this is Delores."

"We've met," Delores says. "It's nice to see you again."

"Give her an apple," Damian says.

Delores holds one in her palm and Onyx takes it, curls her trunk to her mouth. "She's crunching." Delores chuckles. "Hear that? She's crunching."

Damian smiles at Rick Lindstrom and me.

Delores pats Onyx's wide, crinkled side. "That's really cute. That's so funny. You're a funny old thing," she says to Onyx.

I was spending as much time as I could over at the houseboat. Sometimes with Sebastian and Bo, sometimes with Tess and Bo, and sometimes just Bo, if Sebastian was working and Tess was at an FFECR meeting—Fathers For Equal Custody Rights. I would bring my homework, and Bo would come and sit down in my lap and I'd put my nose under his neck and inhale his sticky-peaches scent. He would "work" while I did—scrawling big strokes of crayons on paper after sheet of paper, crazily wasteful but quiet. I got to know what he loved—blowing bubbles, trying to haul big things around, saying no, words that rhymed, showing off by dancing, trucks, trucks, trucks. And what he didn't—getting his face washed, when a toy didn't work, when he had to leave somewhere before he was ready, the neighbor's dog, a black lab named Bruce. I learned his good points and bad ones—he threw things, got frustrated and would kick and grab everything he could, and he'd cry forever in a high-pitched half scream. But he was also cuddly, knew way more than he could say, tried to sing, and would bring his blankie over when he was ready to sleep. Plus, God, he was just so precious. His soft skin, and the way he'd sit in his overalls and study something, head bent down, so serious . . . well.

Tess left a key for me, hidden under the cement frog. I got to know Tess, too. The way she would swear and act tough but wasn't. How much she loved her sister, her daughters, her grandchildren, the way her eyes would brighten and her laugh would twinkle when she talked to them. How she disliked the dock cats crapping in her garden. How she'd sometimes write letters to Max that he wouldn't get anymore. How she made the best blueberry muffins you ever had in your life. How she loved her boat and missed her motorcycle she'd left back home, and how she worried she'd done the wrong thing by Sebastian. How she got fired up when she talked about injustice, causing her face to redden.

I learned about dock life. How on Tuesday summer nights the sailboats would race on the lake, the water packed tight with speeding triangles of white and spinnakers of starburst color. How any variety of boats might pass—tour boats with visitors waving; kayakers, who sometimes had dogs in life jackets as passengers; even flat, motored barges with dining tables atop and guests eating by candlelight with linen napkins on

deb caletti

their laps. I now recognized the neighbors—Winston Grove, who was from Australia, and his wife, Trudy; and Gloria Montana, a woman who lived alone and made sculptures and was always having visitors. There were Annalee and Tony, who'd just gotten married. There was Bruce the dog and Jose the dog and Jazzy the cat and Sal and Brickhead, twin calicos. There was a beaver who was building a dam near the start of the dock.

And I learned more about Sebastian. Sometimes love is a surprise, an instant of recognition, a sudden gift at a sudden moment that makes everything different from then on. Some people will say that's not love, that you can't really love someone you don't know. But I'm not so sure. Love doesn't seem to follow a plan; it's not a series of steps. It can hit with the force of nature—an earthquake, a tidal wave, a storm of wild, relentless energy that is beyond your simple attempts at control. Thomas Jefferson fell in love at first sight, I learned from Mom at dinner one night, and so do butterflies and beavers and so did I. And so I had to go backward and come to know the person I loved. I learned he hated shirts with scratchy tags, that he knew everything about cars and read science fiction and spy novels. He could figure out what was wrong with a computer, drew sketches of buildings on napkins and phone books and spare pieces of paper, and often wore socks that didn't match. He hated to get angry, and instead just kept it inside until it came out in a rush that was near tears. His touch was gentle. He used the word "fuck" a little too often after he got to know you well, but rarely swore around people he didn't know. He liked anything barbequed—ribs, chips, hot wings. Sometimes he licked his fingers.

Our talks went something like this:

Me: If you could change anything in your life, what would it be?

Sebastian: I'd have met you sooner.

And this:

Sebastian: I wonder what animals think about.

Me: I do too.

Sebastian: Does an elephant think about heaven? And if he does, are there big, white fluffy clouds?

Me: Elephant angels with giant halos.

Sebastian: Do dolphins think about God, and if they do, does he sound like Flipper?

And this:

Tess: Fresh blueberries. That's one of the secrets. Not frozen—that'll add too much water and make them gummy. *Fresh*.

Sebastian: They're not cheap, either.

Tess: Sebastian, you ought to know more than anyone that some things are worth paying a high price for. Turn on the oven. Four hundred.

Sebastian: Bossy, bossy.

Me: And hand us that bowl.

Tess: You got it now, girl.

See, it wasn't just Sebastian I loved. It was all of them, that snug feeling of right. I craved their presence, their den, their lair, their nest. I loved Sebastian's tousled presence, his bare feet, his arms around me and him kissing me, my back up against a tree, his hand behind my neck, his hands, mine. I loved when he read to Bo, and I would lose the words, forget they had meaning, and would instead just ride with their rhythms, disappear in the

deb caletti

music of his voice. I loved Bo's raw energy, the way he sucked in the world and used it to add to his knowledge. He was developing a sense of humor—calling an object by the wrong name to get a laugh. And Tess. Well, I loved the way she would over-react, loved the way she did everything with energy and heart. When she dug in the dirt, setting geraniums in the houseboat planters, she did it with her bare hands, and when she laughed, it was loud, and when she got into the boat, it was with a solid, sure step. She was *connected*. To her family, to her surroundings, to her life in general. She lived vividly.

And here's what happened. My anxiety—I sort of stopped noticing I had it. I'm not saying there's some simple solution here, because there isn't. I'm not saying if you do X, Y, Z, it will go away, because I don't believe that's even true. It wasn't gone—I don't mean that, and it'd be stupid to think so. Just, I stopped giving it so much attention. I felt more calm. I hadn't lit a patron saint candle for weeks, and they lay cold and still on my dresser, the top of the wax collecting dust. I even backed off some of my studying, which is probably normal for a senior in her last semester of school, but not normal for me. I got a couple of Cs on tests, something Dad would have killed me for, or at least given me the tight-jawed silence, had he known, which he didn't. He and Mom didn't know anything about Sebastian and Bo and Tess. They thought I had more hours at the zoo, and spent the rest of my time with Alex Orlando and gang. In truth, I would go to school, put in my time, head to the zoo. I'd clean cages and wash elephants and hide watermelon and watch Onyx follow Delores everywhere. Then I'd go to the houseboat and stay until the evening. During that time, I had stopped feeling the way I had for a long while—like a hamster on one of those wheels, running, running, running, his heart beating like mad, in his little wire cage. I had always felt like I was being chased, but I was on that wheel, and the only one chasing me was myself. Now, I wasn't looking over my shoulder, or trying to see the future, living for some other time. It was just *now*.

I finally felt a lack of fear, a sense that the most important things were safe. But instinct, as Abe says, is not a foolproof system. Sometimes it is a map we hold upside down. I was lulled into peace by a rocking boat, by the smell of muffins baking, by the love of a young father, and I forgot to imagine a beautiful young woman and her parents, driving in their BMW to an attorney's office, to the expensive building that housed the private detective they'd hired to find Sebastian.

I forgot to imagine all the ways the pieces of your life can be endangered. Just as the beaver by the dock was gathering and building his dam branch by branch, stick by stick, building a new life in a new place, there would be another dam elsewhere being taken apart—piece by piece or all at once, by a predator, by a storm, or just by the daily movements of the water.

We are sitting at a Starbucks table—two, actually, pushed together. It is decorated with swirls and contemporary hieroglyphics, cave drawings done by a factory, painted in black on tan, shiny wood. Michael raises his cup.

"I've got something to tell you guys," he says.

"You're gay," Hannah says.

"Shut up. This is serious," Akello says.

"Tell us," I say.

"I got accepted into Johns Hopkins."

I have a swell of feeling. My heart just fills—pride, excitement, that satisfaction of knowing that someone's hard work, at least, has paid off. I might have been wrong, but I could swear his eyes were teary. My throat closes. I grab his hands.

"You did it," I say.

"I know it. I can hardly believe it," he says. "I got the letter yesterday."

"That is so fantastic," I say.

"You earned it, Michael," Jenna says.

"Hey, if I get sick, there's no one I'd rather have figuring out what the deal is," Akello says. "You're going to be a kick-ass doctor."

"This is so great. This is just so great," I say.

"The thing I never got," Kayla says, "was why it's Johns Hopkins. Are there two of them? I mean, what's with that?"

"I know it. It's weird," Hannah says.

"See, this is what can happen when you work hard," Jenna says.

"To Dr. Jacobs," Akello says, and taps his cup against Michael's.

Michael smiles. Just shakes his head as if the news hasn't yet sunk in. "They've got something like forty libraries."

"Wow," I say.

"Speaking of library . . ." Kayla says.

Hannah laughs a little.

"Shut up, Kayla," Michael says.

"Shut up, Kayla"? From Michael? What is this? Kayla's mouth drops open, her straw halfway to her lips. Everyone is silent. Jenna traces a swirl on the table with her finger. A coffee grinder blasts on at the counter. Somewhere in my stomach, a sick feeling is starting. They all know something I don't. That's what's happening. I can see it now. Maybe there's a part of me that understands what's coming. Instinct buried. Buried no longer, because now is the time to look. Here it is.

"Really," Akello says. "You are such a bitch."

"Go back to where you came from," Kayla snaps.

"What's going on?" I say.

"Nothing. Ignore them," Jenna says. "Come on, you guys."

"Don't you think she should know?" Kayla says.

"Kayla, don't," Hannah says.

"Know what?" That sick feeling—it's moving. Working its way from my stomach to where it knows it belongs—my heart.

"Your mother and Mr. Dutton."

"What?"

"Shut up!" Michael says. "Don't even listen to her."

"Michael," Hannah says. "You know, maybe . . ."

"Someone had their tongue down someone's throat, is what I heard," Kayla says.

"What?"

"Brittany Hallenger caught them," Kayla says.

What I feel then is the ground, and it seems like it has been moved, taken away. My head feels strange, too, like I could black out. Like there's no oxygen, suddenly, an important connection from lungs to heart to brain snipped.

"Let's go," Jenna says.

"Come on, Jade," Akello says.

"We're not finished," Kayla says. "Lunch isn't even half over."

Michael and Akello get up. Jenna, too. I go with them, and we get in the car and leave Kayla and Hannah sitting there. We go from the cool air conditioning to the sunny May air, the stifling heat of the car smelling of warmed vinyl.

"I don't want them in my car," Jenna says.

"I don't want them in my life," Michael says.

"I hope she chokes on her fucking Frappucino," Akello says.

No one speaks on the ride back. No one speaks, and Jenna squeezes my hand, and Akello offers to carry my backpack. Which means it was true. What Kayla had said back in the café, it was true.

I sit through Biology and Government, and I get through by trying to focus on each and every word that is said. If I look out the window of the class, I'll see my mother's car in the parking lot, and I cannot, cannot, cannot (count the words on my fingers, starting with my thumb) think of that, or of the library or of Mr. Dutton, *do not, do not, do not*. I walk home. I don't take the bus. I count sidewalk tiles. I don't go to the zoo, can't face the elephants and their warmth and love and family life right then. I don't know what to do. I have no idea. I just open the door of my house, and it seems like a strange door. One of those bizarre moments when a familiar object seems completely foreign.

I have no plan. Maybe my backstage mind has a plan, because I drop my backpack to the floor with a thud when I hear her in the kitchen. *Her*, not Mom. Just *her*. In the kitchen—our kitchen, Dad's kitchen, this family's kitchen.

I am in the doorway. She's emptying the dishwasher, of all things. I don't know why this seems so extraordinary and why it pisses me off so much. The dishwasher—it seems so *innocent*. It's innocent to put away our glasses and forks after kissing another man.

"Good day at school?" I say. The sarcasm drips from my words like an icicle from a rooftop.

"Yes," she says. She turns, eyes me warily. She holds a plate in her hand.

"That's what I heard. I heard you had a *really* good day." The anger—it's there. Suddenly, it's there, in a boiling rush. So much anger, it scares me. I don't know how much is there, how much I have inside. I didn't know that rage could sweep up like a wave, washing over everything else, drowning good things. It is bigger than I am. God, it's *huge*.

"Jade. What is the matter with you?"

"You *disgust* me."

She just stands there with her mouth open.

"Mr. Dutton and his *books*. The *librarian*, for God's sake. What a Goddamn *sex symbol*. You were *seen*, do you know that? Seen and talked about. You embarrassed me. You *humiliated* me."

"Jade." She is frozen there, shocked. Holding that plate. She has her jeans on, and the white blouse, opened too far at the neck. Silver jewelry. Is that what she wore? Was there more? Had she slept with him too?

"Who saw?" she says finally.

"Who saw? Who saw? That's what matters here?" There is guilt in those words. "Are you having an *affair* with him?"

"Jade, no! It's not that! It's not . . . what it seems."

"Oh, what—you were rehearsing for the school play? You're probably in my school play now, too, right?" I want to cry, but I don't. Anger is taking all the space. It overtakes every piece of me.

Mom's face twists. "I'm sorry." She bends over, grasps the

deb caletti

plate to her stomach. A sound escapes: grief. Just this cry of grief.

My heart wants to feel pity, it tries to, but I shove it away. Goddamn her. What was she thinking? How could she want to wreck our lives? "'I'm doing this for you, Jade,'" I mock. "'I'm doing all of this for you.' For me. Right." My voice rises. I'm yelling. My throat is raw with rage. "You were doing it all for *you*. It was never about me. You, you, you! If you wanted to do something for me, you would have left me alone. You would have let me have room to *breathe*."

I am screaming at her. This is not me. This is some cyclone inside, a furious evil person. I turn and run. Up the stairs to my room. I slam the door so hard I can hear one of the pictures that hang along the stairwell wall drop to the floor.

I sit at the edge of my bed. Clutch my pillow. My heart is pounding so hard. For a moment, I fear I won't catch my breath. She'd taken my air, yes, she had. I concentrate. Desert. Calm. In, out. Goddamn her. In, out.

"Jade, please." Her voice comes through the door. None of this is happening, which is a good thing. It's at a distance. It isn't my life falling apart.

"Get away from me."

"I want to explain." Muffled voice. Crying.

"Explain to Dad."

I count this phrase on my fingers. *Explain to Dad. Explain to Dad. Explain to Dad.* Breathe.

"Nothing happened. Nothing is going to happen. Jade! Jade, I was so lonely. I am so lonely." She is crying hard now. "He was . . . a friend to me. Okay? He took interest in me."

"Obviously," I say.

"Please," she cries. "Please . . . My life. It's always been so . . . decided."

I say nothing. I pick fuzz off of my bedspread. Build it into a pyramid.

"Your dad . . . I've been . . . alone. A long time. Roger was kind to me. I felt like . . . I remembered I was a human being. A woman."

I don't want her to say that. I hate that she says that. Right then, I hate that word, *woman*. It sounds dirty.

"I'm going to tell Dad," I say. "Of course I'm going to tell him. He should know." I don't know if that's true or not. That I will tell him. That he should know.

"Jade, no. I'll tell him. I'm going to tell him." She is crying. "Let me." Her words come in bursts. "What happened today— it was my fault. I'm sorry someone saw. I'm sorry I did it. That was all that happened. I swear to you. That was all. It won't happen again. I love you. I love all of you."

She is sobbing, hard. "God. Oh, God," she cries.

I rise from the bed. I open the door. Mascara drips down her face, which is red and puffy and small-eyed. Tears have damp- ened her blouse. Pain radiates from her body in waves. Maybe I should put my arms around her. Maybe I should, but I don't.

"I'm sorry for you," I say.

And then I shove past her. I take her car keys, swipe them off the counter. Hey, otherwise she might use them to see her lover, the librarian. I get in the car. I get the hell out of that place that's supposed to be my home.

I drive until I reach the water. I park the car, but by then it has already started. It's too late. I grip the steering wheel, fighting

deb caletti

the feeling of no air. No air and the reality of what has happened are colliding forces, a shaking earth causing animals to flee and buildings to fall, and the sea to rise in one overpowering wall of water. I guess I manage to get the car door open, because an eternity later, Sebastian is standing there, the mail in his hand.

"Jade?"

"I . . ."

"Are you all right? What's going on?"

"I can't . . ."

"Come here. Come here. It's okay."

He helps me from the car. "Panic. I can't . . . Breathe."

"It's okay. It is."

He holds me to him. Strokes my hair. I think I might throw up. I can't throw up. It would be horrible if I threw up. But I might. His hand is firm, rhythmic. He strokes my hair. "Breathe with me," he says. "There, now. Like this. It's okay. See? You're okay. Everything is fine. I've got you."

The desert. His arms. The timeless, endless desert. Love, timeless and endless, too. Breathing, in and out. I start to cry. And he just keeps me tight in his arms and kisses my hair. "It's all right," he says.

Tess is home, but heading out. She changes her mind. She hangs her little knapsack-purse over the chair and pours me a glass of ice tea with a slice of lemon and listens with a care that is both efficient and gentle.

"Lost hearts," Tess sighs.

"Don't be sorry for her," I say. "After what she did."

Tess sighs again. Bo wakes from his nap in the other room,

calls out "Da!" and Sebastian goes to him. "Jade," Tess says after a while. "You know how much I care about you. But you want everything to be either black or white. I've noticed this. You want to put things into separate compartments—right, wrong, good, bad. But not much works that way. Even black and white—mostly, it's just shades of gray."

"Are you saying what she did was okay? 'Cause if that's what you're saying, I don't agree."

"It was hurtful, yes, it was. But right or wrong? Was your dad wrong to spend so much time alone? Was your mom wrong to feel lonely? Were they wrong to grow apart?"

"They have Oliver and me."

"I don't know. The older I get, the more I just see how we've all got the same struggles, and then all I can feel is compassion."

"She chose to kiss that man, and that was wrong." I don't understand how Tess can't see this.

"And where is the beginning of that wrong? Where is the start of that thread? Good luck finding that. Go back eons. Did she do it because of him? Did he do it because of her? Because of their parents? Because of their parents' parents? Because of some deep, archaic need?" Tess is getting a bit worked up. Her eyes are blue and focused, and she leans into me so close I can smell her clean, laundry-soap scent.

"Maybe she did it because she made the choice to."

"Does the river make the choice to erode the rock?" Tess says, eyes blazing.

"I feel like I've walked in on open-mic poetry night down at the Flamingo," Sebastian says as he rejoins us. Bo is sweaty from sleep. Still groggy, his head rests on Sebastian's shoulder.

deb caletti

"I'm trying to tell her that everything is so interconnected that it is often impossible to sort out who impacts who, and how."

"'Every action has an equal and opposite reaction.' Or something like that, right? I got a C in physics," Sebastian says. He winks at me.

"More like we've got this big knotted ball of history and behavior and needs and drives."

"Sounds like a mess," I say.

"A real tangle. But, oh, what a lovely one."

"I'm angry at her," I say. "I don't want to try to understand her."

"Right," Tess says. "You're pissed and you want to lash out but it's too hard to hurt something you understand."

"Yeah," I say.

"Well, when you're ready for compassion, that's where to look. The way we're all just creatures doing the best we can."

Tess leaves to do some errands and attend her FFECR meeting. Evening comes and Sebastian makes me scrambled eggs, and I read Bo's favorite story over and over to him before Sebastian calls halt and Bo disintegrates and finally winds down to sleep. I don't want to go home. Sebastian puts Bo to bed and I do the dishes. I am putting the milk carton away when Sebastian appears in the kitchen, takes my wrist, and brings me outside. We sit on the dock for a while, watching the ripples in the water, the city lights dancing on waves. It gets cold, so Sebastian goes inside and gets some blankets. We lie on the hard wood dock and wrap ourselves in the blankets and look up at the stars. I settle into the crook of his arm. I hear crickets, the drifting voices of someone's television, canned sit-com laughter. The water smells seaweedy, and a twinge of melting butter still clings in the air.

"Today . . ." I say. "In the car . . . My anxiety. I'm sorry." I feel the shame, inching around my insides.

"What are you sorry for? It's all right. I'm sorry you have to deal with it. It seems awful."

"It's like being held underwater," I say.

"God, that's got to be tough."

"I'm embarrassed."

"Embarrassed? Are you kidding me? I have a *kid*. You still accept me."

"Of course. He's part of you. He's great. Anxiety's not great."

"But it's part of you. Jade? I love you. All of you."

My heart soars. I find his hand in the dark. "I love you, too," I say. I want to cry. Happy cry, sadness, acceptance. The whole knotted ball that Tess was talking about. He loves me and I love him, and it is simple and immense, too.

We are quiet for a while. The dock creaks and groans with a passing wave. "You know, you handled it just right. In the car. It helped," I say.

"I'm glad." He turns toward me a little under the blanket, and his breath is warm in my ear. "Bo, sometimes he gets himself worked up, and he just struggles. . . . If I hold him, and just rub his back, or his head . . ."

Sebastian strokes my hair. We start to kiss. We kiss for a long while. His hands are gentle.

I guess that's the only thing that is necessary to know about Sebastian and me on that hard dock, the blanket around us. He is careful, so very careful with me. Then, I realize the importance of having another person who sleeps beside you, the survival-necessity of having a shoulder to shake awake during the middle-of-the-night terrors, those times when it is dark and you feel too alone.

I come home really late that night, and the house is quiet and dark. Milo doesn't even wake up to greet me, but when I go upstairs, the bathroom light is on and Oliver is coming out, his eyes all squinched up from the shocking blast of fluorescent brightness after dream darkness.

"Jeez, Sis, you scared me."

"Oliver, flush! God, don't be gross."

"I was sleeping!"

"If you're awake enough to pee, you're awake enough to flush."

He peers out of the slits of his eyes at me. "You're just getting home. You have your coat on."

"Congratulations, Sherlock," I say.

"You're going to be in trou-ble," he says.

"I'm eighteen, remember? I don't even have to live here."

"Don't say that," he says. "You wouldn't leave me."

I suddenly want to hug him, my little brother in his p.j.'s and with his sleeping hair. "How was tonight? Was everything okay?"

"Mom and Dad stayed in their room all night talking. I watched *Titanic Mysteries* on TV. I opened a new bag of Doritos and ate them for dinner and no one even said anything. Why is Mom crying?"

"I don't know, Oliver."

"He's being a butt."

"I don't know." I've had enough talk tonight about laying blame.

"If you ever don't live here, you can take me with you," he says.

I do hug him then. There had been so many changes, just in one day. I feel new and old at the same time. I feel like the first person ever to make love to someone else. I almost want to cry, from the loss of the old, from the moving forward. Part of me wants to hold on—it's going so fast.

"Jade, you're squishing me," Oliver says.

CHAPTER SIXTEEN

Animals lie, and they do so when the benefits of the lie outweigh the risks. Piping plovers fake broken wings and hobble around in acted-out injury to distract predators from a nest, and apes will hide food when other apes walk past. Monogamous European passerines, most notably the pied flycatcher, will hide their mated status, pretending to be "single" in order to possess several unknowing mates in several locations . . .

—Dr. Jerome R. Clade, *The Fundamentals of Animal Behavior*

Everything in my house felt careful. Like we all understood that we were in a fragile place, and care was being taken not to break us. Door handles were twisted so that doors could shut quietly, steps were soft, voices low, and eye contact was avoided. Anger was too dangerous—anger would have shattered the hairline cracks snaking through our glass. Everything felt held in midair, just waiting, in temporary balance, in suspension. Like those surfers in *Riding Giants*, or Jake Gillette's parachute as he leaps off the skateboard ramp. We all moved carefully, slow moves, a Queen of Hearts in hand, gently placed on top of the card house. Will it hold? Will it fall? Nothing went forward or beyond, except for Dad and the building of his train set. He kept hammering and sawing, and the sounds coming from downstairs were both persistent and somehow mournful, a reminder that going forward always meant loss, too.

Even Milo was quieter lately. He would stretch, rump in the air and front legs reaching out, then he would lie back down again, his chin on his paws, paws on his blankie. His toenails clicked more quietly and slowly on the wood floors. He would sit patiently while his food was being scooped, his chin up, eyes watchful.

That night, after Milo eats, Oliver tosses Milo's old stuffed hedgehog in his direction. Milo wags, leaps after it, and then just slides flat on the rug, the hedgehog held between his paws.

"Give it here," Oliver says. He wears his white karate uniform, with its wide and swingy pant legs and cuffs, its thick, stitched belt. He claps his hands, but Milo just looks his way and stays put. Oliver makes a quick grab for the hedgehog, but speed is unnecessary. Milo lets him have it. Oliver dances the hedgehog toward Milo, gives the hedgehog an enticing growl, but Milo only sighs through his nose.

"What is wrong with you people," Oliver says.

"For your information, Milo isn't people. Milo is a dog."

"You're all acting dead or something. When are you going to start talking to Mom again?"

"I'm not *not* talking to Mom," I say.

"That is just . . . bullshit." He tries the word out. Says it as if he's just robbed a bank and is showing off the loot.

"Oliver."

He apparently likes the sound, and so he says it again, adds a flourish. "Bullshit. Mega-bullshit. I don't like what's going on here. It's like everyone's under a spell."

"The White Witch?" I suggest.

"Always winter and never Christmas," he says.

I think about this. He is right in a way. We are under a spell. Lies are delicate. You have to hold your breath around them.

"Hi-yah!" Oliver karate chops the hedgehog, but Milo merely rolls on his side, exposing his white stomach in a display of canine submission.

"So you haven't told anyone about Sebastian," Abe says. "Mom, Dad, Jenna—no one? Why is that?"

"You. I just told you."

"Besides me." He taps his pencil on his desk.

"No one else."

"Why?"

"I don't know. Maybe I don't want their interference."

"Does their knowledge necessarily equal interference?" Abe asks.

"Some things aren't their business."

"Agreed."

"Like sleeping with him." I test the waters. I look at Abe, but his face is still its usual calm self.

"That's a big step," he says. "How did you feel about taking it?"

"It was a positive experience," I say. "It felt right."

"And you protected yourself."

"Yes, Abe. God."

"Jade, these are big things, big changes in your life. Is there a place between letting people take over and shutting them out completely by keeping secrets?"

"She certainly has hers."

"Mom."

"Yes," I say.

"That may be true, but what about you? What do you get by lying to them? What are the upsides?"

"I keep them from charging in. They won't get it. There's no way they'll understand it—Bo and all."

"So, you manage the situation by trying to manage them."

"Right."

"And this can go on for how long?"

"I guess until someone finds out and freaks out completely."

"What are your other options? You're eighteen. You'll be graduating in a few weeks. Are Mom and Dad going to decide every relationship you have?"

"They'd like to."

"What happens if you give them a chance? Is there the possibility they might surprise you? They've surprised you lately."

"This is Mom and Dad we're talking about, here. They will *flip out*. Do you know what could happen if they found out? If they told someone?"

"So, it sounds like they find out either way. You tell them and they flip out, or they find out and they flip out worse, since you lied to them. Can you really control the outcome, how they're going to feel and how they're going to react, by lying?"

"It's working so far."

"So far? Jade, remember: Secrets have a shelf life."

A week passed. Maybe more. Mom and Dad seemed to be giving each other the small patching threads of kindness—she laughed at his jokes, he offered her coffee when he was pouring. I saw the politeness as forgiveness. I forgot that politeness is also the way we stay safe among strangers.

deb caletti

School was getting that end-of-the-year feeling, that loose, energized excitement that meant some things were ending and others starting. Yearbooks were splayed open on desks and cafeteria tables and steps, and there was that pressure to sum up relationships both deep and never really begun. Lies and promises (*I hope to see you again. Let's hang out this summer! Too bad we didn't get to know each other better*), definitions and secret memories (*You're so sweet! Don't forget about that time with the frog in Lab*). Four years of joint growth and incarceration. Everyone was talking about where they were going and what was going to happen next. We stopped having lunch with Hannah, though I saw she had tried to call me a few times without leaving a message. Michael was trying out his new confidence, and Akello was getting ready to go back home. Jenna still hadn't decided which Christian college she wanted to go to, and my own decision to go to the University of Washington right near home seemed like an extension of the stuck-in-midairness of life at home.

But nothing stays in midair forever. What hangs there will fall, eventually. Sometimes caught. Sometimes shattered. Always irrevocably changed.

"Onyx and I had a falling-out yesterday," Delores says.

Onyx is on her side in the elephant house, being hosed. Delores is speaking loudly over the sound of the water. Rick Lindstrom is carefully spraying Onyx while Delores brushes her.

"I'd have never guessed by looking at her," I say. "She's smiling."

"Well, we had to have a chat. She smacked me with her trunk yesterday."

"Oh, my God, Delores. Are you okay?"

"I'm fine, but I was pissed at her." The sleeves of Delores's blouse that are sticking from her overalls are wet, rolled at the sleeve.

"What happened?"

"I've been getting to know the other elephants. I gave Hansa some apples. I guess Onyx got jealous."

"But you came back today."

Rick Lindstrom shuts off the hose, and my voice is suddenly too loud.

"I told you never to do it again, didn't I?" She pokes Onyx's big, old rough side. "You see, you must never be selfish with your love," she says to Onyx in the mother-of-a-misbehaving-preschooler voice. "I care about all the elephants, but you are my special one."

I don't know if Onyx understands Delores's words. Maybe, maybe not. But her tones and rhythms must be universal, because Onyx lifts up her head, pokes the air with her trunk.

"Be still," Delores says to her.

"Delores, I think you are a natural," I say.

"A natural."

"Yep."

"I think you may be right," she says.

I help clean the outdoor enclosure for most of the rest of the day, but the volunteer chart says I'm helping Damian weigh the elephants next. I look for him in the elephant house. Usually, he's there before I am, with his stack of charts and plastic tub of treats for good behavior. No Damian. I am surprised to find his office door closed, which it rarely is unless he is having a meeting with Victor Iverly. I tap softly.

"Yes?" he says.

"It's Jade. I was waiting for you at the scale."

"Oh, dear, dear, dear," he says. "Come in."

I open the door, and see Damian facing the window in his swivel chair. He doesn't get up. He keeps his face turned from me.

"I wondered where you were. Nothing's ready."

"I've had a distressing call," he says. He folds his hands together. They look like they're getting comfort from each other.

He swivels toward me. His eyes, usually brown and dancing, are sad and flat.

"Are you okay?"

"My brother called. It's Jum. My Jumo." Damian's voice wavers. "She . . . He went to visit. He is worried about malnutrition. She is not eating. He asked Bhim about her weight, her eating habits, and he just shrugged. He asked Bhim if he had examined Jumo's molars. You see, if there is a disease, a growth, it impairs chewing. Jumo is too young to show the ravages of age in her teeth, so it is likely something that can be helped. If he would take the time. He doesn't care, you see. And I have abandoned her."

"No, you haven't," I say. "You still love her."

"I am her mahout—she is like my child, Jum. My little one."

"What can you do?"

"From here, nothing." He shakes his head. "Nothing."

Tess can't contain her excitement. "Whoo-ee," she repeats. "Look at that. Look at him. What a specimen. What a beauty."

"Ish," Bo says.

"Indeed, it is!" she says.

"His eyes give me the creeps," I say.

Bo pokes his finger against the slick, cold scales, scrunches up his face.

"Really," I agree. "Blech."

"Copper River salmon!" Tess sings for the zillionth time. Tony, one of the houseboat neighbors, had caught several the day before and given Tess one. She is hopping around as if she had just unscrewed a Coke lid and found out she'd won a million dollars. The fish lies on some spread-out newspapers on the counter. His eyes are teeny glass paperweights, dull and unseeing, his tail thin and floppy, his middle thick.

"I'm becoming a vegetarian," I say.

"Wait until you taste this. You'll think you've died and gone to heaven."

"I'm happier when I don't think of my food as formerly living," I say. "I'm happy to think it all came from Safeway. Food shouldn't look at you."

"Circle of life," Tess says.

"If you sing, I'm leaving," I say.

"Ish, ish, ish," Bo says. Poke, poke, poke.

"Bo," I say.

"The fish doesn't mind," Tess says. She flaps his tail up and down in a fake swim and Bo squeals.

"Well, I hate to say it, but I can't join you. I've got this last big paper for Humanities, and I need my computer."

"Coward," Tess says. "Chicken. Bawk, bawk."

"Awk awk," Bo says. "Ish."

"No, that's not what a fish says," Tess laughs. "A fish says . . . Hmm. Nothing, really."

deb caletti

"They just make those kissy-lips," I say. "Like this." I demonstrate for Bo. He tries to copy me, and purses his lips with this face so adorable, I could just eat it. I ruffle his hair. "Man, you're cute," I say. "You are so cute, you should be illegal."

"I can't believe you're going to miss this. Copper River salmon!"

"I really shouldn't have even stopped by. I just wanted to say a quick hello."

"I don't know what's keeping Sebastian," she says.

"Just tell him hi for me," I say. "And have fun with your fish."

"You don't know what you're missing," she says.

I walk down the dock and head up the steps to the street. My usual routine is to take the 212 bus that drops me off at home, or to have Sebastian drop me part way. I'm almost at the stop, down the narrow street, when I see Sebastian's car. He waves, pulls over to the side of the road. He rolls down his window.

"Don't tell me you're leaving," he says.

"Humanities paper," I say. I kiss him through the window. A stuffed Armchair Books book bag is on the passenger seat, along with a half-empty water bottle and a partial bag of barbeque potato chips.

"Damn. Now I'm really pissed I had to stay late."

"We'll have some time this weekend?"

"Yah. But I miss you now," he says.

"You're having Copper River salmon for dinner. He's lying in the kitchen. Fish corpse. Tess is beside herself."

"Thanks for the warning."

He takes a strand of my hair. He caresses my face with the back of his hand. "I love you," he says.

"I love you, too," I say.

For a few weeks, every time I saw Mom's car in the driveway, I got this sickening attack of messy, unsorted emotions. It was like looking at some automotive equivalent of shame. The car had been in the driveway a lot, too, as she wasn't spending so much time at school. She was planning our graduation ceremony, of course, along with the other PTA ladies, like Mrs. Lenderholm, with her Porsche and brown hair roots showing through the blond; and Mrs. Thompkins, who, when she left a phone message, treated you like you were five and unable to spell a challenging phrase like "please call." But Mom usually worked from home. Maybe she had been embarrassed into hiding. Maybe she was avoiding Mr. Dutton and the dangers of his passionate temptations—overdue book fines, paper cuts, heartbreak.

Funny thing, on that day, her car just looks like a car. A regular, aging silver Audi, a vehicle that had done great things (like get me my driver's license) and bad things (like break down on the first day of school once), but that mostly was pretty reliable and had nice cup holders, too. I barely even notice it.

Mom's just sitting there when I open the door. Sitting on the stairwell with a white envelope on her knees. Her hair is pulled back into a small ponytail, and she is wearing Mom clothes. Jeans. A T-shirt with a zippered sweatshirt over top. She'd moved from being a woman-woman back to a mom-woman.

"Well, Jade," she says.

"Jeez, Mom. You scared me."

"I could say the same thing about you," she says. Her voice is uh-oh icy. Oh-shit icy.

I don't say anything. She just stays there and looks at me. I hold my backpack in one hand. I don't set it down.

"Something came in the mail for you," she says. She hands me the envelope. I drop my backpack finally. I can see that the top edge of the letter had been torn open, the contents read. I almost don't want to take it, but I do. I reach out, turn the envelope over.

University of Santa Fe, it says. I slip the paper out and unfold it. *We are pleased to inform you . . .*

I'd forgotten about it, that was the weird thing. I actually look at the words and have to urge them into meaning. I feel a surge of relief. *This* is what she's freaking out about? I can handle *this*. This was a betrayal that had an explanation, or at least one that I could blame on someone else.

"Oh!" I say.

"I guess there are things you aren't telling me, Jade."

"No." Yes. "I mean, this is just because Abe . . . Part of my homework was to apply to some other places. You know, not near home. I'm not planning on *going*."

"Jade, there's a lot you're not telling me."

My inner attorney tells me to keep quiet. Not that I can speak, anyway—a bolt of cold fear has shut my mouth. She knows. About Sebastian. My backstage mind realizes this. I want to run. I feel like throwing up. All I had to lose rushes forward, shows itself. My cheek burns where he had just touched me.

"I said I wasn't going. I had no intention of going. That wasn't even the point. I forgot about even sending it. . . ."

Her eyes look hollow. They have brown circles under them that I don't remember seeing there that morning. She still just sits on those steps. "You never told me. I was really hurt by that, Jade. I went to find you. I wanted to know why you'd kept this from me. I went to the zoo, but they said you'd left already. No one knew where you'd gone. I saw Jake Gillette in the parking lot. You know Jake?"

"Everyone knows Jake."

"I see him around school. I try to be friendly to him because he seems lonely."

Jake Gillette. *This* was who ruined my life?

"He was there, with his bike and this little ramp he'd made out of wood," she continues. "I asked him if he saw you this afternoon, or knew where you went. He said he saw you all the time. That maybe you went off with the guy that has the baby, like you usually do. What the hell is going on, Jade?"

My mother isn't the swearing type, same as Dad isn't. Maybe she'll swear at the aforementioned Audi, maybe at Dad under her breath every now and then. But not often.

"What is going on here?"

I don't know how to start. I don't know how to explain it so she'll understand. "I can't talk about this right now," I say. I need time to think.

"Do you think you have a choice? Is that what you honestly think?"

I leave my backpack where it is. I try to edge past her on the stairs. I want my own room. I want to light a candle, look out my window, watch the elephants wander on my computer screen. "Let me by," I say.

"No," she says.

"Let me by!" I shove past her.

"I want some answers!" She follows me up the stairs. The PTA ladies should see her now. Stomping up the stairs, shouting. This isn't in the parenting books, now, is it? This isn't part of the four-cassette pack of *Parenting with Love and Logic* they sold at the PTA meetings. *Now, Junior, this behavior makes me sad.*

"It's none of your business."

Oliver stands in his doorway, hands over his ears. I make it to my room, slam the door.

"As long as you live in my house, it's my business!"

She flings open my door. My heart is wild. Hers must be too—her chest is moving up and down as if she'd just climbed something steep. We stare at each other. It's amazing how much I hate this person that I love. Twice now, over a few weeks, our relationship had suffered deep gashes, the claws and teeth of a tiger tearing into solid, strong hide. I know her so well, yet she is a stranger standing there. I see things in her face I haven't seen before. More wrinkles around her eyes. A looseness in the skin of her neck. When was the last time I had really looked at her? Where had this time gone? It was a question I'd heard my mother ask often, a question I felt now, for the first time.

"You're wearing lipstick," she says. Her voice is quiet. "Not gloss. Lipstick."

I nod. I stare at her and she stares back at me.

"It looks really pretty." Her voice is almost a whisper. "Really pretty." Her eyes are filling with tears.

I swallow. I don't know if I can speak. "Thank you," I say, but the words are full of grief now, too. My throat gathers tight, tears roll down my nose. She puts her palms over her eyes, lets out a pained sound.

"I'm sorry," she cries.

"I'm sorry too." I sob. She comes to me. We put our arms around each other. I can feel her body wracking, and she likely feels mine.

"It's just . . . ," she says into my shoulder, her voice high from escaping a throat closed with grief. "You're not . . . in your little bathing suit in the blow-up pool anymore."

I laugh, through tears.

"You know?" She sniffs.

I nod into her shoulder.

"You're not . . . making me plates of Play-Doh food. Wearing that pink ruffly apron, remember that? You have this *life* I don't know about. It went so fast, I never quite caught up." She sniffs again. "Jade, I really . . ." Her voice wobbles again. She speaks through new tears, a tiny, high voice. "I really . . . I've really loved being your mother."

"You're not going anywhere," I say. I have the high voice too. The back of her shirt is wet from my tears.

"I know," she says. I can hardly hear her, her voice is so small. "But you are."

We just hold each other. I hold her, the young mother who turned on the sprinkler for me to run through, the one who fished for the escaped magnet under the fridge with the broom-stick handle so she could hang my crayoned art, who drove with one arm out the window on the way to the orthodontist's appointment, this woman who loved to organize and who liked kitchen stores and who made great lasagna and who was too afraid sometimes and who wished for things I didn't know

deb caletti

about. And she held me, her baby, her toddler, her young woman who loved animals and deserts and watching the sky and who loved staying organized and who was too afraid sometimes and who wished for things *she* didn't know about.

"God." She sniffs. "Look at us."

"I know it," I say.

"I need a Kleenex," she says. *I deed a Kleedex.*

"We both do," I say.

She makes us some tea. We sit at the table in the kitchen, and she sips her tea and looks down into her cup, stares at the browned string of the bag, sips her tea some more. Her eyes are still red, her face puffy from emotion. My own tea is nearly untouched, except for the warm mug, which I wrap my hands around for the comfort of its heat.

"He sounds wonderful," she says.

"He is."

"His maturity, it's something you like."

"Yeah. It's so different. The guys at school . . . Well, you know the guys at school."

"Like Alex Orlando." She holds her cup by the handle, swirls the liquid inside, a mini-tornado.

"I'm sorry."

"The fact that you've been lying—that's the thing that really made me mad. It hurt. *Hurts.*"

"I can understand that."

"It'd be reasonable for your dad and me to freak out. He's got a *baby*. You know? This is not just you going to the prom. This is jumping into the deep end of adulthood. Sebastian's had . . . He's had deep relationships."

"Had sex, you mean. And you talk about the prom like it's this great big innocent punch-bowl-and-corsage life moment. We don't even have punch bowls anymore. We've got *police*. The *prom's* about sex, for most guys. Definitely for Alex Orlando. You think Alex cares about love and dancing on prom night?"

"I don't just mean sex." She stops swirling her cup. "Not just. Responsibility, too. Of having a child. You're not exactly going to be having a carefree time."

"Can you honestly say that *any* relationship is carefree?" I ask. I consider what I've just said. Mom and Dad, Onyx and Delores, Sebastian and Tiffany, Me and Hannah, Jenna and God—Tess and Sebastian, even. No relationship is carefree—more the tangle that Tess talked about. Complicated, if beautiful.

"Mostly carefree, okay? Before it needs to be otherwise? And why does Sebastian live with his grandmother? Where's his family? What's with Bo's mother? You never said where she was."

"Dead." The word slips out before I have a chance to think. Quick as instinct. Like a python zipping under sand to hide, or the tail of a gecko instantly dropping off to distract a predator. Sometimes, they would be quick. Sometimes, not quick enough.

"Dead? She died?"

"Childbirth." Shit.

"Childbirth?" Shit, shit! "I know it happens," Mom says, "but, Jade, that's really rare."

"I know," I say. My backstage mind has completely abandoned me. I could see it off in the distance, waving its nasty little fingers at me, *Whoo hoo! Jade! Over here!* Childbirth, for God's sake!

deb caletti

"I just . . . Jade, please. I want the truth."

I think for a moment. What comes to me then is Abe, his words. His urging to give this truth a chance.

"Not childbirth," I say.

"No," my mother says.

"Mom, you've got to promise. This is important, and you've got to promise. . . ."

"Okay, Jade. *All right.*" Her voice pulls with impatience.

"You can't talk about this with anyone."

"What is going on, Jade?"

"The baby's mother, Tiffany. She didn't want anything to do with Bo after he was born. She never saw him. Sebastian raised Bo. And then Tiffany's parents, they talked her into getting him back."

"Sebastian?"

"No, Bo. The father, he's some hotshot plastic surgeon in Ruby Harbor, where Sebastian used to live. They've got a ton of money. They can afford all the attorneys they want. Sebastian is the one that took care of Bo. She didn't want anything to do with him."

"What are you saying? Are you saying he took off with the baby? Oh, Jade. Tell me that's not what you're saying."

"You don't understand. Bo doesn't even know her. She didn't care about him."

"Obviously, she does!" Mom pushes her chair away from the table as if it is something gruesome. "Does he realize how he's hurt himself now? What is this grandmother thinking?"

She doesn't know Tess. She doesn't know the first thing about her. It is shocking, really, how fast things can go from great to horrible. I think about my computer and its "system restore."

How the whole thing can revert to an earlier time and place before the mistake happened. "He hasn't been served papers yet," I say. "He isn't in violation of any order. There is no order."

"Yet!"

She just doesn't get this. She doesn't understand Sebastian and Bo together. "He thinks Tiffany will get tired of this. Mom, she's a beauty queen! She doesn't want to be a mother."

"But she is, Jade. She is a mother."

"Knock, knock," Dad says.

My humanities paper is going along just great, as you can imagine. Who gives a shit about exploring history and author motivation in *After the Fall*? I am acting out my own play—*During the Fall*. I have lit one of my patron saints for support, the Infant Jesus of Prague. Patron saint of families and children, which is why he's been chosen. His picture looks a bit creepy, like those dolls well-meaning people buy for you when they visit a foreign country. Those beady, swinging eyes in hard plastic, elaborate dress. But he also wears a puffy velvet king hat with a cross on top. The picture may have been vaguely unpleasant, but the prayer on the back is user-friendly, and it has the essential elements:

1. Kiss-up: *Dearest Jesus, little infant of Prague. So many have come to you and had their prayers answered. I feel drawn to you by love because you are kind and merciful.*

2. Submission, aka I'm Counting on You!: *I lay open my heart to you in hope, as I am at your feet.*

3. Request: *I present to you especially* (and anyone else who's listening, if we're going to be honest) *this request, which I enclose in Your loving heart.* (Insert request here.)

Then, of course, you get the whole thing again in Spanish. The Infant, who isn't an infant at all (and I have no idea where the Prague part comes in), is also handy for colleges, freedom, travelers, peace, the Philippines, and foreign service.

"Come in," I say to Dad.

He is wearing his sweatpants and a Sonics T-shirt. There is something slightly embarrassing about Dad in sweatpants—something loose and childlike. Too *uncontained*.

"God, Dad, untuck your shirt."

"What?" He looks down, checks himself out.

"It's dweeby like that."

"I'm not here to talk about my fashion sense," he says, but untucks his shirt anyway.

"I'm guessing not," I say.

"Can you stop typing for a second?"

I look at him, and he sighs. "This thing, with this boy," he says. My backstage mind is hurriedly stacking stones to make a wall against the assault I know is coming. This is the man who told me I would have to buckle down and apply myself if I wanted to "get anywhere" after I got a B in science in the eighth grade. "Anywhere," I assumed, was someplace with a high credit limit and a BMW like his. "Anywhere" was where you listened to news radio and had a retirement plan and where you took a vacation once a year, which usually meant the falsely enthused idea of "Let's play tourists in our own city!" because your wife was too afraid to fly. This is the man who told me I would one day regret not "getting my cardio," who got pissed when I couldn't help him clean the garage that time they were having the Honor Society picnic. The anywhere Sebastian might bring me is certainly not the anywhere he had in mind.

Dad slings his first arrow at my stone wall. "We only want the best for you," he says. That all-purpose phrase, both barbed and soothing, which may be true but is too often used to cover a multitude of parenting sins, usually involving some sort of overreaction on their part.

"When I was your age, all I had to think about was college and pretty girls . . ."

"And you had to walk to school in twelve feet of snow even though you lived in Arizona."

He sighs again. I wait for him to use Arrow Number Three in the parental arsenal: As Long As You Live Under My Roof. But he only stares at the flickering yellow from my patron saint candle.

"I sound like my father," he says. "I know I do."

I wait. He seems vulnerable, which makes me uncomfortable. Dads shouldn't be vulnerable. Dads leave cave, kill meat, drag home. Dads protect and serve, bring home the bacon, fight fire with fire. Dads fix broken things and remove dead birds from the lawn on a shovel without getting squeamish. They don't hesitate, or look lost.

"Jade, I'm realizing as I get older that I know less and less, not more and more." He sounds a little like Tess, but nothing like Sports Dad. It occurs to me why people are so fond of stereotypes—their simplicity makes you feel the ground is safe and firm, more safe and firm, certainly, than the layers and complexities of the unknown. This man—I don't know him. I'm not even sure how, exactly, to start to know him. "I don't have any answers for you," he says. "Honestly, I don't. All you can do is make the best decision you can at the time after looking around from where you stand. That's all I can ask."

deb caletti

"That's all?"

"Yep."

"Okay." I'm relieved. Actually, I'm kind of shocked *and* relieved. He really doesn't have the answers, and he's not expecting me to have them either. There's something so, I don't know, *human*, about that. I feel a lightness that comes with a release of expectations. This vulnerability—maybe it's okay after all. Maybe we can just be human together.

"Is there anything I can do?"

"If Mom tells anyone about this . . . I asked her what she's planning to do, and all she'll say is, she needs to *think it over*. What does that mean? I've asked her not to tell anyone, but she just says she can't make that promise." God, oh, please, God, Infant Jesus of Prague, and everyone else.

"You want me to make sure she doesn't?" He gives his head the smallest shake, chuckles. It's the kind of laugh one gives when a friend asks for a favor—to spy on a boyfriend, to help them cheat on a test. The laugh of the stupid request, of the impossible. "I can try," he says.

He is right to give that laugh, I know, and that's what keeps me awake that night, long after the printer spits out the last pages of my paper, which is somewhere around one A.M. He has tried to get her to do lots of things—travel, ski, meet other couples. And she has tried to get him to do lots of things—understand her, hear her, accept her for who she is. The possibility that he would sway her is small, finished years and years ago, and this may mean I have ruined Sebastian's life, Bo's, Tess's, my own. Actions and their reactions, all right. I fall asleep finally, but have disturbing dreams. Tsunamis and hurricanes, the doors flying off of airplanes.

I wake about six in the morning. The sun is already out, the sky blazing blue. I watch the changing forms of the punctuation clouds—the casual wisp of a comma, an apostrophe, the curve of a question mark—turning now into seagulls flying.

CHAPTER SEVENTEEN

A caged animal will come to fear his freedom. When first taken captive, put behind bars, he will fight and attempt escape. Finally, though, he will resign, and once resigned, the doors of the cage can be opened, but he will cower within . . .

—Dr. Jerome R. Clade, *The Fundamentals of Animal Behavior*

I go to school that next day, and then put in my time with the elephants, weighing them, cleaning the outdoor enclosure with Elaine. I hang out near Hansa, just because she makes me feel good, the way she sniffs my hair and hunts in my pockets for apples. I don't see Damian, and leave straight for home afterward. Jake Gillette, the traitor, isn't in the parking lot, but Titus gives me his usual "hang loose" wave.

I call Sebastian and tell him I won't be coming over. My paper, I say, although I had turned it in that afternoon. It's the first time I've lied to him. I keep our conversation short—*That paper . . . crazy last days before graduation . . .* because I'm afraid I might tell him everything, panic him for no reason. Maybe I'm just delaying the fact that he will inevitably hate me for putting him in jeopardy as I have.

I also want to hurry home because I think if I stay near Mom, hover, watch, that maybe I can prevent her from doing anything crazy. She would have to look at me, remember who she would hurt. If I let her out of my sight, she might forget that.

It might make it too easy for her to do what she feels is right.

Hawthorne Square is engaged in summer—Mrs. Chen is washing her car, her baby, Sarah, in a playpen on the grass. The fountain has been turned on, and little Natalie Chen is surfing her Barbie in the waves, *Riding Giants* style. Old Mrs. Simpson is filling the bird feeders hanging off her porch, and I am surprised to see my mother in the front garden of our house, her knees in the dirt, her hands around the roots of a geranium plant.

"Hey," I say.

"Hey," she says. She positions the geranium in the hole she's made, pushes the dirt in around it. "How was school?" She doesn't look at me. Natalie shrieks as her arm gets drenched in the fountain. *Don't get soaked now*, Mrs. Chen shouts, her own shorts wet from the leaking hose. I notice Milo standing in the window. Looking out with a face so devastated, you'd have thought we'd all gone away on vacation and left him behind.

"Good. You know."

"You get your paper done?"

"Had to stay up until one, but, yeah."

She stands, brushes the dirt from her knees. She rubs her nose with the back of one gardening glove. "Stupid allergies."

"Really."

"Jade, I think we better have a conversation."

"All right." Sunshine makes the lawn and the flowers and the bricks of the buildings look new and optimistic. I hear the music-box notes of the ice cream man driving up the street, playing "The Entertainer." But it's black dread that edges up my insides.

"Can you run in and pour me a lemonade? It's getting hot out here."

"Sure."

Oliver isn't home yet, but Milo jumps around my legs and barks with nearly-abandoned-now-I'm-not joy.

"Relax," I say, but someone needs to say it to me. I feel a little light-headed. Am I light-headed? Am I going to faint? I think I'm nauseous. I stop with one hand on the refrigerator, trying to see if I'm nauseous enough to throw up. I can breathe, though. I am breathing, yes. In, out. In, Jade. Out. No, my heart isn't pounding, it just feels . . . It hurts. It feels like it might be broken.

I remove the cool pitcher from the fridge, clink ice into two tall glasses, and pour the liquid over the crackling cubes. This is what she used to do for me. Pour me a glass of lemonade in the summer, so that I could have it as I sat on a towel on the grass of our old house after running through the sprinkler. Lemonade, and those boxes of animal crackers with the circus train on the side, the elephants and giraffes and hippos inside. That red box with a string for a handle.

I carry the glasses out, pushing open the door with my foot, hedging sideways so Milo can't escape.

"Oh, thanks," Mom says. She's sitting on the porch step, her gloves tossed near her feet. She reaches for the glass and rests it against her forehead for a moment.

"It's warm," I say. It's what you do when you can't say what you need to—you talk about the weather.

She takes a drink of lemonade, and so do I. It's cool and sour-sweet.

"Jade—I just want to tell you that I love you." Those words—sometimes they aren't what they seem. Sometimes we say it to hear it said. Sometimes they're an excuse. Sometimes, an apology.

I'm quiet.

"You're not going to like what I have to say." She sets her drink on the brick step.

Dread, creeping blackness. Heart . . . yes, there it is. That heavy ache. Breaking. I can only think of one thing: I think of Bo, first with no mother, then taken from his father. I think of Bo, twice broken.

"No," I say.

"Jade, you can't keep this child from his mother. She has a right to be in his life. He has a right to have her in his life. It's wrong for you to take part in this."

"You don't understand. You don't know anything about this. About them."

"I called . . ."

"No!"

"I called directory assistance. For plastic surgeons in Ruby Harbor."

"No, no, no."

"There was only one. I left a message. An anonymous message, Jade. No one will know who called."

"How could you?"

"He can't go on like this."

"How could you do this!" I scream. I see Natalie Chen with her Barbie turn around suddenly. My hand is around the glass, wet with condensation. I throw it against our house, where it shatters.

I want out of there. I turn then. Oliver is just coming up the drive. He has his backpack on, and is carrying a large brown grocery bag, stuffed full. They've just done the end-of-school desk-cleaning ritual, I can tell, and he has likely walked home happily with his reclaimed treasures—glue sticks and half-dry

deb caletti

markers, crayons with the paper rolled off, stubby pencils, bits of loose glitter and pieces of artwork taken down from the classroom walls, staple holes in the corners. That was always a good day in elementary school, bringing home your stuff, the ice cream man playing as you walk. But now he just hugs his bag. He looks stricken.

I run past him. I head for the bus stop, the 212, but change my mind and go to the 76 station instead. I realize I've left my backpack and cell phone at home in the hall, but I dig in the pocket of my jeans for a dollar, get some change from the guy inside. I push open the folding door of the phone booth. That cramped sticky place where bad news is delivered, because only bad news has the urgency required to stop here. *I'll be late, honey. I'm lost, honey. I'm never coming home, honey.*

"Sebastian?"

He's at the houseboat. He's outside on the dock—I can hear the motor of Tess's boat in the background.

"Jade! If you finished your paper, come over. We're getting in the boat."

"I can't . . ."

"Your voice sounds funny."

"Sebastian," I cry. "I'm sorry."

He tells me to come over. He asks me to meet him. At the end of the dock. Where we would have some privacy. He needs to go now. He has to tell Tess quickly.

I am almost too ashamed to go. I wait for the 212, ride in silence in a seat by myself until a guy with an army jacket and body odor slides down beside me. I grit my teeth, feel deservedly punished. I get off the bus, walk to the dock. I wait at the end, near the street. No Sebastian.

It's like the old days, when I would wait for him, not knowing if he would ever appear. Sea boy and desert girl, the boy in the red jacket who was mourning something. Now I knew what. Now I would mourn too.

I wait and wait, and finally I hear the *thwat-thwat* of tennis shoes running on wood, see him, my Sebastian. "Jade!"

He's out of breath. "God, I thought you might not wait."

"I'm so sorry." I start to cry. He puts his arms around me. The hurt party is comforting the guilty one, and something is wrong in that. I can feel his heart thumping beneath the cotton of our T-shirts.

"It's not your fault."

"It is."

"No, it's not. It's mine. I'm the one who did this. I'm the one who's put us in this position. It's going to happen. Tess says it's the chance you take every time you get close to anyone in this situation."

"She's mad. She's furious, if I know her."

"At me. At herself."

"What are you going to do?"

I'm afraid I know the answer. I don't even want to ask.

"Mattie, Tess's sister, has another place. She's got a couple of rentals, where they like to vacation. There's a renter in their place in New Mexico now, so it looks like Montana. Besides, it's by a lake."

"You shouldn't even be telling me."

"Jade. Look at me." He holds me away from him, takes my chin in his hand. "I love you."

deb caletti

"I love you, too. Sebastian, I do."

"Jade, I want you to come. I want you to come with us."

The moment, it's as if it is suspended in midair. I look at him. Sea boy to my desert girl. He holds me with his eyes, and it is easy. So easy.

"Yes," I say.

"Yes? Are you kidding? Yes?" Sebastian grabs me to him. Kisses me hard. "I want you," he says.

"I want you, too."

"Oh, my God, I can't believe you said yes." He's talking fast now. "You said yes, oh, my God. I was so afraid you wouldn't. Couldn't. Oh, God, we've got to hurry."

"Okay," I say. I'm not sure what I feel. Sad, angry, excited, thrilled! Everything is colliding too fast. "What do we do?"

"We're leaving tonight."

"Okay," I say.

"Meet us back here. It's going to take us a while to pack. Say, midnight? Start of a new day. Start of a new life."

"I'll be here."

"You should probably let them know. Your family. Talk to them, write a note, something. Make sure they know you're all right. That it's what you want. So no one has to come looking."

"I can handle that part."

"Jade, I love you. I've got to go." He kisses me again. "Bye. God, you said yes!"

"Yes," I say.

This is what I do. This is what someone who is going to run away does, if you can call a legal adult a runaway. She walks to Dairy Queen. She steps into the coolness, where everything is red and white and there are big plastic pictures of mountainous glops of ice cream covered in various mildly gruesome-looking sauces. Where there are two boys working behind the counter, wearing paper triangle hats and flinging rubber bands at each other to get her attention. She sits at a table across from a mother with a baby in a high chair, the baby with a chocolate-covered chin, and another child, sex indeterminate, holding a wobbling, heartbreak cone. It's going over, and when it does, the kid's gonna scream. Above all, she wonders if we feel more regret for the things we do or for the things we don't do.

I sit in that Dairy Queen for over two hours. I count how many people have Chocolate Fudge Supremes, how many have dipped cones (chocolate and butterscotch), how many have banana splits (fewer than you'd think), how many have Brownie Delights (a lot). I could tell you the figures if I hadn't thrown away the napkin with the pen slashes on it (pen borrowed from boy number one. Pen snitched from Horizon Home Mortgage by someone) on my way out the door.

I walk back to the bus stop, several miles. I count sidewalk tiles. Then lampposts. I count off the words one mother had said to her kid in Dairy Queen (One Blizzard, one Peanut Buster Parfait, neither on my survey). *Justin, you are going to be the death of me,* I count, starting on my thumb until I end on my pinkie. I sit in the back of the bus, like the troublemakers do. I stretch my legs out on the seat. *People pleaser?* I say to Abe in my head. *Ha!*

It's just after eleven when I get home. Oliver is asleep, Mom is in her room with the light off, and Milo is curled up on the couch where he isn't supposed to be. The only one awake is

deb caletti

Dad, as I can tell from the the line of yellow light under the basement door.

I step carefully to my room. I avoid every creak in the floor, and I know where they all are. I knock on my doorframe three times, oh, so softly. My mother has put my backpack on my bed and I empty it. I stuff it full of clothes, summer things, which don't take much space, and a sweatshirt, which does, so I decide to wear it. Same with jeans. I think about taking a patron saint candle, realize it's stupid. I remove my wad of money from my underwear drawer, zip it into my pencil pouch. Address book. Small photo album. Picture taped on my computer of Hansa and Chai and Damian. Really, it's all I need. I sling my backpack over my shoulder. Creep back into the hall. But the light is on now in the bathroom. The door is open. There is the sound of peeing. Floodgates.

Oliver appears, with his aboveground-mole eyes. He squinches at me.

"Flush, Oliver."

"I forgot. I'm asleep."

"You need to go before bed," I say.

"I did!"

"It sounded like Niagra Falls."

"I'm thinking I just have a too-happy bladder," he says.

I want to laugh; instead, a loss so great overtakes me, I almost cry. He shuffles down the hall. His hair sticks up badly in the back. His pajamas have baseballs on them.

His back disappears into his room. The darkness swallows him up. And that's when I know I'm not going anywhere.

PART FOUR:
Toward a Lava-Lamp Sky

There comes a time when an elephant clan must split up. Sometimes this comes after the death of a matriarch, when bonds weaken with the new leader. More often, it is a simple necessity during a drought or the feeding season, when the group is too large to successfully find nourishment, when it is better for their survival to break apart than to stay together. Sometimes the reasons are social—positive experiences in another clan may result in an individual's decision to "leave home," to establish themselves and become members in a new herd . . .

—Dr. Jerome R. Clade, *The Fundamentals of Animal Behavior*

"You know, even if you go to him sometime, there's the chance you won't stay together. Maybe a good chance. This is your first important relationship. The beginning of the story, not the final answer. If you went sometime, there'd be that possibility—that you don't know the end result, but that that's okay anyway," Abe says.

"What do you mean, 'if'?" I say. "It seems . . . out of the question."

"If," Abe says. "It's a beautiful word. *If* is a key to any locked door."

I graduate with my class, wear the cap and gown, shake with one hand, take the diploma with the other, smile for the photo.

I make a late-night confession to Jenna and Michael about my relationship with Sebastian, keeping my boundaries drawn about some parts, as Abe suggested. I cry, and Jenna hugs me, but it all seems to suggest a conclusion I don't feel. I basically live at the elephant house after graduation—between trips to the airport, that is. Good-bye to Jenna, heading to Colorado Christian University; good-bye to Akello, heading home to Uganda; good-bye to Michael, off to Johns Hopkins. I'm hollowed out, the one left behind. I realize that there is a stretch of freeway, a few miles between the airport and town, that is so laden with sadness and bittersweet joy, hundreds and thousands of comings and goings and the loss of change and moving on, so much emotion seeped into the pavement and the surrounding earth on those trips of dropping off departing loved ones, that it should be called the Zone of Heartbreak.

I started classes at the University of Washington in the fall. The large campus lined with cherry trees and brick pathways and ornate buildings studded with grimacing and grinning gargoyles was overwhelming at first. I read my map and handled it, except for one near attack when I walked into a class of three hundred students, stood at the top of the aisle, and felt like I might fall. Fall? Fail? I slept until eight, arrived late sometimes because I could, imagined I was one mere Copper River salmon in a sea of them, spawning and swimming upstream. I was happy to be indistinguishable. Happy to move because others were moving, following their direction. That way, I didn't have to think. I wouldn't have to think about Sebastian at that house on the lake, about Tess making pancakes on Sunday morning, about waking up to the smell of bacon and how much Bo was growing in my absence. I could concentrate on the professor's

deb caletti

voice booming from the microphone, *If we take Williams liter-ally, we may think he means that life itself is a process for discov-ering meaning* . . . I could focus on the words in thick textbooks and on formulas and diagrams instead of playing over and over again the sound of Sebastian's voice on the phone when he called me from Goat Haunt Lake, the crackling faraway sound of it, the *What? I can barely hear you*s. The *I miss you*s. If the per-son in front of me at the campus café reached for a dish of Jell-O, so would I. If I had allowed my mind to open to my own wants and desires, my insides would remember to keen over each of his sentences spoken over distance. The pain of being without him—butterflies crashing against rocks. I would then remember that other phone call, those words: *I can't come, Sebastian*. His own: *I know. I understand.*

My mother's single action on the phone that day was apparently enough to soothe her conscience. She didn't pursue it further, which meant she would be no match for Tess. My mother and I made necessary peace. We didn't speak about it. We just let time do its little thawings. I didn't have enough energy to be angry, and she seemed sad, herself. I had thought it was because of our wobbly relationship, her loss of purpose after my graduation, leaving only Oliver for her to shadow. But then my father finished his train set.

"Come and see," he said. We all tromped down the stairs, Milo racing to get in front and making our passage down per-ilous. We stood in front of his miniature world, now completed. The tiny people in the tiny town, the cars, the shops, that stretch of road going out, out into the forest, to a house by a river. It was beautiful. Mom started to cry. The next day, he told us he would be moving out for a while. It would be a trial separation.

They needed time to think. He had already found a house to rent. On the shores of the Snoqualmie River, on the east side, out by North Bend, where there was no big city and restaurants in every cuisine, where his commute would be over an hour each way, but where the trees got thick and the river tumbled wild and cold. He could fish there. He'd forgotten that when he was a kid, he'd liked to do that. He would teach us, too. Fishing, the expectation of good things.

"Are they getting a divorce, Jade?" Oliver asked.

Desert, cactus, lands from the beginning of time. Ancestors who survived, who were hardy and strong during every moment in the history of the earth.

"I don't know," I said.

"They can't get divorced. They have us."

"Oliver, there's something you need to know—are you listening? You know how to handle this. You can handle anything that comes your way and be okay. No matter what."

"Flask of Healing."

I tapped his chest. "Here."

Delores took to baking. She'd bring in cookies and brownies and oat bars. Muffins and breads and cinnamon rolls.

"You're too thin," she'd say. And she'd leave a second plate on Damian's desk, sticky, gooey, enticing nourishment, sometimes still warm, covered in steamed-up Saran Wrap. She was taking care of the fatally ill again, the heartbroken. Jum had pulled through her last scare, but Damian had gotten word she wasn't eating again. Our elephants were flourishing, though. Onyx was as bonded to Delores as Flora to her tire. Hansa was growing large and strong, and Tombi and Bamboo had tossed a new tree trunk into the electrical fence in spirited enthusiasm.

One day not long after my father had packed a few Hefty bags of belongings into his BMW and showed us his place for the first time (*You have no furniture*, Oliver had said. *It's like camping*, he had answered. *In a house.*), Damian calls me into his office.

"Jade. I just want to tell you that, first, I have really enjoyed coming to know you."

"No," I say. I know what he is telling me. But he can't. I refuse to hear it.

"But, Jade, I must."

"No. No, you can't."

"I have to."

"Everyone is leaving." I start to cry. I can't help it. Not Damian, too.

"Oh, little one," he says. He comes around from his desk, puts his arm around me. He is strong, from all those years of working with elephants, training them, caring for them, loving them.

"You can't go," I sob.

"I must go back to Jum. When you raise an animal, you love it like your own child. I know her thoughts, her needs. She wonders where I am, and I can't bear it."

"We need you too. Damian, *we* need you." My heart hurts. I don't know how much more hurt it can take.

"You know that elephants have your pain, my pain. They're not separate from us. Their bonds last a lifetime. I must go to her."

"No . . ."

"You, you see?" He takes my hands, grasps them firmly. "You are not vulnerable anymore like you were when you first came. You are living up to your name."

I am quiet. I don't know what he means.

"Jade," he says. "You don't know this? Jade, the substance—its nature. One of the strongest materials. Stronger than steel."

"I don't feel strong," I say. He *can't* leave. He can't. It's too much.

"Ah, but you are. You needed your herd as a vulnerable calf, but now you are so much stronger. Like Hansa!" He laughs, but I don't feel like laughing with him.

"You don't need your herd to protect you," he says. "But Jum, her herd is too small. Only my brother and his wife. I have money to buy her from Bhim and bring her home."

"I will miss you. You have given me so much." I am crying hard.

"And you, too, have given me. I am so proud. Now, you are a real mahout."

In the spring, the cherry blossoms rain down on the University of Washington campus like snow. They lie on the brick paths in drifts, as the gargoyles grin in nice-weather mischief. The air is sweet with the perfume of a girl in a summer dress, the water of the lake sparkly like it's keeping a nice secret. The elephants are happy too. Rick Lindstrom, who looked funny at first behind Damian's desk, put all the things he'd learned in grad school to use. He added auditory stimulation (classical music, cowbells, chimes—Onyx vocalized like crazy at Mozart; Delores preferred Vivaldi), built an enrichment garden full of treats, had us all hang ice blocks with bits of frozen vegetables inside (heavy!). He brought in a backhoe to dig a mud wallow (a big ditch filled with water—Tombi liked the hose, too), and had Elaine and me drape one of the pine trees with bits of fruit, like

deb caletti

it was Christmas. Pictures accumulated on the walls of the elephant house. First, the photos of Damian with all of us around his "Best Wishes" good-bye cake, and then photos sent from faraway, with exotic stamps on the envelopes. Damian, wearing a turban now, smiling broadly. Jum, with her trunk around his waist; Jum, grabbing the hem of Damian's wife, Devi's, skirt. A new stone house. Damian with his brother. Jum in the river with Damian hugging her neck, his pant legs rolled up to his knobby knees.

I would drive Oliver out to visit Dad. We'd wind through the trees and bump down his gravel road. The river that his tiny house was on roared and churned, and you could hear the rocks under the water tumbling against each other. We would walk down the riverbank with him. Sometimes we would just walk, not talk. Other times, we would ask him questions, and he would tell us things we didn't know. How as a child he wanted to be an astronaut; that at age eight he had fallen in love with his third-grade teacher, Mrs. Edwards; that he had taken art classes in college. He bought a bed. Then a couch, and a table and chairs. Self-help books, which I gave him a bunch of shit about, were stacked up, travel guides, too. He wasn't black-and-white to me anymore, nor was he hazy shades of gray. Instead, it was more like he was beginning to have bits of color; jigsaw pieces with fragments of pictures I hoped would one day make a whole. Stereotypes are fast and easy, but they are lies, and the truth takes its time.

We'd drive home and Oliver and I would be both sad and quiet, until one day I'd had enough of the funeral and told Oliver we needed a french fry taste test. We stopped at a bunch of fast-food joints on the way home (five was all we could handle), ordered a large, and compared and contrasted. McDonald's—hot and soft and salty; Burger King—bumpier, crunchy; Wendy's—wide, thick; and so on. The winner: this little place called Hal's, where your face broke out from the grease just driving up to it. Every ride home from then on, we'd stop. Funerals are happier with fries.

My mom cried a lot and spent too much time closed up in her room. But right around the time the cherry blossoms started to fall, she came out. Spring, renewal, new life, second chances, air so delicious you wish you could drink it. She started seeing a counselor, got a job as a library assistant at Oliver's school. She made a friend there, Nita, and they went to a concert together—Mom voted with Onyx and liked Mozart.

One day I come home from the elephants and no one is around. The doors and windows are open, Venetian blinds clack serenely against the sills.

"Mom!" I call. "Oliver!"

"Out here!" she yells.

"Sis! Come on! Come out! Hurry!"

I would have been alarmed, but his voice is excited. The kind of voice you get when the UPS man drops off something large and unexpected on your doorstep.

They are in our tiny backyard. Mom has Mozart playing softly through a speaker, which is pointing out our kitchen window.

"My God, you guys. What are you doing?"

"Having a ritual," my Mom says. "My counselor says rituals are good. They help us move from one place to another, marking change in an important way. This is an Oliver ritual."

Here's what I see: our old rickety ladder, the one that Dad

used to hang Christmas lights (with someone holding onto the legs), sitting on the small piece of back lawn. My mother and brother, beaming and grinning, my mother's forehead shiny with sweat. Milo with his tongue lolling out, panting as he lies on the grass in a bit of shade. And our fir tree. The previously ignored fir tree, save for the times it was cursed at for dropping needles on the roof, looking somehow majestic. Sporting gear hangs from its branches, same as the pine tree in the elephant enclosure with its frozen treats. All kinds of sporting gear. Football helmets and kneepads, shin guards and soccer shorts. A basketball jersey, warm-up pants, shoulder guards. A hockey stick is falling through several limbs. Balls of every variety sit under the tree like presents. Even a jock strap dangles from the tip of one branch.

"Wow," I say.

"Look at the top!" Oliver is almost shouting.

"Well, not quite the top. As high as I could reach. Our uppermost point," Mom says.

A plastic protective sports cup, turned upside down. It has a pinecone on top, for extra decoration, I guess.

"The pinecone was my idea," Oliver says.

"We're celebrating the fact that Oliver need not do any more sports, if he doesn't choose to," Mom says.

"I wanted to burn it all, but Mom said no," Oliver says.

"We thought about burying it, but it seemed too morbid," Mom says.

I look at the tree. Take inventory. "Wait," I say. "What about karate?"

"I like karate," Oliver says.

Not long after, during finals week, I get another call from Sebastian.

"Forgotten about me yet?" His voice crackles and snaps.

"Never," I say.

"We're moving again," he says.

I lean against the warm stone of the library in the university's Red Square. My face has been tipped to the sun, soaking it in as I soak in his voice, but now I snap my chin down. Some guys in shorts and no shirts are running through the fountain, throwing soaked foam balls at each other.

"Tiffany?" I say.

"No. Mom says she's been quiet for a while. It's actually just so remote out here that Tess and I are at each other's throats. There's no FFECR, or any other meeting for her to attend, and no work for me. People have gun racks. Mattie's renter in Santa Fe got transferred. The only thing is, it's got a pool, which means we won't be able to let Bo out of our sight for two seconds. But anyway . . . Tess is nuts about the idea, because it's got a big arts community. Theater. I know I can't run forever. Sometime I'll have to go back. But for now . . . For now, this is where we'll be."

"Santa Fe," I say. The desert. An acceptance letter, sitting in an envelope tucked in my underwear drawer. It is a coincidence. A big coincidence. Maybe big enough that you could call it a sign.

We hang up, and that night at dinner, I tell Mom. And Abe, well, he was right. She *could* surprise me.

"Jade, you need to go," she says.

CHAPTER NINETEEN

And then, after the elephants separate for the good of the herd and each other, they will sometimes later reunite. There is no doubt they recognize each other, even after long periods apart. Mothers and daughters and sisters. New sons. They raise their trunks in salute, bump and dance in greeting, entwine their trunks in warm embrace. They bellow and trumpet sounds of joy and triumph . . .

—Dr. Jerome R. Clade, *The Fundamentals of Animal Behavior*

I travel through the Zone of Heartbreak, and decide I should rename it—the Zone of Bittersweet. I am both happy and sad, and the feelings go together like a pair of hands clasped. Mom drives, Oliver and Milo ride in back. I'd said good-bye already to Delores and Hansa and all of the elephants. I rubbed their trunks and gave them apples from my pockets. My heart broke to see their saggy behinds as I looked over my shoulder before leaving the elephant house. Abe had hugged me, gave me Dr. Kaninski's golf mug— "Golfers Do It With Balls"—with a slip of paper inside, a referral to his friend and former college roommate in Sante Fe, Max Nelson, *who plays kick-ass rugby and has anxiety himself*, the note said. I gave a last wave to Titus at Total Vid. I visited Dad before I left. *I am proud of you*, he'd said, his eyes filling, something I'd never seen before. And then I watched the elephants on my computer screen one last time, their swaying, prehistorically huge forms. I touched my fingers to the screen. We are all tied together, even if we don't want to be. Animals and people. People and people. The trick is to face our necessary connections and disconnections. Humans, we need to go away from each other too, sometimes, same as they did. Sometimes, humans need to go away to study elephants. In my bag was a textbook, *The Fundamentals of Animal Behavior*, for the class I was most excited about being enrolled in at NMU.

The night before I leave, I can barely sleep. I am so heavy with the ache of good-bye. That morning, I am full of hugs and good wishes and have a stomach that feels like it could explode with nerves. My heart, too, is newly filled and nearly breaking. Tears are there, just waiting. This is what sets them off: Oliver's hands in his lap, Milo's collar askew. Mom's profile. The speed-limit sign. I remember Saint Raphael in my bag, my one chosen traveling companion, patron saint of travelers and happy meetings. Patron saint of joy. *Raphael merciful—le pido un viaje seguro y una vuelta feliz.* Merciful Raphael—I ask you for a safe trip and a happy return.

I kiss Milo good-bye. I hug his beloved, furry self. He waits patiently in the car as Oliver and Mom walk me in to the airport. We all do mostly okay, until I have to leave them.

"Sis," Oliver cries.

"My girl," Mom says. Tears roll off her nose. "This. This is the hardest thing I've ever had to do, letting you go. Oh, God— I almost forgot." She reaches into her purse. Hands me a small bag. "I was thinking about what you told me . . . What Damian had said about your name." I reach my fingers through the tis-

deb caletti

sue paper, pull out a necklace from which dangles a small jade elephant.

I don't hold back my tears, and I don't give a shit who's watching. Nature is never static, I understand. Change is ever-constant, clouds zipping across a sky. It is dynamic, complicated, tangled, mostly beautiful. A moving forward, something newly gained, means that something is lost, too. Left behind. It is something Mom knows, Dad knows, Tess knows, Damian Rama knows.

But I, like nature itself, am strong and resilient. Over the eons, pieces of me had been brave, and I can be brave too.

I put the necklace on, and we hug good-bye again. And when it is time to walk down that narrow airplane aisle, I breathe, in and out, slowing the heavy hand on my chest. I breathe and picture the desert. I picture deserts and savannahs, elephants and humans; change, taking place over thousands of years. My heart is breaking; my heart is rising. I picture the landing of that plane, firm and safe, the doors opening onto ground I would walk forward on, toward the backdrop of a new, wide, lava-lamp sky. I buckle my seat belt, read the plastic safety card, am comforted to see the old lady across the aisle, reading her Bible, a crocheted bookmark on her knees. We lift off, and I grip my armrests. I close my eyes and remember that we can hold too tight, we can fail to let go, we can let go too easily. I peer out the window, which feels cool to the touch. Below, my past life looks like Dad's train set. Tiny houses, small winding roads, water you could fit into a cup and drink.

We soar higher, climb. The miniature town below disappears

as we lift above the clouds. Life and our love for others is a balancing act, I understand then; a dance between our instinct to be safe and hold fast, and our drive to flee, to run—from danger, toward new places to feed ourselves.

Turn the page for a peek at
another novel by Deb Caletti:

The Fortunes of Indigo Skye

You can tell a lot about people from what they order for breakfast. Take Nick Harrison, for example. People talk about him killing his wife after she fell down a flight of stairs two years ago, but I know it's not true. Someone who killed his wife would order fried eggs, bacon, sausage—something strong and meaty. I've never served anyone who's killed his wife for sure, so I don't know this for a fact, but I can tell you they wouldn't order oatmeal with raisins like Nick Harrison does. No way. I once heard someone say you can destroy a man with a suspicious glance, and I'm sure they're right. Nick Harrison was cleared of any charges, and still he's destroyed. Oatmeal with raisins every day means you've lost hope.

And Leroy Richie. Just because he has so many tattoos, you can't think you know everything about him. Up his T-shirt sleeve snakes a dragon tail, and around his neck is a woman with her tongue that reaches out toward one of his ears. But he orders Grape-Nuts and wheat toast. He's not just about tattoos when he cares so much about fiber in his diet.

We've got two regulars at Carrera's who do the full breakfast—eggs, side meat, three dollar-size pancakes. That's Joe Awful Coffee and Funny Coyote, and it's just a coincidence that they both have strange names. Joe's name, I guess, was given to him years ago—he can't remember why, because he says his coffee was just fine. A big breakfast makes sense for him—he was a boxer about a thousand years ago, and he still feeds himself as if he's preparing to get in the ring wearing one of those silky superhero capes (why they make tough guys wear silky Halloween costumes is another question altogether). And Funny Coyote. Can you imagine going through life with a name that sounds like you're being chased by Bugs Bunny? She's American Indian, about twenty-eight, twenty-nine, with short black spiky hair you get the urge to pat, same as a kid with a crew cut or those hedges in the shapes of animals. She eats everything on her plate, sweeps it clean of egg yolk with a swipe of pancake. Then again, she goes a thousand miles an hour when she's manic, so she probably needs the calories. She calls what she has a "chemical imbalance" because it sounds more accidental and scientific than a "mental illness." A "chemical imbalance" is no one's fault. She comes in to write poetry, pages and pages of it, not that it's ever quiet in Carrera's.

Trina, she gets pie and coffee, which fits her, because she's as rich as custard and chocolate cream and warm apples with a scoop of vanilla. She's about Funny's age, but she's all long, blond hair, lace-up boots, fur down to her knees. She leaves lipstick marks on the rim of her cup, the kind of marks that make a life seem full of secrets. She has this white and red classic Thunderbird. Nick Harrison says it's a '55, but she says it's a '53. You don't care what year it is when you see it parked by the curb. Jane, who is my boss and the owner of Carrera's, says it attracts customers, so she likes it when Trina comes in.

I know about breakfast, mostly, because breakfast was always my regular shift. Usually, I worked several mornings before school, and then the early weekend hours, meaning that my own breakfast was reckless—anything I happened to grab on the way out. A handful of Cocoa Puffs, a granola bar, my brother's beef jerky. I'd have been at the café all day, but right then, where this story starts (where I'm *choosing* to start—most everything before was nothing in comparison), I was at the end of my senior year. I still had to clock in what was left of my school hours, and Carrera's isn't open for dinner. After I graduated, though, I wanted to work full-time there while I decided "what to do with my life." See, I loved being a waitress more than anything, but apparently, it's okay to *work* as a waitress but not to *be* a waitress. To most people, saying you want to be a waitress is like saying your dream is to be a Walgreens clerk, ringing up spearmint gum and Halloween candy and condoms, which just proves that most people miss the point about most things most of the time. Waitressing is a talent— it's about giving *nourishment*, creating *relationships*, not just about bringing the ketchup.

Anyway, before the Vespa guy, I could tell you very little about who wanted tuna salad and who wanted turkey on white and who wanted minestrone, but I could tell you about what people craved when they first woke up, what they lingered over before they got serious about making the day into something.

So, what did coffee say? Just coffee? Coffee served to you, a bill slipped under your saucer when you were finished? When anyone could whip into any Starbucks on any corner and get coffee in under five minutes, what did it mean when you decided to wait for a waitress to come to your table, to refill your cup, to ask if everything was all right?

That's what I wondered the day I first saw him. Because, here comes this guy, right? He pulls up to the curb one day on his orange Vespa. He's no one we've ever seen before, and not the type we usually get in Carrera's. He's wearing a soft, navy blue jacket, and underneath, a creamy white shirt open easily at the collar, nicely displaying his Adam's apple. And jeans. But not jeans-jeans; these are not wear-around-the-house jeans, or go-to-the-store jeans or even work-at-Microsoft jeans. There's something creative-but-wealthy about them, about him in general with his longish, tousled hair, and dark, soft leather shoes that are too elegantly simple to be inexpensive. All in all, sort of hot for an old guy in his thirties, which sounds freakishly Lolita, but still true. His face is narrow and clean-shaven. He smiles at me, lips closed, and says, "Just coffee." He smells so good—showery. A musky cologne, or maybe one of those hunky bars of soap that are supposedly made out of oatmeal but probably aren't made out of oatmeal.

Jane looks at me with raised eyebrows, and I raise one of my own, a trick I can do that neither my twin brother can, nor my little sister, ha. I'm the only one in my family, far as I know. It makes me look slightly evil, which I love. Jane's eyebrows are asking, *What's the story?* Mine are answering, *Hmm, mystery and intrigue.* We've never seen this guy before, and just so you know, when you go into a small café that mostly fills with regulars and you're not one, you'll likely get talked about after you leave. It's part of what I really like about my job. Juicy gossip and lurid conjecture. Love it. Joe Awful Coffee raises his old eyebrows too, but Nick's too busy sprinkling sugar onto his oatmeal to even notice the new arrival.

I bring the man his coffee. The glass cup clatters slightly against the saucer. "Thank you," he says. Murmurs—it's one of those soft, polite, well-dressed thank-yous that legitimately qualify as a murmur. Who murmurs anymore? And then he just looks out the window. Stirs his coffee with a spoon. *Tink, tink, tink* against the edge of the cup. Smiles up at me when I pour a refill.

Just coffee. My guess is that he has things to think about. Things that are too deep for a double-tall-foam-no-foam-lite-mocha-hazelnut-vanilla-skinny-tripleshot-decaf-iced-extra-hot-Americano-espresso type place, where every person can demand and immediately get their combination of perfect in a cardboard cup. Where everyone only pretends to think deep thoughts and discuss important subjects but it's all a piece of performance art. Maybe he needs to get past all that distraction of wants and desires and greedy-spoiled-American-hurried-up-insta-gratification and just sip coffee.

I don't know. But he stays for a while. Almost to the end of my shift. I smile, he smiles. My tip is more than the coffee itself.

"Did you see his shoes?" Jane says. "Italian." I'm pretty sure she knows nothing about this. Jane is a regular jeans and FRIENDS DON'T LET FRIENDS VOTE REPUBLICAN T-shirt wearer. Running shoes. I know she went to Italy a long time ago, and that's how she got the idea for Carrera's, but I hardly think it qualifies her as an expert on men's shoes.

"Fast track," Nick Harrison says. He'd been paying attention after all. He gets up, wipes his mouth with his napkin. Fast track—this *is* something Nick knows about. He used to be a big shot in some architectural engineering firm before his wife died and he used up all his money on lawyers. Now he works at True Value down the street, mixing paint and helping people pick out linoleum. When he reaches for change in his pants pocket, he always has one of those metal tools they give out free to pry up the paint lids. Now he wears nice-guy plaid. According-to-the-law plaid.

"Fucking beautiful Vespa," Leroy Richie says. He's sitting at a table by the window, the newspaper spread in front of him. He scratches a heart wrapped in vines, which is inked onto the underside of his wrist. "Anyone know what a 'lowboy driver' is?"

"If you don't know what it is, I'm guessing you can't do it," Jane says. She frees a stack of one-dollar bills bound together with a rubber band.

"How about a 'resolute trainer'?"

"Someone serious about training?" I take a guess.

"Hey!" Leroy says. "Pilates instructor! I could do that. I've got balls."

Leroy works for the Darigold plant in town, which is why he's up so early, but he's always looking for a second job to make more money. For retirement, Leroy says, though he's maybe only thirty. People aren't too quick to hire him because of the tattoos. *They think tattoos equal drug addict,* he says. *Like all needles are the same. Like even art has to have its designated places.* Darigold hired him years ago, when all he had was a falcon on one shoulder. Now, he told us, the only place he didn't have artwork was on his bald head, which is a picture you didn't especially want to imagine, thank you.

"He's getting on the Vespa," Nick Harrison reports. "Starting it up. There he goes."

I look out the window to watch too. I watch the back of his suit jacket disappear down the street, the flaps whipping softly against his back. It's like we've been touched by something, but I'm not sure what. Maybe it's just the twinge of thrill that comes with a stranger's story, all the possibilities that might be there until you find out he works at a bank and plays golf. Or maybe it's that down deep hope-knowledge that someone or something is bound to arrive to save you from your drab existence, that maybe this is it. We're practically *promised* that, right? That our lives will at some point go Hollywood? That excitement will one day arrive, just like a package from the UPS driver? I don't know, but I can just feel *it*—this static, popping energy buzz. The kind that comes when there's been an epic shift in the tectonic plates of your personal universe.

After work I go to school (blah, blah, blah, nothing, something, more nothing), and after school, Trevor, my boyfriend, comes to pick me up and take me home, where he'll have dinner with us. Trevor stops me right outside in the school parking lot; he kisses me and our tongues loll around together, like seals playing in water. I'm not into public displays of affection generally, but right then I'm just so happy to see him. My hands are on his shoulders, which I like to feel because, back then, Trevor delivered refrigerators and washing machines. He's got these muscles that won't quit. He's still kissing away when he separates from me suddenly, his brain catching up to the rest of him. "You changed your hair," he says.

He looks at me, and I put my hand up to my head. My hair was still short, but I'd gone from brown with yellow highlights to a rusty orange. My friend Melanie did it for me, and she's good at it too, even though she never messes with her own color. She always says her dad would kill her, but personally, I don't think her dad would even notice.

"It looks gorgeous," Trevor says. You can see why I keep him around. I could turn it blue and he'd say the same thing. I *have* turned it blue and he's said the same thing. He grabs a hold of the beads of my necklace, pulls me to him. He rubs the beard he's trying to grow against my cheek and we kiss again. No offense to Trevor, but we all know he has reluctant facial hair. He just can't grow a beard. My legs do better. We kiss a little more, which is something he *can* do, and then we walk over to his car and he starts it up. His car has the low, hungry rumble of a muffler barely hanging in. It's an old Mustang convertible, and it's kind of a piece of shit, but Trevor always says it's a *Mustang*, which apparently means it can be a piece of shit and still be something great.

Trevor pulls up in front of my mom's house. We walk up the porch steps and past the hanging flower baskets, the flowers already turning crunchy from spring sun. Mom's gardening skills are less skills than good intentions. She'll come home all happy from Johnson's Nursery, carrying those low-sided cardboard boxes full of wet, bright flowers, and a week or so later, the plants will be as thirsty as Trevor after moving refrigerators on a hot August day. I squeak on the garden hose before we go in, tip it up into the baskets. The flowers are so dry, the water basically gushes out the hole in the bottom, but at least I like to think there's maybe a few good karma points for effort here, and I don't know about you, but I need all the good karma points I can get.

Inside, my little sister, Bex, is sitting cross-legged on the floor and watching TV. She had a little crush on Trevor then, and usually she'd have gotten carbonated at the sight of him, jumping up and jabbering away. But right then she's focused on that screen.

"What're you watching?" I ask.

"The news." She plays with the ends of her long braids, crosses them under her chin.

Sure enough, CNN. More images of small huts and tiny villages washed away by flooding waters, concerned-voiced news anchors with the kind of perfect hair that has never actually been close to tragedy. The fourth day of nonstop disaster coverage. "Bex," I say. "Look. It's beautiful out. Go outside and play. Ride your bike, or something."

"I can't," Bex says.

"She's grounded!" Mom shouts from the kitchen.

"Still?" I say.

"Too long, you think?" Mom shouts again. Trevor and I go to the kitchen, where Mom has started dinner. She's wearing jeans and a white T-shirt with hanger bumps on the shoulders. I smell onions, the bitter-sweet tang of them frying in butter. Her long hair is tied back, strands around her face frizzly from steam. "I don't know about grounding. What do I know about grounding? Bomba and Bompa never grounded Mike or me. Hi, Trevor," she says.

"Hey, Missus," he says, which is what he calls her even though she's not married. My Dad was living in Hawaii with Jennifer. Mom called Jennifer her "step wife."

"That's 'cause Uncle Mike was perfect and the only rebellious thing you did was marry Dad," I say.

"Bomba loved your dad," Mom says. "*Loves.* So even that wasn't so rebellious." Bomba, my grandmother (who earned her name when I was a baby and couldn't pronounce "Grandma"), lives in Arizona, where she and Bompa moved a while back to make their retirement money "stretch." I like the idea of that, money stretching, the way you take a pinch of gum from your mouth and pull. Bompa died about seven years ago, when my parents were getting divorced. He said he got colon cancer from all the smoke my dad blew up his ass, but really, he liked the joke so much, he'd use it with various people—insurance salesmen, his brother-in-law. I look at the picture of Bomba that's on our fridge, stuck there with a magnet from a pizza delivery place. She's sitting in a blow-up kiddie pool with her sunglasses on, her boobs all water-balloon saggy in her swimsuit, and she's reading a magazine. She taped on one of those cartoon bubbles, and has herself saying, "Bomba, luxuriating in the pool." I miss not seeing her. Without Bomba, we have all cookie and no chocolate chip.

"Why's Bex grounded?" Trevor asks.

"She had to go to the principal's office," I say. "This girl at school—"

"Lindsey," Mom interrupts.

"She *hates* Lindsey," Trevor says. "Suck-up. Teacher's pet." Another reason Trevor is great. He keeps up with all that stuff. He pays attention.

"Yeah, that's the one," I say. "Lindsey told Bex that Bex couldn't karate chop, so Bex proved her wrong. Knocked her on her butt."

"Oh, man," Trevor says.

"Oh, man," Chico, our parrot, says from his cage in the corner. If you have any brains, you stay away from Chico. He'll lure you to him with nice words, like *Come here, Sweetie,* or *Give me a kiss* and he'll make smooching sounds. But then when you get close, *snap!* It gets the vet every time. Trevor snitches a baby carrot from the counter, and Mom gives him a look, shoves the knife over for him to chop some instead.

"She's lucky she didn't get expelled," Mom says.

"Still, she's been grounded for a week," I say.

"I like being grounded!" Bex shouts from the other room. As you can tell, our house was pretty small. Privacy, forget it.

"That's not the idea!" Mom shouts back. "See? What do I know about grounding," she says.

Mom finishes browning beef and adds garlic, and the whole house gets rich with the blissful, hypnotic meld of butter and garlic and onions. She's making a Joe's Special, one of her top-three favorite meals at her favorite restaurant, Thirteen Coins, somewhere we go only for a special treat, since it's pricey. Okay, actually we went there only once that I can remember, back when she and Dad were still married and she didn't have to worry in the grocery store aisle over whether she should buy shower cleaner or not. In the old days, fabric-softener sheets you tossed into the dryer and already-made juice in bottles (versus the frozen kind you mix with three cans of water) were not considered luxury items. We could get the ice cream in a round container and not in a square one.

I hear Severin, my brother, come home. Severin, Indigo, Bex—my father had this thing for individuality in names, according to Mom, which basically means, *If you don't like it, blame him.* Severin says hi to Bex, and then his bedroom door shuts. Mom adds the eggs and spinach, which may sound gross, but it's not. It's amazing. My mother is great in the kitchen, but if you really want to understand Naomi Skye, the person, you need to look at the complicated relationship she had with her old Datsun then. First of all, every smell on the road—a street being tarred, a fire, some tanker spilling exhaust—would elicit this panicky reaction along the lines of, *What's that? Do you smell that? Is that my car?* She'd roll down her window, sniff, sniff, sniff, until you said, *Mom,* relax! *See the flames coming out of that building? The fire trucks? The plumes of black smoke over there?* And then she'd hold a hand to her chest and breathe a sigh of relief. *Thank God,* she'd say. *I thought I was going to need a new engine or something.*

Then, second, there was that pesky little red "engine" light that flickered on the dashboard. This was a sign of certain doom, which she completely ignored. If you pointed it out, she'd say, *It's fine. It always does that. It'll go off.* And then, finally, there were the windshield wipers. We'd be driving along, and her windshield wipers would be going even though it'd stopped raining twenty minutes ago, or maybe even the day before. Still, they'd be *ke-shunk, ke-shunk*ing and she wouldn't notice until you said *Mom! Your wipers are on!* and she'd give this little surprised *Oh, right!* and shut them off. See, a triple threat existed in Mom; it's still there, really (and will probably be there always, no matter what), some anxiety-denial-distraction combo that expressed itself most clearly as soon as she was behind the wheel of that old yellow car. *That's what happens when you're a single mother and work full-time in a psychiatrist's office and are raising three kids and trying to find the time to get the laundry done,* she'd say as she sprayed Febreze on some shirt in lieu of actually using the washing machine. I don't know about that, but I do know that even if she's a bit scattered, she's great with food. She knows how to feed us.

There in the kitchen, Trevor agrees. "Mmm." He groans with smell-pleasure. His own mom runs a day care in their house, so he was lucky if he got hot dogs cut up into little pieces and Cheerios in a baggie.

"Tell your brother and sister that dinner's ready," Mom says.

"Bex! Sever-in!" I shout. "Dinner's ready!"

"Indigo, God." She sighs. "I could have done that." Which is what she always says. "*Go* and *tell* them."

"God!" Chico says.

In a few moments, we're all around the table, pouring milk, passing rolls. Mom liked us to sit and have that meal together. *We will not be one of those families that eat in the car on the way to somewhere else. Where sports practice and meetings and trips to the mall are more important than being together,* she would say. *I want us to share our day.* Trevor was the one who really got off on this, since his mother didn't hear a word he said unless he was dripping blood and had to go to the emergency room.

"Top of the line built-in model," he says, "and they aren't even gonna *use* it. It's for the *catering kitchen.* The place the caterers go to make a mess in so guests don't see." Trevor had delivered a refrigerator earlier that day to some people on Meer Island.

"The Moores have a catering kitchen," Severin says. "And this whole room where Mrs. Moore can practice her tennis swing in virtual reality. I saw it at the Christmas party." Then, Severin worked after school for MuchMoore Industries, which I'm sure you've heard of, but if you haven't, it's this company that sells digital cameras and image transferring. They'll print your name and photo on any object from greeting cards to wallpaper. Severin's my twin, but you'd never know it. I got blessed with the part of Mom that'll reach into her purse for a pen and will pull out a tampon, and I got blessed with the part of Dad that's dissatisfied with social constraints, and that's maybe just a little dissatisfied in general. The way most people feel on Sunday nights is how I think he feels a lot of the time. This led him to get fired from his job at an advertising firm, after he submitted a proposal for a major account, Peugeot, with the slogan, "Got Peu?" After that, Dad left advertising for good, moved to Hawaii, and opened a shop that rents surfboards.

Bomba, who loves me, claims I *dance to my own drummer,* and I'm sure she's got this wrong, because it makes me sound like I'm flailing around in the focused psycho-ecstasy you see in groupies in the front row of any concert. But Severin, he doesn't dance to his own drummer. He walks in a straight line. He got the parts of our parents that remember to buy stamps and that love books and that plan for the future. Severin's one of those guys who have looks and height and brains and a sense of purpose. He worked for MuchMoore, hung out with the Skyview kids from our school, and he could fake his way through the truth that he didn't fit in with them. The fact that girls like Kristin Densley and Heather Green called our house all the time and that he got good grades didn't piss me off, though, because Severin's this really nice person. He treated Trevor like an equal even if Trevor graduated from the alternative school. Severin, my *brother*, talked to me at school, even if no one seemed to grasp the idea that we were related. He's the kind of guy that also does nice things for no reason, like once he replaced a broken string on my guitar as a surprise.

"Two kitchens to clean, is all I can think," Mom says.

"*They* don't clean them," I remind her.

"No, they just hire immigrants at less than minimum wage," Mom says. She sounds like Jane, my boss.

Bex takes a swig of milk. "There are people without *homes* and *food* now, let alone refrigerators," she says.

"Detention's over, Bex," Mom says.

"No, wait. Seriously," Trevor says. His face does get serious. But serious in a way that makes you want to laugh. "What would you do if you had that kind of money?"

I know that Trevor is someone who asks a question because he's dying to give you his own answer, and I am a good girlfriend, so I say, "What would you do?"

"I know what *I'd* do," he says.

"Start your business," I say.

"What's that saying? 'Give a man a lemon, he eats lemons for a day; teach him to make lemonade and he'll always have something to drink'? I'd invest in myself," Trevor says. You can see why

I might be lacking a little faith in Trevor as a businessman.

"Nunderwear!" Bex shouts, raising a fist to the air. This is Trevor's latest brilliant plan. He'd had other ideas before, but this time he's *serious*. The last time, he was serious too, but he's forgotten that. Nunderwear is based on those days-of-the-week underwear, only with Nunderwear, they'd all read SUNDAY. Trevor's got this whole product line of gag gifts he wants to sell under the business name Lapsed Catholic Enterprises. He's sure other lapsed Catholics would find them just as hilarious as he does, and he doesn't even smoke anything (anymore). He wants to make those little packets of cheese and crackers using communion wafers, called My Body Snack Pak. Then he has the Pope's Hat Coffee Filters, which he actually sketched out on a piece of notebook paper. Shaped like the pope's hat, they'd come in a pack of fifty and fit any standard electric coffeepot, for using or wearing.

"You guys laugh, but you won't be laughing when I'm rolling in the dough."

"If I had that kind of money?" Bex says. "I'd give it away to the needy. To people whose houses have washed away, just like *that*." She snaps her fingers.

"CNN isn't good for kids," I say.

"I mean it," she says. Her blue eyes look directly at me. She's eleven years old, so I suspect her submersion into disaster coverage will fade as soon as she's in her sixth-grade class painting papier-mâché tribal masks they've made out of strips of the *Seattle Times* and Gold Medal flour and water. "I would."

"Severin?" Trevor asks.

"Easy. College."

"Like you're not going to get scholarships," I say.

"You have no idea. I get Bs! God. I'm up against these kids who've taken every SAT prep class, who've hired college counselors that have been working with them since they were zygotes, searching out scholarships and filling out applications. . . . It's nuts. And they don't even *need* the scholarships."

"What's a zygote?" Bex asks.

"I told you, we'll work out something," Mom says. But she doesn't look too sure, honestly. She stares down into her plate when she says it, picks at her salad with her fork as if the solutions are hidden somewhere under the lettuce.

"What's a zygote?" Bex asks again.

"When the egg and the sperm—"

"Oh gross, never mind," Bex says.

"Can we ditch the sperm talk at dinner, please?" I say.

"What about you, Missus?" Trevor asks. His mind is still on rich people. "What would you do if you had lots of money? Lots and lots of money."

"College. For Severin and Indigo and Bex."

"I don't want to go to college," I say.

"So you claim," Mom says. It's an ongoing argument between us, and now when the subject comes up, Mom stops it cold with some statement that indicates her irrefutable superior knowledge about my real desires. She doesn't get that I don't know what I want to study, and that it therefore seems a waste of money. I'm not going to be one of those people who spend thousands of dollars getting an art history degree and then end up working in a dentist's office.

"Okay, besides college," Trevor says. "Don't you people dream big? Swimming pools?"

"I'll take a pool," I say.

"Famous people, parties . . ." He's trying to bait me.

"Hun-ter E-den," Mom sings. Okay, so I had a little crush on Hunter Eden then. Who in their right mind didn't? My friend Melanie actually went to one of his concerts and met him, because her dad's PR firm handled Slow Change. Yeah, I'd have liked to handle Slow Change. I may not have wanted to dance to my own drummer, but I wouldn't have minded dancing to my own guitar player. Not only did I find his playing to be amazing and inspirational, but he was sexy enough to melt ice, like he did on the body of that girl in the video for "Hot."

"Okay, okay. Front-row tickets, backstage pass, after-concert party. Then I'd die happy," I say.

"I could sing you 'Hot'," Trevor offers. Everyone laughs. Even Chico does his *eh, eh, eh* laugh imitation. "It wasn't *that* funny."

"You still need something for yourself, Mom," I say.

"College *is* for myself," she says. "You can take care of me in my old age."

"Diamonds!" I joke. Mom is a nonjewelry person. If she ever gets remarried (which was looking unlikely since she didn't even date) she'd probably rather strap a hefty Barnes & Noble gift card to the third finger of her left hand than a ring.

"Dahling," she says. "No, I like the blue ones. What are they? I always think topaz, but that's not right."

"Sapphires," Severin says. "How about a trip somewhere?"

"Zygote City," Bex says.

"A Jenn-Air built-in Euro-style stainless with precision temperature management system," Trevor says.

"No, I know," I say. Bex looks at me and smiles.

"I know too," she says.

"Toilet seat!" we say together.

"Eh, eh, eh," Chico says.

"Come on, guys, it is *not* that bad," Mom says. She was wrong, though—it was. It had a thin, shifty crack in it, and you had to be careful how you sat down, or it'd snip you in the ass. If you stumbled to the bathroom in the middle of the night and didn't stay alert, you'd get a zesty wake-up pinch.

"We've got the only toilet seat in all of Zygote City that bites," Bex says.

"I promise, I'll get it fixed," Mom says. "Add it to the list." Microwave oven: out of commission since Bex put a foil-wrapped Ho Ho in there. Why she wanted to warm it up is still a mystery. Vacuum: worked if you only used the hose attachment and didn't mind spending about twelve hours hunched over the carpet like you'd lost a contact lens. Iron: black on the bottom and leaking water.

"Gold toilet seat," Trevor says, as if it's decided.

"Or one of those padded ones," Severin says, and grins.

"Those give me the creeps," I say.

"Me too, but I don't exactly know why," Mom says.

Freud, our cat, saunters in from the living room, stretches his hind legs behind him. Bex dangles her fingers toward the floor and Freud nudges them with his triangle nose.

"Here, kitty, kitty," Chico says evilly. He makes smooching sounds.

That was what my life was like, before I got rich.

Jordan's father has done something terrible. . . . Ruby's in love with a dangerous guy. . . . Cassie's stepfather is going mad. . . . Jade is afraid of everything until she meets Sebastian. . . .

Girls you like.
Emotions you recognize.
Outcomes that make you think.
All by Deb Caletti.

The Queen of Everything

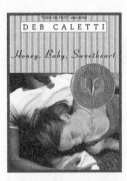

Honey, Baby, Sweetheart
National Book Award Finalist

Wild Roses

The Nature of Jade

Published by Simon & Schuster

PULSE it

Did you **love** this book?

Want to get the
hottest books **free**?

Log on to
www.SimonSaysTEEN.com
to find out how you can get
free books from **Simon Pulse**
and become part of our **IT Board**,
where you can tell **US**, what **you** think!

SIMON
PULSE